The Five Lives of
Ms Bennett

Helen Hagemann

Oz.one Publishing ©

For my grandmother who taught me the value of stories

I want the reader to feel something is astonishing. Not the 'what happens', but the way everything happens.
Alice Munro

Oz.one Publishing ©

TABLE OF CONTENTS

Prologue

Alice's Fifth Life

Maggie's goodbye post-it, I'M OUTA HERE, remains on the fridge. With no effort to remove the piece of paper, Alice wonders why the brevity of her goodbye smarts a little. She feels low. Perhaps it has something to do with the weather this year, May, June and July being the town's coldest, wettest months. The sky is drenching the night, raining continuously during the day; lightning, thunder, dark clouds spilling waterfalls, a sky show having its way. The wind whips under her frail umbrella and skirt, and rain drums into a storm-water drain on the drive, sliding sand and debris. Why the cloud-author is in such a mad tizz this year, she doesn't know.

On the first fine day, Alice moves some of Maggie's unwanted furniture, a chest of drawers painted white, an electric fan, a bookcase and a black Ikea chair. She clomps around in a pair of Maggie's Japanese scuffs. From the wardrobe, she sleeves off a tight parka, a size ten barely reaching her elbows. In the kitchen, she stacks bowls, glasses and a dinner set. On the windowsill, two China dolls remain. Against the bed-head and bare mattress, four pillows with matching pillow cases. Maggie's collected life. Alice leans back in a chair and gently unfolds her scrapbook. In the last newspaper cutting of Maggie's band, she isn't smiling. She succeeded in Perth's Indi scene, but would her music take off in Melbourne? Did she leave because of her father? Of course, she didn't expect her to stay in these nuisance grounds, parents living separate lives on either side of a driveway. Alice was annoyed by the last melodrama, Max telling Maggie that he was going to die. She wished he'd stop playing with his daughter's feelings. Didn't he know she was fragile, getting over Tim, another new love skulking back to a previous girlfriend?

After two weeks, the house is buckled in silence, Maggie's old acoustic lying in its case under the bed. In the shed, Alice sorts through her things, looking at her daughter's dreams. Attempts at photography, black and white slides, the bottles of developer discarded. In one box, Maggie's self-published CD's. In another, her hand-written songs, music and gig list. She's packed away her collection of science fiction, and a large volume of fairytales.

The books remind Alice of the old house in Swan Road. She can still hear the children's boisterous laughter, machine guns rattling, all the tantrums, Crowded House and REM up loud, Maggie's jubilant stomp and spin as bright as a star, Alice following her to most gigs, her band playing two year sessions at 'In the Pines'. She can't forget hours at the end of their bed, Maggie tuning a new song between her fingers. Before a radio interview, dragging both parents outside on the porch, rehearsing old songs, and familiar chords stroked with love. Then a new tune floating across her father's face lends him a rare smile.

The last song leaves Alice feeling hollow-hearted, the guitar balanced on Maggie's lap on her father's front porch, fingers placed on a lulling chord, the blankness clearly visible on Max's face.

In this side-by-side living, Alice finds household items dumped at the front door, and at night Max's rhythm and blues and jazz CD's thump continuously through the garden. A recurring dream wakes her in the morning, sensing a lion's hot breath dripping on her cheek. He is old and slobbering, pinning her in rows of lettuces, ghosting the mortar and brick. When the shadow of the animal distills in the morning light, Alice knows the beast. Max is that rocking shape, snorting in the shadows, huffing his breath in and out, as if ready to kill.

Maggie leaves a photograph of herself amongst a collection of cards and bric-a-brac in the shed. Her burgundy-rinsed hair, curled behind her ears, looks more like a boy's. She has the cat's plumpness tucked into her lap. She wears a Japanese-lettered green top, and her black three-quarter pants show signs of Toshi's long white fur.

Amongst her music and scrapbooks, she finds more reminders: a baby book, her chubby pinkness in the well of a cot, ruched blankets behind her legs, a teething dribble soaking her jumpsuit. Alice has packed old skirts and jackets into a laundry basket. But she's thinking about the biography of Maggie's life: her dancing concerts, first rock band at high school, heart-to-hearts about boys and puberty. All the recent talks on feminism more precious than ever before.

Later in the week, Maggie rings excited by a two-storey townhouse she is going to share with four others in North Carlton. She talks for two hours. It's like she's won the Melbourne Cup.

Alice adds Maggie's photograph to the collection of frames on the coffee table. The other photos of prior generations she keeps in a sturdy envelope. She thinks of them as little opals, changing colour each time she looks. She's glad she saved the Temple Bay albums, emptied out the dresser drawers in her mother's Tweed Heads apartment. It didn't matter if the family joked about her magpie habits. The tattered fawn envelopes, marriage certificates, birth certificates, letters, were precious machinations of the past, too easily forgotten and irretrievable later on. Snapshots of great-grandparents, grandmothers, grandfathers, uncles and aunties at parties, cousins at the beach and ones taken in front of the Harbord house, show facial features that have either emerged or seem to resemble her.

Alice spreads them on the table like a span of playing cards, picking out the best loved. Some are spotted with rust, others surprise and delight. Most are dog-eared, raising so many questions: Who was that? What year? Where? What part of Sydney? Alice doesn't recognise them all. Maybe it was Aunty Vera or Aunty Alma. Her dad looks so young in a three-piece suit, soon after getting engaged, her mum in a crepe dress, so figure flattering. Here they are again alighting the Manly ferry, a matching pair, Lauren Bacall and Humphrey Bogart donning suede hats. In Alice's hallway, their wedding photograph doubled, regarding itself in an opposite mirror. Her mother's long parachute-silk gown whisked creamily at her feet.

The baby photos fastened in little black cornices stare back at Alice. On her christening day, three pages of wasted Kodak film reveal the peeling Sunday school hall, the yard, the Minister's house next door, his rose arbor, the church's front steps, scattered hymnbooks, and a flowered altar. In the group photos, a congress of ancients gather around, great aunts in the foreground clutching their white gloves and purses while the Minister splashes a psalm of names. On the front porch at home, high at chest level, Gran holds a six-month-old Alice, the long train of lace and ribbon of the christening gown billowing over her forearm.

A young Gran, half smiling in a mosaic frame, decorates Alice's kitchen shelves. Edith is attractive in steel rims, with dark homespun hair knotted at the nape. A bodice decoration sits snugly at her chest, like a velvet doll. Alice can't make out whether it's a lock of hair, a black-ribbon brooch or false necktie? Gran radiates health and inner-beauty, a woman Alice only ever knew as old. Her string of names still astounds: Edith, Adelaide, Edwina, Rachael, Alexandria. And her deft fingers would have sewn the lace bodice, cuffed sleeves on the ivory dress. Was this a special occasion? Was she in love, about to marry? Perhaps she couldn't wait for afternoon, a lazy park stroll near a raucous waterfowl lake, parasol in hand, twirling the name of John through her lips, a man who would never disappoint, never touch alcohol, leave her nothing from his life, save good memories, and the short duration of himself.

Part 1

Grandma's Chocolate Tin

Memo 1:   *Store matches near the chip-heater for convenience.*

Unfurling the bat-wings of cellophane, Gran pops a butterscotch sweet into Alice's mouth. 'Leftover from the Saturday pictures,' she says.

Today they're sitting on the back veranda, staring into the white fields of each other's eyes, giggling, sucking and slurping on the lolly, shifting it over the tongue, making a walnut pouch in the cheek. Alice sits close to Gran, cuddling, her hand resting inside her cardigan. Gran wraps one arm around her for a quick squeeze. Alice can't be bothered straightening and pulling down her caught undies, so she moves off the cool veranda step, shuffling her bottom onto the flare of Gran's rose-petal dress.

Inches away, white horse orchids nod new blooms, bantams and pullets trail the fence-line. The two new ducks waddle under the fruit trees, scraping their beaks on sheets of corrugated iron, remnants of her dad's extensions. Princey is digging a bone under the lemon tree, exposing more of its thick roots. It's a balmy March afternoon, seventy-two degrees. No wind ruffling her skirt, just a little tickle in the tall backyard trees two houses away. Dad's aviary is an incessant box of chatter, rainbow lorikeets, Weiros, budgies and cockies, strolling perches and dropping tail feathers.

It's four o'clock in the afternoon and Edith lifts several skeins of wool from the line. 'We're going to wind these into balls, and I need your hands out like this.' Edith holds her arms out like two ends of the clothesline.

'What are you going to knit, Gran?'

'A twinset. Should be enough wool.'

'Where'd it come from?'

'It was a cardigan I knitted for your grandfather.'

'Please, please, tell me about Grandpa. About the boat!'

Edith wraps her skirt between her knees, placing the lumpy wool at her side. 'Well, when the fish were biting at Christmas all the holidaymakers used to take the good boats out. They were gone by six. Your grandfather got tired of that, so he bought one. We loved it. It was big and roomy. We caught lots of bream and jewies. Two weeks later, we were fishing round the point at Wilson. I turned to get a sandwich, pour a cuppa and there he was, slumped across the oars. I thought he was dozin'. But he'd gone.' She falters for a moment, wiping a doll's bonnet over her face. 'I couldn't shake him.'

Alice hears the repeated stories, but it's her grandmother's mouth she needs to watch. She knows nothing about death, but thinks it's like burying the old cat Timmy under the lemon tree. She once drew her grandfather floating up to heaven holding a balloon. She sketched him flying down, looking at her at the beach. Another time, she sat him on a motorboat amongst the seagulls sunning themselves on a flagged tarpaulin.

Alice likes visiting the beach every day, swimming, whirling a rubber ring. Sandcastles and mud-pies are her specialty, and watching men twisting cylinders into the moist sea earth, trading bloodworms from wet hessian. After a swim, with her friend Heather, they throw seaweed at one another, running shrieking along the foreshore. Concentrating hard, they each score points scaring seagulls or soldier crabs. The girls like painting, and so they collect limpets and mollusks, leaving them to dry in polka-dots and stripes on the laundry windowsill.

Alice waits for her grandmother to bring out the chocolate tin of photographs, each time passing the same three. Gran searches methodically, raising another print half way into the stack. It's John at the washstand, rolling his sleeves over a pump handle.

'I reckon that pump looks like a rooster,' says Alice.

Gran laughs. 'You was a naughty little thing, Alice. When we wasn't looking, you used to tease our rooster. We locked the gate. Then lo and behold, you wiggled your finger into the bantam cage.'

'Did they bite me?'

'Yep. They thought your finger was a big fat worm. Reckon Tom Gettoes heard you wailing up at his place.'

'Is that why you killed and ate all the chooks, Gran?'

'Well, no. But the other thing was,' she continues, 'you put a crayon up your nose. We was doubled-over with hysterics until your mother found she couldn't get it out.'

'Up there, like a boogie,' she giggles.

'We could see it all right. Anyway, it was thanks to Doctor Fox, he got the tweezers and out it popped.'

Alice remembers her chalkboard and chalks, drawing on the veranda, but not storing a crayon up her nose.

The two females move further up the steps, Gran sorting her mementoes like pennies. She passes Alice a postcard of five firemen standing stiffly in a row, legs at army ease, bodies in their best bowties, caps and suits. The fire engine, housed in a weatherboard shed, pokes its nose as a minor image in the frame. Alice points across the men's shoulders at the braced wooden-door, a brass bell, and an axe handle locked behind glass. Gran explains that they were proud of their new engine, a 1920s International.

When a cracked photo is drawn from underneath the pile, the old woman withdraws into other corridors. Three men in full uniform, double-breasted velvet jackets and high boots, bow their heads. Particleboard lies beneath their feet. Steps lead to battered doors. In a side annex, minor scorching. One man is smoking a rollie. The rest look pitiful, shoulders and mouths drooped. Alice thinks the burnt building resembles the black-stick house along the Esplanade.

She waits for Gran to call her nickname; twirls her three bangles, watching for signs that Gran's eyelids have lifted. Alice has come to know this scene, like the charcoal in the grate, sparking a new flame with just a little prod. She counts her grandmother's stitches, the number of times the right forefinger loops the wool, clicking her heels forward and back, tapping her leather shoes on the concrete path. In this place together, they are apart. Alice bumps her grandmother, making her drop stitches. In the silence, she picks at blades of buffalo grass, crisscrosses them like a paddle-pop raft. The old straw hat balances on the geraniums. She thinks Grandpa might soon jump back into the picture.

'Is this where you had the pump?' asks Alice, pointing to the old tank-stand. More clacking, the scrunching sound of wool escaping as Edith unwinds the ball from her knitting bag. 'I used to play under there, Gran. Look here, Gran.' Alice taps the tank stand with a long piece of doweling. 'With matchsticks. I lit one.'

'You didn't want to start a fire, did you?' Edith raises her eyes over the rims of her glasses.

'Nah. Not really.' Alice sprawls close to her grandmother and snips at the clover with the scissors. 'Did you ever see a really big fire with Grandpa in that fire engine?'

'No, women weren't allowed.'

'Oh.'

'It was bad luck in those days.'

'Why?'

'There was always bad luck.'

'I like firing matches. Whoosh!' she giggles, imitating the strike.

'Don't you dare, Alice, or I'll tell your father.'

Alice twirls her pink hoop until it catches on her cardigan. She leans back on the top step, placing herself inside the plastic toy.

'I made 'em plenty of cups of tea in my day,' says Edith, resting her skeins. 'They was always awake because of me.'

'Was that your house there, Gran?' says Alice, holding the photo.

'Yep. See those roses out the front, every colour of the rainbow. I loved that old house and garden. Trouble was, it was too far from the beach.' Edith wrestles an aching foot and straightens. 'Fire Station used to be an old barn till they renovated it. Your grandfather spent long hours in there, checking and re-checking the equipment, tuning the pumps and making the truck ready, just in case. It was one problem after the other.'

'Did he burn his fingers?'

'He got his whiskers singed plenty of times. I remember the big one. It was a miserable job. Half the Spit Junction was burning. Like a wood-yard, your grandfather said, full of timber ready to go.'

Alice imagined a bush fire like the logs that tumbled and fell in the lounge-room grate. She liked the sound of snapping wood that sent sparks up the chimney. She was glad, too, that Gran was still making scones and cups of tea for her, that everything was much the same; except, they didn't have a fire engine to climb on, or a garden of roses.

'I don't know why, but he kept these journals.' Edith lifts the book from the bottom of the suitcase, dog-eared pages falling from stitches. 'Here's a good story,' she says, balancing the large book across their knees. 'It'll help you understand your grandfather.'

Warringah: Griffin Road, 1934. Minor property damage.
When we got there the hill along Griffin Road was yellow and smoky. Left Laurie and Bill in charge of the hose checked out the back of the sheds. The fire was already frisky in the button grass. Luckily the lantana and eucalypts further in hadn't gone up yet. A lad from the factory rolled up with his truck to help the owner remove some crates from a big stores shed. A few fences needed to be soaked. I got the volunteers onto that one. A strong nor-westerly blowing didn't help things much. The stacked drums, full of petrol, kerosene and turpentine was our biggest worry. We could hear the petrol simmering inside, the drums swelling with the heated pressure. All the boys and I could do was try and keep the drums cool. We were under control as the other men outside and further up in the long grass begun to get onto the fire and we won the fight.

'Oh, goody, they won.'

'Yep. They won that day, but the next week there was all hell to play. The storekeeper, old Snowy, came skidding up on his motorbike in front of the house, while I was in the yard. Well, he rang the bell and woke the men. The fire started down at the Surf Club where they kept all the surfboats and boards. There was a fish and chip shop, a tackle shop. The whole lot might have gone up.'

Alice waits, as her grandmother wipes the moist ridges of her eyes.

'There were people everywhere, sirens wailing, women, old fellas, boys outside the double doors. Of course, they weren't allowed in. They just ran with the fire truck all the way up Evans Street, dogs yapping at the tyres. I noticed your grandfather was having trouble with his pants and belt, but didn't take any notice. The men soon found he wasn't well. He was slumped over his office chair; coat half off, ledger books all over the floor. In the panic of it all, they took him to the doctor's first. Had to wake him up. Doc kept shaking their hands. The boys said he was pleased it wasn't his place going up.'

Edith passes the wool to Alice and places it on both wrists. 'He never forgave himself that day. When they left him, the rest of the crew had terrible trouble. They couldn't get the hose to work. There was something wrong with the hydrant pressure. The surf shed burnt to the ground. They got there too late, Petal.'

Edith is silent for a moment, letting the balls of wool roll in her lap. 'That's why he left his job at Rowlands and the Brigade and we came here to Temple Bay. He bought a boat, and well ...'

Alice rubs against Gran's dress. For an hour they sit in the fading sun on pillows, shifting only their limbs now and again. With every taut pull and release of wool from the knitting bag, Alice imagines a fish inside hooked until it lets go. Eventually, she lies back on the porch boards and buries her head in her sleeve.

Edith

Memo 2:   *Girls need to be taught knitting, sewing, crochet, rug-making, and all other homely duties. This will help gain confidence, self-esteem, and a sense of accomplishment.*

In the stillness of the afternoon, Alice senses Gran's presence, her nylon dress in a static cling, her breasts smelling of Lily of the Valley talc. She turns once, feeling the warm brushstroke of Gran's hand, removing lines of hair from her mouth.

She waits, listening for the familiar sandy drag of the Paddy's Market suitcase across the floorboards. As the locks click, a musical curiosity fills her head, dizzy now from a sudden uplift, radio playing and dad's buzz saw droning in the shed.

Gran's varicose legs slap together as she lifts her onto the large cane lounge. She watches with interest as Alice searches inside the suitcase, decorating arms and chest with knotted pearls, beads, brooches. The mother-of-pearl combs, hair clasps, brushes with worn bristles piled at her side. She smooches up to her cheeks, insisting that it's time to string more necklaces with the pearls from the button box. Swirling hands inside the varnished wood, she sorts the round pearls from the glass eyes, counting them on the sliding lid, raising more until the plastic buttons and butterflies sink to the bottom.

In the following days, Gran takes Alice fishing. They catch the ferry across the bay, and Gran slings a line off the Araluen rocks. They wander the shoreline, Gran in a knitted twin-set, Alice in rolled pants dragging a stick at the waterline. They gingerly step over rocks and barnacles, patting and prizing grey-black shells, searching for a possible gem inside.

Alice follows Gran, listening to family voices inside her head. *Your grandmother's an angel. Sent down from heaven.*

She thinks about Gran's special powers. The quick slip of the hook from the fish's mouth. The bucket flapping with three silver bream. The necklace of scales she leaves on the shore. Crouching in the shoals for mollusks, Alice giggles into her curled hand, thinking about Gran's floppy bedtime smile. *Gran, your teeth remind me of stars. They come out at night.*

***

The next day, Gran and Alice settle on the veranda's floorboards to play Chinese Checkers. There's a whirring sound of bees, the drone of the timber mill across the street, and Edna, her mother, clattering the sewing machine. As the shade inches across the nasturtiums and rumpy bunches of hydrangeas, Alice stretches out on the decking, piling the bridge with pillows. She loves the veranda, especially its protection from the strong southerly buster, and with just a hint of sun left in the afternoon, the boards warm like a radiator.

Sitting crossed legged, Alice copies Gran dunking Anzac cookies in her tea. She tries to scoop up a biscuit before it falls and swims. Holding one hand under the other, she manages to keep the fourth one intact. Now she can't speak, and nods to Edith to go first. 'Um, I'm having the blue this time,' she says, finally.

With the tea tray stacked in the kitchen, Alice winning every game skipping several holes at once, Gran strings the beans. Alice squirms in close. 'Was your old house in a forest, Gran?'

'No, Petal, we lived in Newcastle. It was a timber house, but we were miles from the mill. I remember the road to town and school.'

'Did you play Draughts and Monopoly?'

'Oh no. We had cubbies and a couple of dolls between us.'

The bean skins curl on Edith's dress. Alice joins them in a daisy chain. She is silent now, making up new rules of the game, pretending that Gran's sisters are sitting close, her eight-year-old arms moving 'their' green marbles across the board. She won't let the boys wedge into their space. They have to go around the back, play swords or chasies. She doesn't want them to tip the doll's pram over.

Alice listens to Gran's words with excitement, sensing the rush of air, hearing her sisters yelling, running through the bee-covered clover. Under the grey light of an iron roof, Gran makes a cardboard lean-to, ordering Mary and Edie to hide from the boys. Alice tries to stare deeper into her grandmother's house; at the muddy footprints on the front veranda, listening for the flies and Christmas beetles tapping on the louvres. Gran builds momentum into her story. Stained clothes and stockings jumble on a washstand, her only pair of shoes left in the hall. The ceiling has gaps and spiders. Birds nest in the rafters. The sugar and flour jars are empty. There's a fire-grate with only two coal halves in the wood-box. Gran sprints with the girls into their bedroom, slaps her body on a metal bunk, dimpled with thin blankets. Her sisters are fighting over a dress. *It's mine! No it's mine!* Tug-o-war. The straps rip. The dress is shoved into the pile on the floor. Gran's mother, Louisa, calls out, *Dinner!* Watery soup, bread and dripping. *Someone pass the pepper and salt.*

'Err yuk,' says Alice.

'One Christmas, Uncle Bill came with a duck wrapped in butcher's paper,' says Gran. 'He flung us two pence. So, me and me sisters went for the bread and bought a bag of sweets with the change.'

Alice imagines a young Edith popping a remaining toffee into her mouth. 'How come you only got one, Gran?'

'Well, with thirteen of us, that was all that was left.'

'You could have bought a whole bag of lollies for yourself, Gran. With bottles like me and Jimmy.'

Helen Hagemann

Baby Boomer

Memo3:   *Giving birth to a baby is one of the most rewarding and fulfilling roles a woman can undertake.*

Alice Bennett. The world is waiting for her name. She has removed herself from beautiful rooms ruined by alcohol, and although she is the first in her family to divorce, nothing feels this good. The graves are thrumming. She can hear them chatting, thinking *what fun*. All the family women before her, lying in the dust of their punitive lives. Louisa, her great-grandmother, dying in childbirth aged thirty-nine, along with the baby. She bore a total of fifteen children. One set of twins still-born, another pair surviving. Alice hears Gran's whispers, *I had to mind the toddlers, clean their dirty bottoms. There was no time for being young.*

24

Although the house is voiceless, Alice is rustling shoe boxes, blow-drying her hair, ready to go to work. She has the week pictured in her mind, chatting to readers, making coffee, sorting and stacking books. Jerry, another librarian, sends her attentive emails. He gets cosy, but courage is beyond him. Obvious signs, like flirting with every blonde, reveal that he won't walk out of the maze of marriage. Alice senses he wants some sort of hearth with an imitation flame.

Gran's soft melodious voice returns, *I was twenty-nine when I got married. Lucky your grandfather came along when he did.*

Alice wishes she could find a similar man like her grandfather, the same sobriety. Now in endless evenings spent alone, she misses Maggie and all her harebrained schemes. Managing the band, setting up a business, bringing the guys over for a jam. When the house filled with sounds of a banjo, brush drums, new-country steel guitar, Alice liked the attention from the boys when she made pizza. She always wanted days like this, if only she had a halfway decent husband. He'd been such a nuisance, tapping on the window to move their cars.

From the first moment after wheeling in her suitcase, Maggie had said, 'Why do you think I'm moving in Mum, because I know the kind of scene dad will create. I'm here to protect you. He won't be able to take things out on you, not while I'm around.'

'He refuses to cut my side of the lawn. I have to do it.'

'Get a lawn-mower man.'

'He comes to the front door, shoves letters at me and stomps off. I wish he'd just put them in the letterbox.'

'Tell the cunt to fuck off.'

'I wish he'd move away. He can afford to. I can't.'

'Send him a list of things you don't like. Do it, Mum. Right now!'

'Well, you better hang around for a bit, while he reads it!'

Back to the Sixties

Memo 4:   *The way ahead for a young lady is the traditional way of life: love, marriage, housework, home and happy days.*

The polisher moves over the floor, back and forth. Alice's mother is scandalizing the morning with dust from shaken mats and scatter rugs. Gran trickles Marveer over the furniture, wiping the china cupboard's long surface with an old singlet. Her mum emerges from the centre of the house with a dustpan and broom, only to re-enter with a squeeze bucket and mop. Slosh, slosh. The floorboards in the hallway dry into shapes of the world.

Once, when Alice was little, she over-soaped the veranda's boards, turning suds into clouds, water into weather. The bucket spill rained down on ants and a tiny ladybeetle. Testing her mother's patience, she ran screaming through the house, running away from Jimmy;

the loose floorboards in the passage see-sawing an answer to her mother.

The whole house shuddered under larger boards, her dad extending the veranda, renovating the bathroom, and sleep-out. On a timber joist, near the hot-water heater, he carved his children's lives in wood. On Alice's birthday, holding a ruler flat above her head, he marked her age and height. At nine, she was half an inch below Jimmy's mark, boys at school jokingly calling him Squizz or Shorty. Her dad reckoned he needed fertilizer to grow, while little Kevin passed her four-year mark at three.

***

Eleven o'clock, and the strong aroma of cooked pastry, baked apple and cinnamon locates every nostril in the house. Alice rubs her bare legs, rocking the old wicker chair from side to side. The leftover apple stalks trickle freshness. 'Yippee!' she squeaks. Mum's pie sits on the veranda bridge to cool. Her hands hold out a bowl, a wooden spoon leaning like a flagpole in a mixture of butter and sugar, 'Only half made it to the oven last time, Alice. Just stir, no licking!'

As soon as her mother's back is turned, Alice swirls a finger through the cake mix. This is the best part of cooking, letting the buttery sugar dribble its moisture on her tongue. And summertime, the best part of the year when the yard fruits are ready for bottling and jam. Gran's washed out all the tins, telling Alice and Jimmy to pick mulberries. During the week, Jimmy gave Alice a knee up to collect the fattest ones, dropping them into a bucket. She flapped out her bare feet to remove all the squishy muck collected from underneath the tree. On the back lawn, she loved stretching her biscuit-gold limbs, smiling and giggling, opening her lips on a dark cavern of fruit.

As the sun pleats its light into the body of the house, Alice squeezes in between Gran and mum. On the back step, they're snipping mulberry stalks and cutting passionfruit.

With hands inside their pockets, jockeying for a place, dad and Jimmy look for a foothold into the house. 'Go through the side porch,' Mum says, in a slow weary way. 'We're working here.'

Inside, the house hatches small noises, a suction release of the refrigerator door, clanging glass, bottle cap tinkling into the sink. Resisting his groans, the women hand out spoons, apple pie and cream. Except to dad. Since taking on heavy tank building, he'd rather fold himself in an armchair, his sleepy breath inhaling cigarette ash and stale beer.

'Guess what we're going to do this afternoon, Petal?' says Gran.

'Paint.'

'No, crochet.'

Alice brushes crumbs from her lap, and follows Gran from room to room, collecting baskets, knitting bags and pattern books. She likes arranging the veranda, moving the cane chairs, using the glass coffee table to store her pencil case and Gran's sewing basket. She imagines herself a little butterfly dusting her wings over the floorboards, fluffing petticoats, choreographing her landing of bare toes under a full skirt.

Edith sits on the floor beside her, pushes an ivory thread and needle forward over her forefinger, quickly working a circle of single shell stitches. She hands it to Alice, and they repeat the pattern, *hold the thread over the finger, dip and drag the cotton through, hook again and pull through the two loops.*

The dog drops his saliva-coated ball. Conversation floats on and on, orders at the shop, smocked baby wear, old-fashioned wooden needles, Gran going to school in a sulky. The horse tied up to a fencepost in the dust, sun on their backs as they jiggled the reins home. Alice insists that Heather's riding school is smelly like dad's manure. Mum flares, nudging Gran. 'God, it was awful the other night. Bob had to empty it before the cart man came.' Gran just flicks her boot at Princey's rolling ball.

Alice pulls at her cotton spider lines. No amount of unpicking will help. She shoves the mess back into the knitting bag. Gran has deserted her and is plucking leaves from the vegetable garden. 'Here,' says Gran, holding out two chubby fruit, her old straw hat deserving a closer glimpse. There's a crown full of bright strawberries in green pixie hats.

The sun splinters light into a silver colander and metal dish of water. The bouncing fruit sparks a memory for Edith. 'We were shelling peas one night, waiting for the old boy to come home. My mother had a colander just like this.'

'Did you have strawberries back in the old days, Gran?'

'No, just weeds. Long grass, of course, the horse used to chew that. You know I can remember that horse as clear as day.'

'Did you ride him?'

'Well, there was one time Dad tied him up outside the pub. We waited and waited. His tea was getting cold. Lo and behold, we heard the horse chomping and pulling the long shoots from underneath the front gate.'

'Like this, Gran?' asks Alice, ripping out the buffalo.

'Yes. Well anyway, the sulky was empty. The horse had found its way home without him. Must have got sick of waiting outside for the old boy. So, that night me sister and I had to go back into town and fetch our father. I was always scared of him when he was drunk.'

'Did he drink lots of beer like Dad?'

The women glance at one another. Edith pats Alice on the head. 'You're lucky your father only drinks beer. My father was a heavy rum drinker. There was never any money in our house when he got stuck into the rum.'

'It's all the same, Mum,' says Edna.

'No. Bob's mild compared to your grandfather. He used to get real dark, like a bomb ready to go off. He was a mean bugger. I'll never forget it.'

'Well, all I ever do is carry out Bob's beer bottles. Hate to think what Betty Parker would say if she saw all those bottles stacked to the roof.'

'Jimmy and I rang the bottlo yesterday. We should get about five shillings, I reckon.'

'You'll have another lot next week at the rate your father's going, Love.'   Alice's mother disappears into the snowy back of a double sheet. With a doll-like peg at the side of her mouth, she sips back the spit. 'Save your money, Love. It's the only way you'll ever get rich.'

Alice waves her skirt up and down. 'But I love freckles, cobbers and jellybeans. Yum!'

'Now that your mother's busy,' says Edith, 'I want you to sit still for a moment. I have something to show you.'

Alice locks her chin into her hands on the porch boards. She can see her grandmother's loose underclothes as she hoists herself up, a little tickled pleasure rising on the old face. Alice knows she is up to something, throws the ball one more time to Princey, and leans back, listening to the familiar click of the suitcase.

Gran eases a knife-edge along a tin's rusty lip. Alice likes the noises around her, the squeaky springs, Kevin banging a plastic hammer, the dog grinding his teeth into the ball, her mum at the washtub outside. On her high bed, with her toes in Gran's crocheted blanket, she lets out a suppressed shriek as the Sydney Harbour Bridge lid flies across the room, *A la Cazam – Boom Bam!*

Apart from some old documents and airmail envelopes, there's a small blue book. Edith brushes it with her hand. On the outside it is dark blue, while inside it is a bluish-grey, ruled with faint red lines. Edith turns the pages and points to the last brought-forward column. 'It's up to ten shillings. It's for you, when you're a bit older.'

'Can I spend it?'

'I'll show you something. This column is where you take out, and this one adds up. If you take out all the money you won't have this little book anymore.'

It made sense to Alice. She liked the feel of the little book.

***

With a new tin from the Commonwealth Bank, Alice begins searching for tray-bits in one of the twin tubs of the washing machine, and in her father's pockets. She takes soft drink bottles back to the shop, runs errands for Betty Parker and Mr Miles at Number Twenty-four. On her bed, she sorts through the mound of cash like Scrooge McDuck in his money-bin. When the tin is full, Alice passes it to Gran to bank. She doesn't think about her skinny chest, while she bounces Gran's aching body on the bedsprings, nattering on and on, turning the pages of the little blue book.

***

It's Christmas and with some help from mum, Gran cooks a rich boiled-cherry pudding. 'It's loaded,' she says, carrying it to the table.

'How come you got the biggest slice?' asks Jimmy.

Alice parts the cake with her fork, watching Gran's face. 'Well, I'll have the hardest time looking for the money then, won't I?'

The family pick at their food, as Alice breaks the silence. 'Oh, no! I got the button.'

'Fooled again,' says Jimmy, laughing and clutching his stomach.

Altering a lumpy load in her cheeks, Alice spits out a combination of fruit and custard on her plate. 'I think it's a two shilling piece. Ha, ha. I've got more than you, dillbrain.'

'I've got one and six. So how much have you got now?'

'This year it's the biggest score ever. Three *whole* shillings.'

Gran clears the table, while Alice scrapes the coins with a knife. She's recounting, noticing that she has two shillings more than her brother. And while Jimmy never notices what women do together, Alice catches her grandmother, smirking at the kitchen sink, drawing what looked like a one-pound into the dusty windowpane.

***

Somewhere through the late hours, while lying back on her crossed arms, Alice hears the shuffling of cards. Sometimes, the women play for matches or small coins. Straining her ears she hears Gran grumbling, her mother protesting about cheating. On one occasion, Alice wonders why a whole game has gone quiet. Muffled words sound like 'Gran's oyster'.

Alice likes sitting at the edges of her grandmother's body, waiting for a hand to come down in a cuddle or a kiss on the cheek. She's ten next birthday so she doesn't get this kind of attention anymore. Sometimes Gran gets cranky and yells when she bounces on her bed, or pulls her knitting needles. Despite the grumbles, the old woman shuffling a daily path back to bed, Alice props herself up on pillows next to Gran, writing her school compositions.

For a long time, Alice doesn't notice the preserving pots raftered in the shed, or hear the sad whispers at night. She can only take Gran a cup of tea, sit and comb her hair. Sometimes, they go over the photographs in the tin, the growing columns in her bank book. On occasions, Alice shows her a sketchbook full of dinosaurs, a big picture of Notre Dame, and Big Ben. Her latest is Grandpa fishing in the bay, circling another boat in front of Gran from a figure eight. Closing the book, Alice pats Gran's hair, telling her that it's too tight. That's why she's got a headache.

In the next few weeks, Alice plays quietly on her own, caving herself inside the wardrobe with blankets, or selling plants in her fernery shop. Under the tankstand, she arranges brick shelves, setting up her posters and coloured pencils. When it rains, she sits beside the warm copper, blackening the cement floor with bits of charcoal. Although she gets into trouble, the laundry is where she stores her paint pots and shells.

The kitchen is the best place. A double window, overlooking the driveway and bushes, frames the daily walk of neighbours along Carramar Road. The corner stool has the right outlook to catch the weary world of Betty Parker, or René descending the doctor's steps. When the Vickerays bring two-day old chips, Alice divides them into equal paper portions, and when old Milesy leaves Readers' Digests, comics and books, she senses charity working through glass. This drifting caressing world is so comfortable, she likes swaying in and out from school, leaning against the sink, milk in hand, watching the women's mouths taking in gulps of air. Wiping away tears, and shrieking with the pain of belly laughter, they finally allow Alice to ask 'what? Tell me. What?'

'Betty... Betty Parker,' puffs her mother uncontrollably, 'put carb soda all over a cake she gave us instead of icing sugar. We've just waved goodbye at the window. She wanted it back.'

'She's all in a dither,' says Edith.

The women convulse into hysterics.

While laughter streams into their eyelashes, and words drift through the house, Alice is on her bed, twiddling her ankles, turning the pages of Mickey courting Minnie. Her mother appears at the doorway, smirking. 'Alice. We want you to go to Manning's. We need some butter and eggs. Your grandmother and I are going to make a – ha! Oh, dear, oh dear. A cake.'

Back on her bed in Jimmy's dressing gown, Alice can't be bothered reading her story for homework. She wants to go back in the kitchen, listen to Gran's stories about Alf Manning, his deafness, mixing half a dozen eggs up with axes. Tomatoes with potatoes. 'ALF!' they yell. 'HALF A DOZEN TOMATOES.' They're laughing, laughing so hard it goes under their breath, only to rise again on ditties about the neighbours. René's migraines returning since the handsome new doctor arrived in town, Betty Parker going on about Jesus when they already know what's to come; sucking and slurping back spit like Mr Pendlebury's false teeth.

Now she has to read some silly book. What is wrong with Dick Tracy? He gets up to some tricky adventures. *Robinson Crusoe's* interesting, but *Tales of Pennelope Strange?* What a dumb book. She hides it in the bushes between the shed and toilet. She'll tell Miss Cartwright she lost it. However, Alice expects that at the end of the week when Miss Cartwright asks two or three kids to read, one of them will be her.

'So, Alice Bennett,' says Miss Cartwright, on Friday. 'Stand up and tell the class what you thought of Pennelope Strange.'

'Not much.' Alice wiggles out of her chair, stands beside her desk and leans to the side, one hand resting near her ink-well. 'Oh, sorry. I forgot the book.'

'Well you must remember it. We all want to know the story, don't we class?'

Alice turns around and faces grinning faces. 'Uh, oh,' she says, looking at the floor. 'Okay then. Well, what happened was…um…well, Pennelope got lost see, and there was this other kid…'

Alice rambles, heightening and lowering her voice; turning now and again to her classmates. She describes a little girl (much like herself) inside a dark wood, tripping along dense paths, swirling and dancing, ducking dark shadows and shapes, until a tree turns into a monster. She is scaring herself with her own fairytale.

After ten minutes, Miss Cartwright holds one hand in the air. 'Stop!' she says 'Alice, that's nothing like the *Tales of Pennelope Strange*. You didn't read it, did you? I like your story, but sit down young lady. Next time read the book I have given you.'

Outside, it takes several minutes for Alice's face to cool and relax her scrunched face after grimacing at every kid in her class.

***

Harvest Festival arrives, and Gran zigzags the final trim on Alice's Sunday school frock. It has taken her two weeks to make, often grumbling and cursing the buttonhole machine. But Alice is proud at church, people queuing with preserves, jams and seeds; everyone smiling at her, crammed into the choir platform with other children, hymn book in hand, her taffeta and printed organdy overlay making her feel like an apricot rose. After comments about her beautiful dress, Alice delivers the same response, *My Gran made it.* But when the festivities are over she races up the lane, pelting the dress under the laundry tap, lathering the Creaming Soda's aerial spray with her tears. She can hear her mother's voice, 'Alice, come here!' Her raised hand under the large cherry blotch.

'Don't worry,' says Edith. 'It was a party. She couldn't help it. I can sew a pocket over the stain.'

Leaning back on the laundry door, Alice can't explain the rush and thump inside her chest, Grandma saving her from a smack, the dress from the ragbag.

Alice knows she is like her grandmother, kind and thoughtful, with soft grey-blue eyes. Both love shopping, Alice at the lolley counter, Edith at Paddy's Markets in Sydney. One Friday, the moon was out when Gran arrived home, her old suitcase and umbrella placed eagerly on the cane lounge, locks snapped, newspaper unwrapped. *Open Sesame!* Laughter. The women getting ideas with skeins of wool, materials, cottons, bias binding, and lace. Gran told stories about flat-faced boys holding up crocodile handbags with matching shoes, Italian fishmongers screaming over their cardboard tags and ice.

The next morning, the women measure each other, their sleeves touching, the intended garment held close. The tape is stretched one way, then another. *No, move it a bit. Try it against the grain.* Alice imitates Gran cutting through the material, pulling the cotton edges from the brown paper pattern. *All you have to remember when buying material or making a dress for yourself Petal, it's twice the width and double the length.*

With their voices deliberately bright, Gran and mum discuss dress sizes and big bottoms.

'We're all pear-shaped in this family,' says Gran.

'Child-bearing hips, Alice,' her mother continues. 'You'll have them, too.'

'But I don't want a big wobbly bottom.'

'Not much you can do about that, Love. It's already planned.'

Alice watches the women closely, draping floral prints, their nylon frocks sparking with electricity. She thinks about the shelf of their hips, her mum's dip at the waist, a rumpy curve to carry Kevin, the washing or ironing basket. She unfolds her notepad, runs a pencil down the page into two round hips. She can see the strength in her mother's legs like pillars. She imagines that 'child-bearing' must be like Samson in the Old Testament, pushing the stone blocks of a large temple apart with his bare hands. She couldn't think of anything more heroic than that.

'How's your knitting coming along, Petal?' asks Edith.

'Want me to get it?'

Alice holds a large piece of cardboard in front of Gran. Various colours of a thin scarf lean skywards towards tufts of cotton wool.

'Oh, my Lord,' says Edith, running a finger through the curling stitches. 'What have you gone and done?'

'It's Jacob's ladder to heaven,' says Alice, proudly pointing to her two glued wings as angels. 'Grandma, later on, could I please make something on the sewing machine?'

'Oh, I don't know about that. Goodness knows what you might do to it.'

'I promise I won't break it.'

From her bits and pieces, Edith wraps a yard of blue cotton around Alice. 'This is something you can make yourself.'

Swinging the material over the kitchen table like a cape, Edith lets Alice use the big scissors while she presses her fingers on the pinned pattern.

At the machine, Alice can feel the brush of her grandmother's stockinged feet. Although her legs aren't long enough to reach, she senses the rhythm and vibration of the treadle, the back and left foot rocking.

Alice copies and mouths the clattering drone of the Singer, pumping her feet into two little mounds under the quilt. She hears her parents whispering again, talking late into the night in their bedroom. Grandma isn't eating. She's at the doctor's; being sent to Sydney for tests, something growing like clover inside her body is giving her indigestion. Alice draws the serpent from the Garden of Eden snaking around Gran's body. She is alone on the back step. Edith is propped up in bed refusing trays of meals, lifting only the soup bowl.

The family is tired and sullen. For days, Alice hears muffled voices in the lounge room. Something about reading a will, getting the house and the furniture. Two weeks after her grandmother's funeral the Duchess and King arrive from the Eastern Suburbs and argue about the sewing machine. 'I'm not parting with it. You never came the whole time she was sick. Now you only want what you can get.' Alice listens to her mother's heightened tears, her dad telling them to 'piss off'.

Watching coats fly down the path, Alice is in the kitchen with her dad pouring himself a beer. Jimmy is teaching Kevin Draughts on the lounge room floor. Her mum is folding away the washing. 'They can have her diamond ring, for all I care. I never want to lay eyes on them, ever again. Good riddance!'

Alice pulses blue material under her fingers, pulls out the machine's two threads and plucks the cotton with the scissors. 'I've almost finished the neck. I bet Gran would have said my scrunched lace was beaut.' Alice holds her right hand on the wheel. 'Mum, what's going to happen to the suitcase with my bankbook in?' Edna pushes the door open, and holding a bundle of cardigans in her hand, pats the bed for Alice to come and sit. She runs her fingers over her hair. 'You're going to have your grandmother's room from now on. Don't worry, Love, about the bankbook, the money's still yours and I'll leave the empty suitcase for you under the bed. Your grandmother would have liked that.'

'Mum, could I just hold the little book one more time?'

The Colour of Hush

Memo 5:   *Sweet twelve and half & never been kissed.*

Gran's stories have disappeared along with her life. Alice doesn't feel like working the sewing machine, so she climbs over the next-door's fence. She likes counting the rocks in the stone path that lead to the laneway, or collecting odd specimens of rope, fishing line, or a plastic bucket left over by holidaymakers. Once she found a pair of thongs that flapped loudly on the concrete.

Spread out in the sparse Buffalo grass, Alice designs little pathways with pebbles, twigs and leaves like a miniature Brownie campsite. During the Christmas holidays, she paints rainbows on every page of her Disney colour-in book. With her new sixty-four paint-set, the Plaster of Paris moulds shine with detail and glaze. Standing back and casting her blue eyes over Donald,

Minnie, Goofy, Daisy and Mickey Alice pretends they are part of the St. George football team.

***

One day during the holidays, Alice asks to climb the tree house that Jimmy and his mate Brian have built in the laneway. The cubby has a door, a tin roof and a platform made from dad's hardwood planks from the back of the shed. They've even nailed ladder-boards up the trunk. But the Smart Alecs are on the deck, yelling, 'Bugger off, Alice! No girls are allowed!'

'Up yours then! I've got something better to do.'

With the sun sending intermittent silver rays through the backyard trees, each day Alice heads for the coolness of the shade and a stack of bottles piled along the Chin's fence-line. She rolls some with her foot, letting the stench of fermented hops leak away. Others dangle wet and sticky labels. She picks out several pint bottles, bearing up the milk sludge to eye-level, wiping the dirt with her hands, clanging the cleaner ones down the path to the back veranda and tank-stand. She can hear the far-off drone of motorboats and likes the way the glass mirrors her big nose and cheeks, the flapping clothesline in the background. She glances at Kevin in his sandpit, making two lane highways with his tip-truck.

Alice's mother, juggling her golf clubs and buggy into the Beetle, yells from underneath the boot. 'Alice! Don't forget to pay the baker. I've left the money in the basket.'

She nods, and in the midday heat decides to move her bottles to the cooler westerly face of the tank. She floods the ground with the open tap, sluicing out the sandy dregs before topping up the water.

Holding her stomach tight, shaking, wiping and stacking bottles, Alice nearly forgets to breathe. Mesmerized by the swatches of colour, the changing shades underneath her paintbrush, she doesn't hear the two boys coughing and backslapping each other behind the outhouse, nor does she catch a faint whiff of their rolled tobacco. She is standing on a crate, lifting the brush, dripping a mass of yellow, red or green goop into the bottles, swirling the water, then standing back admiring her work. There are moments when the bottles resemble Manning's soft drink stand, Lemon, Lime, Raspberry and Cola.

Alice doesn't notice the shadows moving across the tall rye grass, her mother unloading the golf buggy, hosing the car, Kevin and the dog running under the spray. She conducts an orchestra on glass, discovering different sounds in the varying heights of water. If she taps the rims, a high note. On the grooves, a low thud. She listens to the pinging sounds of the tank's corrugations cracking in the sun, and hits the tank-stand's wooden ledge continuing up the rungs of metal.

The melody heightens along with a familiar voice at the fence. 'They want us at the flat for a minute,' calls Heather.

Alice squints into the afternoon glare. 'Which drink do you want to buy, Heather? I've got Orange, Lemon or Strawberry Cola.'

'Alice, the boys want us to play at my place. If we come, they'll let us climb their tree-house.'

'But I don't want to. I'm playing with my bottles.'

'Just leave them. They'll be here when you get back.'

'Do we get to join their club?'

'Soon as we've done what they want.'

The girls walk through the Chin's front yard, heading towards Carramar Road, Alice wiping her paint stained fingers on her red jeans. 'What do they want this time?'

'I don't know, but we'll be the only girls allowed in the cubby. They don't want Judith because she's a bossy-boots.'

When they turn the corner, the boys are skylarking on Heather's lawn. The house on the high side of the street has a large portico, trailing geraniums, and the name *Emmanuel* above the door. The dark house is a portal to games of Ali Baba, surprises in large wardrobes, hide and seek. After school the girls switch the piano over to the Pianola, rolling scrolls of honky-tonk, Winifred Atwell ghosting the ivory keys. Mostly they drag out the dolls, Snakes and Ladders, or Chinese Checkers. Alice likes the way her sandshoes rippled like sticky gum over the kitchen's soft cherry lino. The larder is full of cream biscuits, Saos, cheese and Vegemite, and the backyard has a swing amongst orange, mandarin and loquat trees. Mr Randall owns two vintage cars. The girls often sit in the dark green M.G. pretending to be Mole and Badger from *Wind in the Willows*. The Randall's are hardly ever home. René is either at the doctor's or choral practice, and Heather's father works double shifts at the Kariong Boys' Home.

Alice thinks about the bottles sitting on the tank-stand and hopes they won't discolour or smell. For a moment she imagines old Miles' ginger cat smashing them on the concrete, or holiday arrivals tossing them out.

On an upper level to the road, the boys are karate chopping the spaces between the Randall's pickets. When the girls open the gate, they roll around each other like balls in a pinwheel. Jimmy struggles for air, while Brian hooks him in a strangle hold, bending and moving knees towards the garden. Alice finds she's been tricked. 'You boys are stupid.'

Looking at her, they collapse into a box hedge, four feet and arms lying belly up. Until they spring up facing one another, hands held out flipper-like. They're pumped and sweaty, prodding, corking knees and thighs. Brian whirls Jimmy around, hugging him into his stomach. Facing the same direction, Brian's right foot locks into Jimmy's soft thigh, heaving him onto the ground. With begging hands in the air, Jimmy stands in front of the girls. Brian's flushed face matching the irritation in Alice's eyes.

When they enter the back rooms of an outside flat, Heather cups her hand and giggles into Alice's ear. 'They want a root,' she says, flashing her eyes boldly towards Jimmy.

'You know what rooting is, don't you?'

'Yep,' says Alice, looking puzzled over Heather's shoulder at Brian, his head bent to the floor. She gazes at him, moving her eyes rhythmically over his body, until they catch a quick glance from his.

'Jimmy and I are going to do it in my bedroom. You and Brian can go in there,' says Heather, holding back doorway beads on an old iron bed in the corner.

Alice is alone with a boy she grew up with. They attended Sunday school together with Jimmy. She feels herself drawn along by Brian's sticky hands. She has a delicate sense that he must like her, so she allows his tickling fingers to find their way inside the elastic of her undies. She is silent the whole time, stretching her bare legs like anchors into the shell-like pattern of the bed quilt. He tugs at his shorts and then presses his stomach into the warmth of hers. She likes the way their bare skin touch, his hand turning her head to kiss her beneath the eyes, but suddenly she shifts higher on the pillow and his forehead bumps the bridge of her nose. He holds her face while his thin lips smack into her mouth. It lasts so long Alice can't breathe. Then he's telling her, 'I'm glad you're not wearing lipstick yet. I hate lipstick.'

Brian no longer has a childish voice, he moans and groans like one of Tarzan's jungle animals. He presses hard against her, bumping wildly in the air as if the veins in his arms are about to burst. He is wild and out of control. Alice lies still, thinking about the dogs she's seen in the street. She likens Brian's actions like a male dog doing all the work. She wonders if the soldier crabs that carried one another on their backs are rooting as well. Brian pokes her with his fingers, turning the little mound of flesh in and out, picking a point between her legs where he wants to wade deeper with his dick. She hears Heather's girlish giggle on the back steps, hears the drag of matches. Her brother and her friend have done it, she thinks, and now Jimmy is letting Heather smoke his cigarettes. He thinks he's so smart, like a cool Humphrey Bogart.

Brian continues on and on, mooning over her, swooning and swaying, looking northward into the window, then back again, pushing his tongue into her mouth. His bottom rocks and his thighs circle and probe. Alice lets the sensation wash over her as if the tossed bed is a tangle of seaweed. She is struggling, gripped like a trawled fish. When he breathes out little grunts and puffs of air, she thinks of him caught in a rip, legs cramping in a full roll of surf. Then reaching the shallows, he raises his stringy body up and moans as if coming out of the waves, exhilarated that he hasn't drowned.

When he rolls from her, Alice believes that Brian must love her. She can't remember the last time anyone in the family has kissed her like that or held her so tenderly.

Brian tells her, he's good at French kissing. Images of her Sunday school drift in front of her, the mental picture of Mr Pendlebury in the pulpit, his whispering voice hissing on and on about sin and damnation. She sees her neighbour's lounge room; Betty Parker's wall print showing heaven and hell, Christ walking with the lions. Now here she is on another path, heading towards the gambling houses, where the corseted ladies sit at bar counters, where the fiery furnace entices sinners. He must love me, she thinks. Maybe he's just being nice because she didn't have any tits. Alice wanders around the room, rambling. 'I can't find my pants, have you seen them? My other sandal is somewhere. When is your mother coming home? Don't worry about the cubby. It's dumb!' But her questions are met with a piqued silence, as if her raw flesh, the kissing and fondling of her fanny has suddenly become the lost part of a Chinese whisper.

She scowls and furrows her forehead at Brian. Has he forgotten she is there?

He shrugs his shoulders in front of the bureau mirror, flicking out a comb from his top pocket, peaking black hair into a Tony Curtis ducktail. All the smiles and niceties have disappeared.

'So, it's a big joke?'

Alice runs out the door, past Jimmy and Heather on the steps. She flings herself through the back gate, slamming it shut with her shoulder. Tiptoeing past Mr Gettoes spraying his tomato plants, she skirts Mannings' double garage, halting for a moment to slam the tree-house rope hard against the laddered steps. She moves quickly through the Chin's wire fence, and crouches near the Zamias listening for any noise of holiday arrivals. Satisfied the house is empty, she settles herself inside the double toilet, cupping her face, digging her elbows into the tops of her legs.

She can hear the boys in the laneway, calling to her. They're pitching their voices into the air. 'She can have a free tour of the cubby. She can use the cubby whenever she likes.'

Alice remains in the toilet block in silence, her undies caught in a figure eight at her ankles. She hears Brian talking to Jimmy. 'What if she tells?'

'No, she won't. I know her.'

'She's not home, Jimmy!' yells Heather from the back porch. 'Your mum says she's with you.'

Just a few yards away at the back gate, Alice can hear the boys discussing the Rendezvous or is it the beach? She doesn't dare move or pull on her panties just in case they hear the squeak of the lid, or her sandals on sand.

'She's probably sulking somewhere in a boat,' says Heather.

When the afternoon continues to spread its country silence, Alice wiggles up her panties, washes her hands at the little basin and leaves the outhouse. The sky darkens under cloud, and in the two hours while she's been away from the tankstand the thick paint has bottomed in her glass bottles. She notices the split colours, how the water has turned a milky yellow or pink on top. She wonders what might happen if she puts all the dark shades inside the bottles. Would the rich reds or green stay at the bottom while the inky colour float to the top? She opens the paint tin, oven-hot in the harsh sun. Some of the colours have run, the blues and yellows melting into a variegated-green slurry. She hasn't used the charcoal, grey or black. They're still hard little rectangles. She scrapes a small amount of water into them, and wiping the slush from the edges with a hanky, gouges deep holes with her paintbrush.

The grass whispers behind her. She doesn't pay attention to the ginger cat slinking under the house, a lizard sauntering the piebald stump or ants building tiny moon-craters in the broken concrete. The dog, tugging at the fence and running back and forth along the chicken wire, annoys her. 'Go away, Princey,' Alice shouts. 'Go play with your ball somewhere else, you stupid dog!'

The nature of things no longer interests Alice. She wants to ruin the perfect rainbow colours, so she drips black sludge into each bottle. 'It's just stupid to think you'd stay the same. Now you're black, black, black!'

Bent over the stump, she splashes a sooty paste across the surface of her paint-tin, turning every pristine square to the colour of night. She doesn't hear the jingle of Heather's bicycle, as she fills the bottles with black sand.

'We were looking for you,' says Heather.

'I don't care about the cubby,' she says, defiantly.

'Look, Alice, it's just like playing doctors and nurses. Anyway, Brian wants to talk to you.'

'What for? '

'Oh, come on! Come back. We all want to have a smoke.'

'Did you do the drawback?'

'I tried, but Jimmy's going to show me how to blow smoke rings. Come on, please! I don't want to be the only girl.'

Heather opens a space on the fence with her shoe, pressing the bottom rung of the wire, urging Alice through the opening stretched by her hands and feet. Alice looks back at the black stains on the bleached timber slats. A kind of gravity pulls her along. She'd liked the kissing part, but Heather just laughed about boys' smelly armpits, turning the conversation to dark red lipstick and her new trainer bra. Alice can only wonder about the rubbing motion Brian made between her legs, his sweaty face locked in little clicks, the pearl drops squeezed out and onto her belly.

Helen Hagemann

Part II

The Freckled Gang

Memo 6:   *School days are the best days of your life.*

Another good summer passes. Alice's father packs his tools and ladders in the old Austin and leaves for the country, exhaust fumes puffing bales of smoke in all directions along Ridge Street. The boys in town have gone their separate ways; Rupert Manning joining the army, Brian travelling to Asquith in his Roller Blind van.

Heather and Alice stand defiant in the laneway, watching Manning's station wagon backing out of the garage. Judith's arm trails a loose white sleeve and a piece of paper out the window. 'Here Heather, show it to Alice.'

Alf Manning executes a three-point turn, closely shaving the old gum tree.

'Oops,' says Judith, laughing, ducking her head back into the car.

'I don't know why she's so happy. She has to sleep with about fifty girls. What's the note say?'

'It's her school address and telephone number. She wants us to ring her when she's settled, and *not* to forget her.'

The both girls wave goodbye, yelling in unison to the car horn. 'See you later, alligator!'

'Cripes they're snobs.'

'You're still going to visit me after school, aren't you, Alice?'

'Yeah, I'm still going to eat your chocolate crackles, dummy!'

Alice walks with Heather back to her gate in silence. Things won't be the same. No more neighbourhood kids playing in the backyard. No cubby and definitely no smoking. Turning thirteen isn't the grand rosy moment she expects, especially with Judith attending a prison school.

'We'll see Judith when she comes home on holidays,' says Heather.

'Yeah, but now it's a bit like that old Sunday school hymn, *you in your small corner, and I in mine.*'

Monday morning and the jitters arrive. Jimmy gives Alice a quick lesson in knotting her school tie. Her head streams with lists: exercise books, textbooks, ruler, fountain pen, bus timetable, don't forget the Saos in the fridge, sharpener, Jimmy's wooden pencil case, a few comics. Oh, and just in case it arrives in the middle of PT, a sanitary bag with a woman's essentials.

Packing her Globite, she looks down at something worse than the lino's pattern of scars. Jimmy's boots. Just like her brother's bike, another secondhand antique. Her first day at high school and she has to clod-hop around in cracked leather uppers. Plus there's a hole the size of a two-shilling piece under the right foot where her mother hurriedly glued a piece of cardboard. The left one is worn thin, but she still feels the cool veranda boards against her socks. It would be another six weeks before her dad returns from Gunnedah with his shoebox of wages. There were only two good things that were certain today at Wiseman High School. Wendy Ballantine and Bronwyn Hobbs. The girls from Temple Bay Primary might just help her get over the sulks.

At Manning's bus stop Alice's dreaming begins. She thinks she sees Heather at the Randall's gate, but it's Margaret, her sister, getting the mail. Miss Parker plods slowly up Ridge Street. Alice notices her hair has been chopped back since her father died. Standing there waiting, no one greets Betty. About five people are engrossed in their thoughts. Alice's mind is on the day her Wiseman High School letter came, everyone cuddling, jumping ring-a-rosy. Since then except for the shoes, her face has a slight happy groove. She doesn't dare show too much excitement in front of Heather. Heather only ever liked music, and was at the bottom of sixth class. With all her yellow jaundice and hepatitis sick days from school, she was destined to get the rowdies at Green Point High.

Alice is relieved she isn't going to Green Point, especially since the bodgies and widgies from the Rendezvous attend that high school. She can't stand them in the café, always bumping into her snooker cue, or turning the jukebox key over to Elvis just when she'd paid for *Peggy Sue* and *Chantilly Lace*, Charlene knocking her elbow, spilling her milkshake. As she enters the skating rink every Saturday the same Brando look-alikes blocking the turnstile, hunching leather jackets over their shoulders like they're scratching some sort of itch. Toughies!

Chewing fingernails and spitting them out, like it's their teacher. Alice hears that Skinner's spending twelve months in the Kariong Boys' Home, some of his mates too, for stealing and arson. Now she's free from their farts on the bus, and the intimidating, noisy collapse of numb-chuckers, or a deliberate thud of knuckle-dusters on counter tops. No use feeling like a collapsed marshmallow, she aims to visit Heather on weekends, Judith during boarding school holidays. Perhaps, there's the chance of attending the football together.

Wiseman High looms as a brownstone building with plenty of English and History. If she's quiet and hardworking, she can easily ignore pimply boys who nick things from Woolworths and act half their age.

Alice can't pretend that she'll miss the shoulder height of her friend. Since childhood, she has depended on Heather, saying goodbye every afternoon at her gate feeling like the pink layer in a licorice allsorts, and Heather the whole lolly bag.

Heather's musical house is where Alice learnt everything, even to be wary of her brother Brian. Most of the time he is never there, but the bedroom memory remains. And when he walks in, watching them at the Pianola, his telepathic eyes send a violent, searing look of disgust as if he never had it off with a kid, let alone responsible for her deflowering. Heather makes their encounter worse, flapping her tongue and saying things like, 'Are you two going in to bat?' Alice sighs, turns, and tells Heather to 'dry up!'

On the Green Point platform there's some segregation, but for the most part the boys hang around Bronwyn Hobbs. Since moving from Bankstown last year, Alice has only known her for six months. Someone shouts out 'Alligator!' Now she catches Alice coming down the bridge steps. Limbering up for a run with her mouth in the shape of a scream, she hugs Wendy Ballantine in a gale forced head wind. Alice can see why the boys are hovering. She has these huge tits that lift her box pleats and front hemline.

Alice follows Bronwyn and Wendy into the Ladies. They flutter out their hair and hoist up their shiny black shoes on the bench. They got them in Sydney, both the same; mum did too, in Anthony Hordens. She keeps hers wedged into the floor tiles. The train toots down the track and everyone scatters. Most of the boys still mad-eyed and high on holiday camping quickly sink tickets into pockets. Alice is on a jealous path to the front of the platform. Just a little bit annoyed. Then she's more peeved in the carriage when Dennis Lester dribbles diamonds of spit on her half-read *Tom and Jerry*. Everyone laughs in spasms like a *Looney* tune, a mimicking free-for-all.

After the boys turn seats into tables, they're ready to smoke. Alice knows they're on a mission, anything other than going to school. Marlboro cigarettes and matches glow. But Alice in her unflattering shoes heads for the end seat, with Wendy joining her after an asthma attack. She tells the girls she has to prove herself at school. She's on trial. She doesn't want to let down the family. 'I got here thanks to Jimmy's top school report.'

'Is he some sort of brain?' asks Bronwyn.

'Yeah, but I want to show Mum and Dad I'm just as clever. He's only in the B Class, and I'm doing French and Latin. Don't know how I'm going to go with Geometry and Algebra though, I hate Maths.'

Interwoven in a melee of commuters, in crinkled shirts and slung blazers, like a future classroom of sorts, the whole shebang alights the train. They leave fingerprints, ash and smoke in the carriage, orange pulp on poster walls, and join a single queue through the Wiseman ticket gate in a company of briefcases and papers. Then there's a quiet meander up the hill.

Halfway up Mann Street, Alice feels the cardboard double-shake inside her shoe. At the end of the straggling bunch, she stops to remove the offending piece, throwing it in the bush. Later in the afternoon, after a blistered walk to the train, she practises telling her mother over and over that she isn't going back to school until they shop either in Wiseman, in DJ's or anywhere, she doesn't care where, but she needs to have a new pair of shiny black, lace-up Batas.

Alice's Typewriter

Memo 7:   *Penny wise, pound sure.*

Green Point, Temple Bay and the ocean beach are Alice's playground; a type of cosmos, a pivotal arm of watercourses, inlets, foothills, and peninsula. On the journey to school, the train line divides Temple Bay into mangroves and rugged national park to the west, the town-site and jetty baths to the east. Along the tracks, the semaphore points north to Glenrock, Point Clare, the Wiseman baths, and the Regal Theatre. South is Central Station, the Royal Show, visits to cousins in Balgowlah, the ocean aquarium and the Manly fun pier.

Alice spends the last few hours of her school life dumping reminders of a tough time; cat fights, belligerent boys and her pinching Woolies school shoes. Inside a rusty forty-four gallon drum, third-year textbooks and exercise books spark like a traveling fuse, floating ash as cast-off memories.

She gets the wobbles afterwards, burning her best History books. When she looks in the mirror, a sooty face returns. A piece of charcoal paper stuck on a strand of her hair sends her laughing up the path. She lifts her middle finger up in the air. It has the same effect.

Often at the skating rink, Alice stomps the wooden floor after hearing hilarious 'elephant' and 'fat' jokes. In the spitting seed contests, she blows out more watermelon than pips. A continuous roll on the buffalo grass brings a pain like a belly ache. Her brothers fail to see the funny side. 'You're as mad as a two-bob watch, Alice. You'd laugh at anything. Here laugh at this!' Then they'd march up the path towards the shed, hawking and fluffing elbows like barnyard animals. But their scrawny peg legs and body bent over like constipated ducks only reminds Alice how stupid boys are. She doesn't care. She's passed with all "B's" except for Latin. None of their banter deflates her now. She's as happy as Tarzan on a bunch of good vines.

No sooner after folding the newspaper on her great Intermediate results, she waits with her mother in the Bank of New South Wales in Wiseman. Later, cranking the handle of an adding machine in the Green Point branch. Her laughter continues between chatting to boys in the Commonwealth Bank on exchanges, getting the manager's lunch at the cake shop, then later at night helping her mother string the beans.

In her first six months as office junior, Alice only dreams of one thing. It occupies a window in the Optometrist's next door. Apart from the plastic stands of spectacle frames, an odd assortment of Polaroids, two typewriters have 'For Sale' signs propped in the middle of the keys. Left of the large Remington, a nameplate on a blue portable spells the word "Hermes". Alice strokes the keys with invisible fingers, positioning the base, re-arranging cosmetics on her wardrobe desk. She pretends to type a letter until she notices the price tag. Forty-eight dollars! The amount is more than she earns in a week! Maybe she has to rob a bank to buy it. But not Mr. Pringle's.

Arriving home from a mate's after school, Kevin suggests she gets a second job. At the dinner table, Jimmy will lend her the money but wants twenty percent interest.

'Why, you'll just have to save, love.'

'But Mum, by the time I bank enough money, Mr Cooper would probably have sold it. It'll take me twenty years. What if I don't pay board?'

'No!'

'Mum, it won't be for long.'

'No, you shouldn't have emptied your passbook, and besides you eat too much.'

All through the meal they talk about the bank; Jimmy treading his old path of teasing Alice about Mr. Pringle, the Manager and Friar Tuck, the Accountant. Alice bristles, kicking Jimmy under the table. In retaliation he flicks sugar. When Alice squeezes out a handful, the bowl topples, sending a snowy drift across the tablecloth.

'Cut it out, you two.' Their father covers his hand over his empty beer glass, his third trip to the fridge beginning to show.

Alice watches him open another Toohey's at the sink. Today his guzzling appears to make the veins in his forehead swell. Both her mother and father chat on about his new partner, Ken Gallagher. Apparently Ken is a bit slow on the uptake. While her father stares at his beer, things keep buzzing around in the bottom of the glass. Like not getting his money, the unpaid bills, the biggest contract ever, 'fallen through'.

Alice remains at the table while her father works on a stack of paper, shuffling and re-shuffling correspondence, emptying a shoebox of cheque butts and deposit slips.

Business is starting to interest Alice, especially loans, mortgages, interest rates, savings and debentures. She quickly learns money is a necessary commodity, spending even more exciting, and saving, well, that's harder. But hell! Her dad's business is important and extra special. They can't have the phone disconnected. On the spread of her third piece of toast and jam, Alice is inquisitive about the awful gloom in the house. Can she help? She's learnt something about what to do if a person receives a dodgy bank cheque.

'Do you know his account then, Alice?'

'Yeah, I know Ray Hodges, Dad. Watch out, because Mr Pringle is bouncing his cheques all over the place. He's gone way over his overdraft limit. Plus he's on the black list.'

Alice's father produces a folded cheque from his wallet. Its edges are gritty and upturned. The silky red curls of Mr Pringle's hand writing shows, 'Present Again'.

'Well, what you have to do Dad is bank it again.'

'Just when a man's getting on top, I get a signed piece of rubber, bouncing around Temple Bay like a bloody kangaroo.'

'Mr Pringle might honour it, if he makes a deposit in the next couple of days.'

'He keeps telling Ken and me his government money's just around the corner. Well, I wouldn't mind betting he's spent it already.'

The eight hundred dollars owing could not be ignored. Alice knows her father is toeing a precarious scaffold. One slip with Hodges and he's never going to see his hard earned money. She knows little about his building company, but has witnessed Mr Pringle raising his voice the last time Hodges leaves his office after a long overdue appointment.

She wants to step out of the room, lie down; read a good book, anything than watching the years form on her father's face. Tomorrow, she plans on asking questions, pushing herself a little, for her old dad.

'You're a good girl, Darl,' he says, swaggering off to the shower.

Percy Cooper, the Optometrist, waits silently next to her at the front of his shop window. Alice practises her lunch hour vigil, eating a hot pie out of a paper bag, and typing imaginary letters to friends. She has inserted teal paper from the newsagents, with little bluebirds and berries swirled in the corner. Everything is blue to match the flash in her eyes moving fast along the carriage return of the smoky-blue typewriter.

Percy's white coat flaps in the breeze. 'Is there a pair of sunglasses you particularly like?'

'Oh, no! I'm just checking.'

'I see no reason why you shouldn't come inside and try on a few pairs.'

'It's the typewriter. But I can't afford it.'

'Hmm.' He looks at her with that amused shopkeeper's smile. 'Well, I see no reason why we couldn't work something out. Would you like to pay it off?'

She watches herself looking back at him in the window. Sensing the skill of the typist, her posture rigid, she is thrumming her typing school rhythm beneath her fingertips. Tap, tap, tap. ASDF, semi-colon LKJ. Up and back, and down again, ASDF, semi-colon, LKJ.

The following day after ripping her pay packet open, she splashes two one-dollar notes over the glass-top counter. Percy lifts the typewriter out of the window as if it's a delicate crystal vase, zips up the travelling case, buckling its tiny brass latch.

Tea is going to be late. No time to shell the peas or mash the potato, it will sit as the centerpiece on the dining room table. Case flung open. Caps locked. Embossed blue paper at the ready.

***

That year, no one in the Temple Bay receive their money from building a series of houses at Ocean Ridge, co-authored by Hodges & Co.; all except Bob Bennett and Ken Gallagher, B. & G. Plumbers.

Alice had entered Mr Pringle's office at ten o'clock every morning, waiting for him to handover the dishonoured cheques. That summer month when the bay boomed as a holiday and retirement village, you could have set your wristwatch to Alice's precision. Miss Giggle-Gerty Bennett having the fortitude to look out for Hodges in the foyer checked the teller's box, and surreptitiously flashed her eyes over the activity in his cheque account. When the ledger machine rocked a large sum of money into the credit column, Alice quickly rang her father to come in and deposit Hodges' cheque that Mr Pringle now inscribed 'Refer to Drawer'. Three days later, life and a gentle smile returned to her father's face when the cheque was cleared.

Leaning on the bridge rail over the veranda, Alice believes that their whole feathery garden of flowers is buzzing with applause. Already her father has consumed half-a-dozen beers, watching with amusement as her frown lifts when he finally says, 'I got that old bastard, Hodges.'

'You sure did, Dad.'

'I know it will get around town, but me and Ken will say we were just quick off the mark.'

'Don't tell them I work at the bank, though. Or I could lose my job.'

'Nah! Never. Mum's the word. I appreciate what you did.'

They both look out beyond the bridge into a backyard of rosellas and budgies, garage, tool shed and a purple trumpet vine that trails the outside toilet.

The back lane is her territory, a quick access to the main shops, attempts at driving the Beetle, and always listening to the sounds of her dad's vehicle coming home. The cheque has brought them closer together, and Alice wishes he might spend some time with her, have a milkshake in the Sea Breeze Café instead of several beers in his lounge room chair. She doubts he would ever go, since he has previously told her that *that café* houses a different species. Cockroaches.

Bob pulls a piece of paper from his trouser pocket. 'I've got another one,' he says.

The paper is folded and smeared with a brown skin of dirt. Alice's face drops. Just when she's helped at the bank, spending all that time worrying, the builder's money finally coming through, her dad is going to show her another piece of trouble.

'It's for you, Darl. From Ken and I, with thanks. It's only ten dollars, but it'll go a long way to help pay off your typewriter.'

***

The Bennett household relaxes in their good fortune. The telephone remains and Ray Hodges moves out of town with a little hocus-pocus from finger waving tradesmen. Alice hugs her father for several minutes around his neck the day her final receipt for the Hermes typewriter sits in her purse.

By the time she receives her transfer to the Pennant Hills branch, her father learns of every jerrybuilder and con-man in town, stating that from now on, the business is to keep their jobs small.

Once again at teatime, Jimmy dances his fingers over the sugar bowl.

'And by the way, Jimmy, Mr Pringle and Mr Tuck are very glad that Hodges left town, because...' Alice falters for a moment, her hand inching across the tablecloth. 'Not only did I get my transfer, but a promotion as well!' she shrills, tilting the sugar bowl over Jimmy's head.

Helen Hagemann

Magnet City Orbit

Memo 8:   *Country road, take me home, to the place where I belong.*

The countryside looms past her every morning on the train, the Macdonald River looking as still as bottled water. The river's surface, hazy in the morning, curls a light smoke into the hillsides. The shoals and creeks, collapsed shacks, idle houseboats beckon her beyond the river's edge. As the waterline travels with her, time moves to daylight dreams of exploring the North Shore, the Strathfield line to Central. Pennant Hills is a landscape of box trees and jacarandas. Alice imagines living there, a slow meander to work, or a short bus ride. She has thoughts of sleeping in, a house in an avenue of flowers, comforting her in five minutes after clock-off time.

Once, in the early days of commuting, fashionable stores along the Pacific highway enticed. The head-office

Christmas party was a wild affair, filled with the shenanigans of staff.

Every morning on the train, Alice chats to twins Irene and Veronica from the youth club. Pigeoned in a double seat, Alice clings to its wrought iron edge, swaying slightly, going over theories of why their last tennis night was cancelled. *Boys and too many pranks. They didn't put the net away. Left chocolate wrappers and Coca-Cola bottles on the court*, says the Council.

Alice knows that the girls are tired of managing the key, suffering the council's complaints. Like most twins, they do not dress the same, but have the same expressions. They look after one another, are Catholic, very religious, and wear silver crosses around their neck and in their ears.

When she first caught up with them on the train, bells rang alarmingly. Alice quickly learnt about their travel complaints. *You're lucky if two people leave the train at Green Point, and be careful of the mad scramble. Watch out for the drunks on the way home. Don't put your feet on the seat. Don't expect to sit down until Brooklyn.*

Three years and the city monotony begins to swamp Alice. She is tired of standing, swaying, crushed against seats; the overtime, repetitive jackhammers on the rails. Irene and Veronica continue to warn her about the freezing, biting westerly in autumn. The coldness of a bay blowing across Green Point's exposed platform. Her winter skin is covered in goose-bumps, slumping in the back door at nine. These are the things that Alice wants to strip from her mind. She is so sick of commuter boredom for four hours a day, she consults her horoscope, analyses her charts. She finds the answer in a six monthly forecast, and is quietly amused.

After three months of begging, she hears her friends' excuses. *Their parents won't approve. Not enough money. They'd miss mum and dad.* Alice tries to think positive, searching the morning stars for that slippery moment when their lives will change.

The next day, she boards the train singing, handing the girls a newspaper cutting. Veronica quickly folds it into her bag, she'll read it at work later. Irene, in a voice softer than a nun's, continues to talk about the same old topic of asking her boss for a raise.

The girls squint into the sun, their thoughts quiet as they look out the window. The whole idea submerges somewhere back in Horsefield Bay. Outside, screaming jets of air. Inside, Alice wonders is the subject suddenly obsolete? Is it like that moment when she went to midnight mass with Irene, and the swaying incense and bell ringing captivated? Or are these two philosophies at loggerheads? Perhaps, the wine and bread, the official sacraments are trying to dull the mystery of the stars? At this point in time, obviously a lull is occurring in the intense firmament. She needs more devotion. But hang on! She's electrically charged, has the fiery passion, powerful resources on which to draw, has a great deal of endurance, especially under difficult circumstances. She knows the Herald's rental page is an indication of change. At least, her book 'The Sun & Moon Signs Library' indicated upheaval. Scorpio powers *had* to endure. She's always endured this, this crowded compartment, daily side waltzing, coat hurl, the unsteady ebb and surge of line derailment, making her life late.

Alice shows the girls the zipper-like ladder on her stocking. Another pair gone! When the train relaxes into the station, the girls crane their heads around corners for an empty seat. Then providence intervenes. A workman getting out at Brooklyn, swinging his bag through the queue, clips the back of Veronica's head. She pauses for a moment, then opens her cogent tongue. 'I'm so sick of these morons,' she offers loudly, 'barging past, checking out of *their* favourite seat every morning.' She continues on and on, until the men out-stare her, and with turned backs alight the carriage, their odorous bodies dribbling onto the platform. As the train gathers itself into a membrane of sidling noises, moving from the platform, Irene says stiffly. 'They think they own the place. Who says it's reserved for them?'

'We can get away from these idiots. It's easy.' Alice hefts her workbag over her shoulder. 'If we get a flat on the northern line, it'll be close for all of us. Irene can change trains at Hornsby and be in Wahroonga in no time. How many stations is it, again?'

'Two.'

'See. Told you. It'll be better that this sardine tin.'

'Why not North Sydney? The place is full of flats.'

'Too far, Veronica. I reckon Strathfield.' Alice keeps talking while the train lumbers towards Asquith. The clatter and wheeze of metal is like the slow drag of her day. At this hour in Sydney, anyone is just wiggling a hand out of a quilt, hitting the alarm clock.

Announcing several rental properties in the *Sydney Morning Herald*, Alice nods anxiously, as the twins inspect the columns. They finger the pages, finding suburbs like Manly, North Sydney, Gladesville, Mosman, The Rocks. She listens quietly, nodding her head in agreement; contemplating the last zigzag through the countryside. She is so sick of the perverts and winos on the late night trains. Still feels uncomfortable about the last time rushing to the station after overtime. An old codger, leaning towards her, pointed out all the sexual innuendoes in his dirty *Post* magazine. When the carriage emptied, she had struggled to explain the halfwit to an elderly carpetbag woman who said in a whiney mosquito voice, 'Oh, he's one of *those*, is he?' And she couldn't say anything to passing guards while they whistled close to her hemline. Every time she thinks about the incident, she bristles.

Alice slings her body forward while the girls snatch another newspaper ad. Ushering them towards a window seat, she bends into their talk of borrowing a truck, hiring a television, emptying a shed of vinyl chairs, Formica table, and a maroon lounge. In the gritty atmosphere of the train, Alice doesn't care if her stilettos gouge zodiac symbols into the carriage's lino. The day suspends her in dream, in the clickety-clack of the Wynyard subway, surfacing at Circular Quay. Close to the gateway of harbour and bridge, three girls in red t-shirts contrast the day's white ferry wash. It's a football day. On the Manly Boardwalk, the twins wax lotion into their English skins. In a wrapped hula-girl beach towel, Alice reads the morning's horoscope again. *Just spin out Scorpio and throw yourself into a new challenge.* There's her future in front of her, a bombora of tanned male bodies, so thick, they're crowding the water.

***

The day before moving day, Alice jumps around her room, allowing herself to feel the joy in her head. Being Friday, she avoids the late hours of a monthly cash balance, and her planned trip to Sydney takes on a celebratory air. First, she'll go to Paddy's Markets, try on some red shoes, then wander around George Street or watch a film. She imagines getting back early, packing boxes, bags and emptying drawers, then settling with a good book.

From all her giddiness, she has to lean back against the headboard. Looking across at her wardrobe, her eyes meet the city girl in the mirror parting from the child in her room. That little girl at the beach, brown and skinny, spearing the water from boat decks, swimming hours in the channel, hiring a motorboat with her cousins. She is leaving Heather jumping off the sand dunes near the point her dad fishing from his boat past the channel. She is saying goodbye to anxious days of pimples and hankies stuffed in her bra. Being twenty and alone. Weekends of sleeping in, feeling sluggish and washed out, or sprawled half asleep on the beach. The enticing world of Sydney smells like a scent away. The silent knolls on the headland at home – a lifeless landscape. She can't think of any reason to stay.

Alice removes sandwiches and a frozen bottle of cordial from the fridge. She hears her mother stirring in the bedroom, telling her father to hurry, he's slept in. She carries a glass of milk and a bowl of cornflakes to her room and sits cross-legged in the middle of her bed.

'That you Alice?' her mother calls. 'You're a bit late for work, aren't you?'

'Not going.'

Alice looks up suddenly, her mother's protective hand on her shoulder. 'You all right?'

Yep, I'm going shopping in Sydney. I'll be back for tea. If the Bank rings, Mum, just tell them I'm sick.'

'Oh.'

She hears her mother nattering in the kitchen, 'She's acting funny this morning.'

Waiting, Alice prepares to answer her mother's doubts, and instead grumbles to herself. *I'm not acting funny. There's something I have to do.*

She hears her father talking. 'Oh, leave her alone, Ed. She knows what she's doing.'

Alice hurries over the platform steps, clopping her heels over the quartz stones at the southern end of the station. The first carriage is nearly empty. It feels oddly assertive to stretch her legs and bags across the double seat. The train sputters and slips out of Green Point. A ticket inspector motions at her shoulder to take her sandals off the seat, clips her ticket and disappears through the rattling doorway. She waits until he's out of sight, puts her feet back up and crunches into the icy cordial.

Clouds rumple over the passage of hills. Grasstrees sway from rocks above. Rows of wire-fenced cottages, mangroves and a swampy inlet recede to the right. On the hillside, a lone horse grazes frisking his black-honey flanks in the sun. When the train powers into the dark belly of rock and brick, it seems as if the haystack and stable fly into the mountain with her. In that first roar of wind, the train switching from day to night, she imagines tunneling her way out.

When her eyes adjust to the light, a hollow feeling of darkness remains. She looks out on the rows of oyster leases. When the train slows down at a river town, she wants to whack her heels hard into the seat. A heaviness settles over her, the memory.

Why did he have to use filthy language? She's too young to hear that, seeing a pulsing angry fist. Listening to a man's loose tongue loud and abrasive in the picturesque harbour; the slow ramble of the bay switching to a saga, like the action pages of a sinister comic book.

His fat face is there, reddening, the globe of his belly bobbing through seaweed. She hears the yelling. That's enough to quickly dive off his boat. She wants to take flight, like Daisy, send out an adrenalin of colour, the way waterfowl do, a tangle of low-tide seaweed inhibiting her rhythm. In the deep channel, she stops flailing her arms wildly, her body aching for a dumb need to rest. He's nosing the dinghy towards her, the outboard motor flooding the countryside with its sputtering cough. She hears his foul tongue slurring filth. He's there, closing in, as she scrambles up the sandbank. He cuts the engine, pushes the boat ashore and grabs her arms. Alice pulls away and climbs meekly into the boat.

'Are you going to call the Police?'

'I'm going to do more than that.'

'Where are you taking me?'

'Nowhere.'

'Leave me alone. I...I won't dive off your boat anymore.'

'You little slut, ripping my tarpaulin.'

'That wasn't me. It was rotted.'

He holds her captive now, the boat scudding from the sandbar, across the chop of deeper water. Alice's face is burning. She's a prisoner inside the menacing frames of a Phantom comic. The man is part of the scum of mutineers on a pirate ship, anchored around the point from the Heads. Diana has vanished somewhere into the tall grid of trees, captured or tied to a rock. Phantom is too busy wielding a sword against muggers off the coast of Martinique. Her only chance is to run, escape by water.

Alice scans the tips of the waves. A holiday cruiser shaded by foothills, motors through the deep harbour, passing the first channel marker. She jumps, her body pulled towards the boat. 'Watch out, there's a little girl in the water,' they call. The fisherman steers his dinghy alongside. The mutineer's out-numbered, four against one. He hesitates and in a mad fever churns the rudder in the opposite direction, navigating himself out of sight.

Hauled up by one man on board, and another beside the boat levering her out, Alice is water-logged and shivery. On shore, the men wrap a towel over her shoulders.

'She's all right,' says the Captain.

'We'll be off then, as long as you're okay. I bet you just want to get home. Two streets away, is it?'

'What'd she say, Harry?'

She says, 'the mutineer's gone.'

The men push away in their dinghy, telling her to take care. She hears them say 'nasty fright' and the word 'devil'. She thinks about the bongo drums. Of course, she can't hear them above the boat's sputtering engine. Rounding Snapper Road into the main street, she imagines that Devil and Phantom are asleep by now in their cave, tired out from all their fighting.

She is saved, escaping like Diana from the mutineer.

Her chenille bedspread rustles with boxes and paper, the middle of the bed looking like shredded tissue wings. Alice had enjoyed moments of the day, witnessing an unexpected kindness from the Sydney salesgirls and storekeepers. The pandemonium had been crazy, but handing over money felt good. Now relaxed and in her pyjamas, she removes sets of clothes from wire hangers, stacking them at the end of her bed.

'That you, Love?'

'Yeah, Mum. Come and have a look at what I bought.' Alice raises some strappy, red high-heels, matching bag, and cream stockings. She hugs a seersucker dress into her waist and wheels out a tube of lipstick. At the bottom of the paper, she uncovers a hinged book, the size of a postcard.

'It's a little book of thank-yous. Read the one by me.'

In the silence, Alice watches her mother move a finger across the thin line of her eyelid. 'Oh, that's lovely. You okay?'

'Yep. Just a little tired.'

'Did what you wanted to do, then?'

'I reckon I have.'

'I won't be around in the morning, Love. It's the important match, so good luck with everything. You'll be back before you know it.'

'I will, Mum, just for weekends.'

***

Alice walks around the twins' backyard and peers into the shed. Roller-skates, a ping pong table, a trolley load of National Geographics and encyclopedias, racks of dancing costumes, rest against the door. Veronica hauls a suitcase up to the driver. A salon hairdryer sits at the rear of the truck, its huge head hinting of future hairstyles and dances.

'There's no room on the truck for your stuff, Alice.'

'Not even one little corner?' she enquires. 'Hey, you won't need that old fan, there.'

'If we can't fit everything in, we'll just sell something,' returns Veronica. 'And we forgot to tell you, we're having the large bedroom at the front.'

'Hang on. I was hoping to get the bedroom with the filigree curtain.' Alice follows the girls back through the laundry. 'I wanted the... Doesn't seem fair, Irene! Veronica, why do I have to have the cracked window and broken lino?'

'Well, if I were you Alice, I'd ask the landlord to fix it.'

Alice coughs. *No, I will not, Veronica, thank you.*

The remaining space in the truck is taken up by a dressing table and four chairs. Alice hides as the door swings shut. Down the path, the driver and his mate check the backyard. The truck leaves slowly, disappearing up Spencer Street, the Young's aqua FJ following closely behind. For a moment Alice thinks, *Oh, to hell with it,* still recognising the delicious moments ahead: making house, hamburgers, parties, working closer to the bank away from the silent battle of her parents. A city life pulling her like a magnet with promises of new sky and cute male legs.

For some time, Alice is conscious of the changes in the house. Jimmy working in Tamworth, her mum and dad playing the pokies until late at the golf club. Kevin stays with his mates most of the time, although he doesn't leave home. The town is meaningless. All three girls want bright neon nights, a chance to catch rock bands, live shows and movies.

On previous weekends they caught taxis or double-decker buses around Sydney looking for the perfect pad. For a while they were at cross-purposes, Veronica discovering a high-rise in North Sydney, Irene wanting Pymble close to work, Alice falling for the rosewood Balmain suite. They soon settled for a two-storey in Stanmore instead of a North Sydney skyscraper. The house, a semi-detached terrace, offers the hardness and softness of a city view, front balcony and porch in flaky wrought iron, large rooms with high ceilings. It's not close to the bridge with harbour views, nor does it have embossed wallpaper or hall mirrors like the Balmain apartment, but at least commuting to Central, the Stadium, and Prince Alfred Park Ice-rink is a brief traipse down the hill to the station.

Robert Bennett is not in the Leagues Club or any other pub today. Instead, he's taking orders on the back veranda. Robert, better known to his friends at the golf club as Bob or Old Son organizes his daughter's furniture in the boss's Ford Falcon ute.

'Dad!' yells Alice. 'There's a basket of washing in the laundry, too. That's got to go in.'

Her father emerges from Alice's bedroom, muttering. 'I can't get the bloody base to collapse. Frigging thing won't move. Get me a chisel from the shed will ya, Darl?'

Alice runs back from the shed panting, hands on her hips. 'Dad! We were meant to leave an hour ago.'

Her father ignores her, pouring a glass of beer at the fridge. Alice tucks herself in behind the Singer, pulling and rewinding long strands of cotton, and tidying the pin drawer. She rolls a few pins and needles into a man-size hanky, placing them into a side pocket of her handbag. She wanders in and around small boxes, a chest of drawers, heavy tweed and winter coats hanging on the veranda. Under her arms, she trundles her tennis racket, golf bag and roller-skates down the steps. At the back of the tray, she carefully wraps her blankets and pillows in a plastic shower curtain. Meanwhile, Bob continues to bang expletives into the wire bed-base.

Alice stares out across the lawn, looking beyond the veranda to a house empty on weekends, pimply boys at the cinema and two dead relationships. Once, she got caught up with the local heartthrob from Woolworths. After six months, his heartbeat flapped over a new girl in town. She saw him, lined up with her at the Regal pictures, dressed in white socks and sports shirt. But first, they started the courting thing, car ride to Woodford every Sunday, hand-brake cuddle in the front seat, his hands going down to where she thought he'd be exciting. Instead, he just tuned the radio. Her mother prattled on, 'Ray this, Ray that. Doesn't he look like Robert Stack in *The Untouchables.*' But Alice likened him to his car, sporty on the outside, bland interior. He was just too deep. Then every Saturday night, as she slithered down into a snowy drift of bubbles, all she wanted to do was touch herself under the depth of quiet water.

Despite the powdery surface of the cement ute, Alice stays dressed in her latest black slim waistcoat, white seersucker blouse and black skirt. She looks quickly behind the bedroom door, under the bed, and pulls out two empty drawers from the built-in. Her face in the mirror reflects the puffy rims around her eyes. She can't bring herself to say goodbye to Princey. She can still see her mother on weekends, only if she's not playing Pennants at Everglades. Alice locks the door. 'Don't worry Gran, I'll be back in this room soon. I'll still take care of it.'

Alice listens to two magpies shrieking in the backyard. She is simply tired of waiting, and her stomach fluttering. She knows that the birds' squawk is an omen. If the twins scream at her about being late, she will have to speak up for herself.

Watching her father fix the ute, she thinks about his summer nights out late, the smells of his latest catch. The bay, he often states, is the biggest fish tank in town. This panorama shifts in her head. She can't help feeling a little jealous, the Sydney crowd having it both ways. A world plump with jewfish and oysters, a slow chip on the golf course, then the limitless musicality of a big city. She will miss the soft-stepping people of her hometown, the ancient geometric shapes of the bay, the tides and beach percussing in her head. Once, she visited the Peninsula Lighthouse and its shores in her dad's boat, when he owned a boat. But when school resumed she hated seeing the beach as a sign of holiday refuse. Empty beer bottles flashed in the sun. Garbage bins tilted their load on the grass, and sodden bits of paper and pine needles scoured the shoreline. Fish heads and entrails washed backwards and forwards in a greasy foam. The rowdiness and the showing off in summer annoyed her. Some days she felt tense watching petting teenagers.

So with endless waiting, she plants her feet on the Singer, and absentmindedly moves the machine's wheel back and forth, catching yellow cotton in the bobbin. Her fingers work a habit of picking out thread and fluff. This activity reminds her of clouds and pathways: the Pacific Highway's shapes and colours, the bladey greenness at Somersby Falls. Winding trails to Staples Lookout, spiralling roads, the orange rock that seemed to spring up beside the car. Once on a family trip, their old Vauxhall crawled slowly in a long line of traffic through the mountains. Oncoming lights shining silver on her parent's heads, the dark, then the flare-up again from an overtaking lorry. That was the night they visited their relatives, the Duchess and King in Dee Why who ate their dinner, stowed the meal dishes away, and never prepared another. Her father returned home along the highway, tense and quiet, determined never to visit again.

It occurs to her that Irene and Veronica might also be waylaid, their furniture van breathing close fumes from heavy traffic near Hornsby or Asquith. Alice smacks out a Juicy Fruit bubble. On the sound of the popping noise, Princey lifts his head up from the cane lounge, sniffing the air.

'Good boy,' she says. 'And no, I don't have a chockie for you.' Crazy dog, she thinks. Running on three legs to Manning's, beating everyone. She will miss his cute antics, but not his senseless habit of nosing in her undies' drawer, or wrestling her handbag after work for a biscuit or Fantale. There won't be any of that now. Not the dripping jaw, his mouth stuck hopelessly on a chocolate cobber, snuffling a mounting soreness into the long buffalo grass. The terrible whining, a paw trying to open the door to his teeth.

Pacing the veranda, Alice remembers the albums in the cabinet. Lifting the plastics, she collects the humorous ones first, Aunt Bea in a bizarre black and white bathing gown, looking like some sort of Bette Davis in a rowboat. Her cousin, Colin, caught peeing in the backyard. Her dad dangling a snake over logs on some lonely outback homestead. Alice flips through the old greys, Jimmy in his pram, loads of her dressed in bonnets, her crumpled face outside the Canberra War Memorial. She slips the brown and white print of Gran ready for Paddy's markets under a rubber band. The train always waited for her at the station, they said. She likes the one of Aunty Alma and Aunty Vera cuddling on the back step of their holiday shack next-door. She keeps the Woodford and Temple Bay albums: bodies trundling along the shore with umbrellas, buckets, rods and towels, the one of Kevin (aged three) digging in the shallows near the pool, the crowd behind him at the point, reeling in rods. You can spot the Sydney bathers by their white skin and sandals.

Suddenly her dad's ready. She can't believe it. Everything pokes through a half-pulled tarp. Bookcase and headboard hug the back of the cabin, knotted by two ockey-straps. He's managed to pack all her possessions, glory box full of Tupperware, golf trophies, sewing machine, the blue Hermes typewriter, and Grandma's suitcase strapped and bloated.

Stopping for petrol, and Tally-Ho papers, Alice thinks perhaps things could be worse, a blown head gasket, leaky water-pump, flat tyre maybe puncturing the perfect picture of a daughter leaving. Of course, she's not in any particular hurry.

Along the highway, they both sing to radio tunes. At times, they are silent, the head rocking in the vehicle's momentum, heavy eyelids lost in the imprint of the land.

Alice takes out the rental contract from her bag. It won't do to tell her father they'd changed the first version. Irene and Veronica disagreeing with the landlord's idea of his brother renting a room in the same house. Alice isn't going to divulge that kind of information.

'If I could Dad, I'd take a turn at the wheel.'

'No worries, we'll stop off for a bite to eat soon.' Bob flicks a match, and lights up a tailor-made cigarette. 'Have one,' he says, shuffling the packet at her.

'What?'

'Oh, we know, Darl. Your mother and I could smell them in your room.'

'Well, I'm trying to give them up.'

'Oh, yeah,' he laughs. 'It's not that easy. I've been smokin' since I was fourteen.'

'And you've never stopped, have you?'

'Nah. What for? A man's gotta have some vices.'

'They're easy to get when you're a kid. People keep offering them all the time.'

'I don't really like you smoking, Alice.'

'Well, guess what Dad? I've just been looking at my budget, and now I can't afford to smoke, living in Sydney.'

'Good,' he says, passing her a lit cigarette. 'One final one for the road, hey?'

Alice puffs, looking at her father with a smirk on her face.

Around the next bend the day turns to water, the oil-still river shimmering olive-green in the light. Alice's mind trails back to the little stations along the line. She would have liked to discover the bays and river settlements. Instead, she was in that daily grind of a long journey, hours speeding past suburbs, blank faces with shopping bags, men snoring, the train winding around the watercourses, slipping through the valley on its continual fluorescent hum of rails.

Alice and her father finally reach the Pie in the Sky roadhouse and pull in close to the diner. The only food in town is pastry. There's a squally wind coming up from an eastern foreshore, so they huddle in a latticed shelter. Alice listens to the sounds around her, the highway traffic coming loud and soft, buffeted by large fir and gum trees. The sloping terrain is too high for river noises.

Carriages rattle over the train bridge. At low tide the familiar cultivated oysters expose their dark gnarly beds. Alice has been here so many times, and now she's here again, perhaps for the last time, trailing her feet on the edge of the gazebo shade, judging the meat pie's deceit. It's hot exterior giving no indication of its cold mass inside. She makes a river in the tomato sauce, a weekend path to the Manly Concourse, Nana and Pop standing on the front step, foul gas jetting from their damp house, firing an artificial barrage to her nose. Family is shrinking now, like this retreat from a father she hardly knows. Beyond the park, a paper bag weaves a white signal in the upper draught of cool air. Train and road-bridge stretch across the river like extended Meccano, the hillsides a mixture of mangroves and rocks. She remembers the grassed area of Wiseman's Ferry, several hundred-horsepower Yamahas anchored or at full speed. The time she saw someone in a neck brace, Irene demanding the refund back on the water-skiing.

She enjoys this mind wandering. Spencer and St Albans are certainly quaint, the mountains housing all manner of dwellings from fibro to tin humpies, the flowering bush in the spring. Her last holiday with Irene fades in and out, an invitation from a guy in the Brighton pub in Manly to travel the river. She remembers him pushing the punt away from the reeds, the curled maze of the river, going inland until the MacDonald River petered into shallows and mudflats. She thought back to the bed and breakfast they rented on the Manly Esplanade, the heady intoxication of four days, swimming, lying in the sun, pub drinking; the mosaic of palm trees, Coppertone skin smells, airborne glass, and the accentuated noise of rock music and surfies. It often lifted Alice's mind to think of Sydney beaches, the transition from the quiet to something alive and beating.

Alice and her father walk to the edge of the high embankment above the river. Bob collapses into the grass, stretching his shaggy legs. 'Great train bridge. Your grandmother and old John went to the opening.' He lifts his cupped head towards the brackish water. 'To look at it now, you'd think there was never a space there. This place always reminds me of the old timer with the oyster bottles.'

'Was that his job, Dad?'

'No, he lived on the line, but a bit too fond of oysters. Moonlighted, you might say. Gulped them down when the train went into the Green Point tunnel. He was known to put the empty bottle back. It didn't last long. People soon learned to clutch their bags after that.'

Alice squirms at the thought of an oyster's rawness. 'I only like them smoked.'

'Just what I need,' he says, 'a smoke.' He lights up, lifts tobacco off his lip. 'Ten million bricks,' he says, 'in that tunnel. All of 'em shipped to Green Point. Caused a bit of a fuss at the time, people wanting bricks for their houses. Anyway, it made history, oldest railway tunnel in the state.'

This is meant to soften Alice, trying to make her stay. 'I'm always glad of the first burst from the tunnel, then you know you're practically home.'

'Temple Bay's not such a bad place. Your mother and I moved there 'cause your grandmother and old John enjoyed it so much. I started off with just twenty pound in me pocket. Not much work around, so I got a hawker's license, a tricycle with a box tray. Sold fish and prawns in summer. Rabbits in winter.'

On the jetty below, boys cast silver lines. Two boats look to a future displaying 'for sale' signs. Her dad screws up his pie bag, reminiscing. 'You know, I'll never forget the Harley Davidson I bought from an old geezer in the camping ground. Forty pound it cost, ran on a cup of petrol,' he says, bending his knees, stretching them on the grass. 'I used to sell fresh King prawns along the Esplanade, till the fishing inspector put the kybosh on. So I packed up me gear and went to Murrurundi and Gunnedah doing renovations. You were only little. I had to forget about fishing with Stewie for a while. A man never has enough time. Always at work.'

'You know why I'm leaving, don't you Dad? I want to be closer to work.'

He taps Alice's head in agreement, filling her with savage stories of the big city, drivers at break-neck speed. Warning her about the dangers of the Cross. 'It's got a bad reputation,' he says, 'them *Les Girls* and all that.'

A trawler backs out and turns from the jetty. The slow cruising reminds Alice of her father, moving from one point to another. She hadn't spent any time with him of late. He worked away most of the time, and didn't go to church. He carried his life like a wounded orphan, saying he never had a childhood. Now he's being paternal, hammering her with questions, telling her to be careful in Sydney as if she is placing herself between the devil and all the crazies that roam the streets.

'I'll always be with Irene and Veronica, Dad!'

'Humph.' Bob sucks in his lips and wipes his brow before repositioning his straw hat. 'Come on. Roll me a smoke will you, Darl?'

Back on the highway, they careen bends and damp rock-face the colour of pumpkin skin and flesh. Alice removes the tobacco pouch from the glove box. As the traffic slows near Hornsby, she rolls the paper, juggling the Ruby Red on her lap. During her teenage years, she often smoked a few durries in the back lane with Heather, Jimmy and Brian, pretending they were movie stars. Brian showing her how to do the drawback. He had wanted to play inside her pants a second time, all arms and legs in the back seat of his Austin. Other times, he crouched his fingers between her legs, staring into her face, his excited penis against her. It seemed that her mind was caught forever, carrying that first time memory on and on, under the bed, on top of the bed, two teenage bodies going at it for hours, and later running along the laneway crying. She had buried her secret somewhere deeper than the colour of hush. Alice hadn't met anyone she wanted to marry, not like Heather. But then Heather could talk to any boy at the roller skating rink or down the beach. Yelling after them, 'Hey Bill! How long are you up for from Sydney?' There was no Bill, just a ploy to start talking. Heather liked flirting and when real love came it left as rejection. Once, she heard Heather's begging and pleading on the telephone, later glimpsing her fixed stare at the dial after the click of the hand piece.

The next year, Mrs Randall made a sudden wedding announcement: Alice and Judith 'Bridesmaids', Heather's sister Margaret, 'Matron of Honour'. They dressed in gold taffeta, low necks and bell skirts, Heather in embroidered organza with a wide train. On the day, Alice wondered why she wore off-white. And rolling her hands over her belly in the lounge room, she confided in Alice that her bouquet hid a tiny heart. 'Have to get married now. Can't have a little bastard.'

'Heather, you hardly know this bloke. Where'd he come from?'·

'I work with him.'

'I just hope you're going to be happy, that's all.'

'This way I get out of going to work. I'm sick of paint and wheelbarrows.'

'You need more of a reason than that.'

'Well, I never got the one I wanted, did I?'

Weddings always reminded Alice of Heather's lounge room. One corner stacked with presents, the photographer in another taking pictures of the family, Heather tuning out the noises around her, her nervousness moving to a groan. Her face looked paler than her dress. Even the well-wishers calling on the Randell's new telephone, brought back stretches of time. Heather wouldn't take the calls, she seethed with irritation and no one knew why. She nervously fluffed out her dress, pretending, shifting from one foot to the other. She never wanted this scene; she wanted a dreamy conversation with her old flame. Her emotions were sinking into the pit of her stomach, that little island in the middle of her belly, claiming her for another role.

Alice thinks about that day, wanting to say sorry, sorry for the urgency of growing up and that stupid broken condom. She told Judith that she never wanted to get married, but she knew she was kidding herself. She liked her own company, but the constant teasing always made her feel lonely; neighbours and friend's parents saying, 'How's your love life. Got a boyfriend yet? Watch out or you'll be left on the shelf.' She just wanted to puke.

***

After Hornsby, Alice's head lurches forward in sleep. The sun sending little streams of warmth into the cab. Bob tunes in the radio, the noise of the races and commentator filling the cab. He passes Alice a newspaper. 'Have a look at the tote pages and tell me who's running in the fifth? And see what the odds are for Damien Son.'

'Did ya make a bet?'

'No, I'm no mug. Just like to keep me interest up. I like the idea of winning, that's all. Last Satdee, I got a second in the third, and won a trifecta in the fourth. A man should place a bet, I s'pose. But your mother'd have a fit. You know what she's like. I just wish she'd stop fussing about inside and come sit with me on the veranda, have a beer or something.'

'She doesn't like the noise of the races.'

'Oh, I'd soon turn it off.'

Alice hears the same echo, beer, football and listening to the races. This is the measurement of her small town life, barefoot in the kitchen, marrying some brickie constantly at the fridge snapping bottle tops. She is too young to wither away in a one-milkman town, already concerts and rock-'n'-roll dances disappearing. And in any season, boys at the Surf Club only concerned themselves with one downpour, beer down their throats. She didn't mind leaving the roughies at the roller skating rink, two or three louts in the Rendezvous milk-bar, bums up-ended at a snooker table, but the sound of Roy Orbison's lungs in top treble in *Only the Lonely* and *Crying* would stay forever.

'Where've you been?' Irene stamping, hands on her hips, drags out the word 'been' like a rubber band.

'Sorry. We had a bit of trouble. Didn't you call the landlord for another key?'

'He's in Greece!' blurts Veronica. 'We've been waiting here for *hours*. Our parents had to get back. We couldn't even show them inside.'

'We could take pictures,' says Alice, screwing her face, and pointing behind her hand towards her father. 'Dad will help with the lounge. Where is it?'

'It's in the backyard. Well, we couldn't leave it in the street, could we?'

'Sorry Irene,' says Alice, watching her father disappear down the lane in the ute. 'I didn't know Dad would borrow his old work bomb. Plus we had battery trouble. I knew I should have given you the key.'

The Stanmore Springboard

Memo 9:   *Bright lights, big city, gone to my baby's head.*

Three nights later, the girls stay up till midnight, discussing the house roster, shopping, skating at Prince Alfred Park. 'Think of all the shows we can catch. The Mammas and the Pappas. Peter, Paul and Mary. Yeah, Sammy Davis Junior, Nat King Cole,' they nod.

'I heard Johnny O'Keefe's singing in Bankstown somewhere,' says Alice.

'My boss has given me two tickets to *Romeo and Juliet*. Veronica and I are going.'

In all their talk of leaving home, a new city language speaks of summer sounds. Bondi Beach, Taronga Park Zoo, King's Cross and Luna Park. Sydney beaches lure them with noises of volleyball, soft sand and bronzed tans. *Yeah! Our kind of town.*

When Alice first settles from the long trip, standing on the wrought-iron porch, she finds the sky bluer, her avenue of trees. She had helped her father hustle her possessions and furniture around the back, leaving them in their lounge room. He huffed and sweated the whole time. 'I should have brought Ken,' he complained. 'Everything's so bloody heavy.'

Finishing the twins' load, her father kisses her at the front door. Alone now in her room, Alice is miniscule under tall ceilings. She has her money, keys, and possessions. Why did she suddenly feel odd? Why was that swinging bare globe telling her she'd left something behind?

After work, Alice arranges her room, putting childhood photographs on the mantel. The frames are cool in her hand, almost like the ocean's flappable surface. Images on one photograph appear animated in the sun, making Heather, Jimmy and Brian smile a little broader. They're crouching near pools, damming the channel with buckets of sand. Heather is wading in, raising her arms above the waves. In another, the boys are teasing claws out from underneath a rock. By the time she finishes sorting, a dozen photographs sit on the mantelpiece, including the double-frame of her Masonic ball, Heather and her partner in one, Alice and her date on the right. She could never remember his name, couldn't think what she'd done wrong, the boy's smiling good looks as timid as his mouth staying mute all night. Alice hopes that Sydney will bring a livelier crop of men. In all the months working at the Pennant Hills branch and going skating with her workmates, she hadn't really met anyone.

Two weeks later, Irene, Veronica and Alice pass through the turnstile at Prince Alfred Park. A frosty breeze shivers across the ice. Alice finds it hard to imagine the rink being used as a swimming pool in summer. How did they do it? Did anyone wonder about the massive tiled hole beneath their skates? She imagines how horrible it would be to go crashing into its weakest point, finding an icy sea below.

Samantha and Adrian from the bank wave from the boots' collection counter. They point to Wayne, buying his usual chips and Chiko roll. Alice wants to avoid his burps and pranks tonight, because the European is here again, coming out of the change rooms. As she wobbles on the rubber matting, the rink is a clatter of chrome. She inches up close to him. Under the patina of night and hooded lights, she is fixated on the tapestry of his chin, football beanie exposing a dark Brylcreemed fringe. He's dressed in black. Rolled cuffs exposing dark olive skin. She hears sound waves, the glide of his blades dancing in little clicks, and oh, that body-sway, as if born on skates. She doesn't know his name, but that doesn't matter. Tonight she will invite this Polanski to skate with her in "partners".

Alice jellies across the ice until she finds her balance. Her friends snake in and in out, holding hands, patterning an arc beside her.

'We're all going in the speed skating, later. What about you, Alice?'

'Nah, Ade. I'll just sit and watch.'

'Hoo, hoo! So you're going to perve on me, are you?'

'Adrian!'

Adrian is a tease. She loves that about him; playing the part, while he is a bonafide queer. Sometimes he pays for everything, even her fare in. She wishes their friendship might be more, but then she has to contend with him saying things like, 'that boy's got nice eyes. Did you see the way he looked at me? Oooooh!'

Talking with Adrian is fun. They have a laugh in his teller's box, while she collects the deposits and cheques. She likes being with him on Friday nights, meeting up with the gang from the bank. Now the girls always stay back for coffee, and never have to catch the paper train. They do not miss their old journey to Green Point. Not one little bit. She tries to figure out Adrian, but can't. She doesn't know a solitary thing about men fancying other men. And he hasn't been explicit about it.

Alice sips lemonade and catches sight of her Polanski. She feels relaxed sitting down. Since spraining her ankle at the Youth Club, she felt the weight of the steel blades grinding on their weakest point. If she didn't rest they would ache all night, dragging her into a bad mood.

'Partners' is last on the list. Now it's just the normal mixed session. Her powerhouse European twists in and out of slow bones, angling his body into a perfect stop. He's a mimic on a highway of ice, skimming across the surface like an insomniac seal high on the rhythms and composition of chilled water. Alice remembers the last occasion, trying to impress him. In navy tights and a pleated slate-blue skirt, she had moved closer. Bold enough to skate in front of him, her rhythm swished from side to side. But someone's boot got in the way, and as she tried to do a fancy trick in the crossover, she bottomed out in a corner pool of ice. Her sexy maneuver ended up with her exposing a soaked white dovetail and lace fringe. She had spun-out like an ice-hockey shuttle, a projectile, whacked out of the game.

Again, the pink flush of cheeks reminds her that she isn't the best of skaters. She takes it easy and heads for the Polanski. God, damn! He chickens out and disappears into the toilets.

Adrian whistles past, grabbing her by the hand, whisking her off into the crowd. 'Watch me, gorgeous.' He swivels around and skates backwards in front of her, a little perky smile rising on her cheeks. 'That's the way to do it,' he says.

Alice couldn't help smiling with Adrian around. He was infectious. Persuasive. She would never forget his two driving lessons; the first near a Stanmore park, teasing her, pretending to change gears with her right leg. The second, at the Entrance in an empty street. After handballing chocolate bars and cellophane packets of lollies into the back seat, they both sat in silence. Alice felt sorry for Adrian, his pale face and furrowed expression giving you that 'there goes my-pay-packet' look. She would have preferred a quiet sip on a strawberry milkshake, a hamburger, sitting in the milkbar, anything other than crunching his gears, hitting a curb and smashing his right-back fender.

Images of her last Friday night with Adrian fade in and out, and just like the quiet house, the next day, she feels empty inside. With Irene and Veronica spending Saturdays at the Sydney shops, she tries to combat the boredom. Nothing fills the hole in her heart, not even re-arranging her bedroom, not even lifting the record player's needle on Dylan's, *It's a Hard Rain's Gonna Fall.* Adrian's requested transfer to the North Shore branch is a door closing on her life. He's in love, he says on the telephone, a new boyfriend moving in with him at Ashcroft where he's to start as Assistant Manager.

Alice reminds herself that life is a series of doors. A year later, a surprisingly different door opens on a mysterious voice at the end of the line. A husky, not-to-be-interrupted Theatre Manager telling her about uniforms, cordial, ice-cream, inventories, Minties and Smiths' Crisps. Hearing her dad's old saying, that feet are for dancing and her 'noggin' is for thinking, she makes a quick decision, saying, 'Yes, yes, yes!'

***

In the following months, Alice runs from Central station to the Capitol Theatre. She runs because it is Friday night, and the streets are dark and undulating. While she is too old to imagine monsters, Alice senses grimy men lurking in laneways and doors.

Haymarket is the dirtiest end of the city, and while Irene has scored an usherette's position at the Cygnet further along George Street, she has only managed Candy-Bar Assistant at the oldest theatre in town. She works for two years like this. Summer, autumn, spring, winter, moving through the cold, the wet face of the city, her pointy-toe shoes stamping the railway platform in a diamond print, her white breath curling in front of her. Most Friday and Saturday nights she loads trays of orange and lemon cordial, stacks shelves, tallies the cash register. On certain occasions, Steve, the head usher, allows her to watch the movie.

In the interval rush, with fingers working deftly on paper cups, mints, chips, and ice creams, her mind is on the end of her shift. During the week at the bank, she is elsewhere being rocked by sea breezes, gazing into the quiet starry sky on an ocean liner's deckchair. By the end of the third year, she has just enough energy to give Steve a quick goodbye peck at the door, and with savage insistence tells his hurt face, that in two weeks she will be sailing out of his life on the Oriana.

Helen Hagemann

Part III

Indian Ocean Island

Memo 10:   *Only a gentleman kisses on the first date, and a lady says no to sex on her first.*

Alice struggles to zip up her luggage. It's one large backpack minus the bedroll, pots and swinging cork-hat. It's been a week of rehearsals, what to take, what to wear. Two weekends of selling goods. Picking up the tickets. Emptying out her room, the whole flat. Veronica's engagement party. It didn't matter about Irene's original plan to visit New Zealand; Perth sounded more like a hoot, the Wild West. They figured they could save for the Kiwi Isle another time. Besides the candy-bar job hadn't rendered Alice that much money.

Practically everyone, except her dad, visits Circular Quay to wave goodbye, including her cousin, Lois. Alice and Irene wrestle for space on the promenade deck, waving through a deck of streamers. The loud thrust from the ship's siren has them shouting across water, one hand waving, the other trailing a paper chain along the decking rail. Sydney harbour is puffed out in sunlight, with small to medium sailing craft.

Both girls follow a guide map to their room. A four-berth cabin catches a floor-slide of backpacks. Over masses of carpeted stairs, they head for the coffee and biscuits on the quarterdeck. The itinerary has new capital sounds: Quoits. Ping-Pong. Lucky spots. Magicians. Barry Crocker. Hairdressers. Lunch with the Captain. Crayfish and Scallops.

***

Alice senses the Oriana strong and enormous about her unsteady gait. In the lunging ocean of the Great Australian Bight, she does everything to avoid the green jowls. As she traverses the upper and lower decks, pill bottles sway inside her pockets. They rattle from swimming pool, past potted palms to the furthest viewpoint overlooking the wild grassy sea.

In Perth, the girls emerge from their microcosm of night parties, smelly old men on the dance floor and a smorgasbord of seafood and cold meats. With the certainty of pay packets and uniforms, Alice and Irene alight another gangplank. Irene's dark top-knot moves through a swell of passengers, her tinted sunglasses matching her black clutch bag. People queue beside the wooden prow of a Rottnest ferry. Bikes lined five abreast are shuffled like a pack of cards and handed over to the waiting crowd. Both girls are glad they survived the rough part of the crossing, thanks to the survival skills of the crew on *The Temmeraire II.*

Leaving a multitude of bobbing heads, the slow weave of bike wheels, and a van detailed *Rotto Hostel,* both girls enter a kitchen. They're amongst men now in white coats and black buttons, queuing with a steady line of girls in half-aprons. Amongst rows of checkered tablecloths, Alice carries a tray of lunch plates. She stops beside a young man who is constantly snapping his finger, as if she is the only waitress in town. As she backs through the porthole doors with empty dishes, crumpled serviettes and jam sachets, the young man smiles at her through thick lenses. His iron-blue eyes staring her down. He tries to get a laugh by twiddling and inhaling the table's plastic rose.

The act is repeated daily. If he's not sniffing the rose, he's ordering another ramekin of vanilla ice cream. Alice discovers the secret of her rustic, scented island — its cloisters filled with romance. It seems as if this fellow has the island's reputation on his mind, and is numbering the ways they can be together.

***

They sip Pina Coladas through black straws. Their bodies, bead and drip under a quarter moon; hair and bathers still wet from their nightly swim. Alice decides she won't complain to this German fellow about Mrs. Featherstone making her wash ten windows along a hot northern corridor, or the ache in her arms from lifting heavy trays.

'So, you're not related to Hitler by any chance?' asks Alice, suddenly feeling clumsy about her stupid question.

'Man! Of course not,' he drawls, 'Hitler was Austrian, na? I'm just Max Klauss from Hamburg. Paid my full fare, too.'

'You know, with your blond hair, glasses, and crew cut, you look like a Yank.'

Max wets a finger across his eyebrows, pretending he's someone famous. 'In Hamburg we couldn't get enough of Brando and all those Yankee movies, na?'

Alice laughs at him, as he rolls his shoulders like an actor. 'Anyway, I'm Alice Edwina Jessica Bennett. Edwina's from Gran, and the other two names are from my great grandmother.'

'I like this Alice. Alice in Wunderland.'

'Yeah, I get it all the time. Except now I'm Alice on Rottnest.' She pauses for a moment, trying to find something better to say. 'So, do you have any family in Australia?'

'A brother, but he's a bastard, na? Stole my tax return, first year I am in Adelaide. That's why I came here. I left the lot, suits, jackets, waistcoats, everything German. I got a job in Tom Price and they paid the airfare.'

'I'm from Temple Bay,' says Alice. 'Flatted in Sydney for three years. Worked in the Bank of New South Wales as an examiner. This waitressing, though, has knobs on. I've never worked so hard in all my life!'

The air smells of seaweed. Alice towels her long black hair. Hung over from a previous night of drinking, the cold snap of sea has finally shucked off any edginess or worry. In these few weeks, she has rested her body in the

Basin's grotto blue sea, and wants to glide around the island, listening to holiday noises, the tinkling bike traffic. For now, she will never leave the quiet, sun-baking corners of Rottnest.

Max touches her bare skin, and not thinking of the consequences he cups his hands under her breasts.

'You don't waste any time, do you?'

In the mild intoxication of the night, Max is ready to lay his needs upon her. 'Up north, no coffee, no women, just booze.' He talks in half-formed sentences telling her he's been working twelve months without a break. Alice watches the way he laughs out loud, as he flexes his muscles. 'Hard work, eh?' His language continues in short bursts. She is the first girl to sit and talk to him for any length of time since coming to Western Australia. He arrived on his twenty-third birthday. He's rich, he tells her. Saved all his money, while others drank and gambled. He pushes his fingers through hers, clasping tight, lifting her hand to his lips. They can have a good time together. Dinners at the hotel, hamburgers, *Kaffee und Kuchen*. Trips to Perth. Shopping. He would like to buy her expensive underwear.

Alice yawns. She is half awake from the alcohol, and the previous late night. Max cuddles close, his fingers searching the shape of her breasts. He whispers German dialect into her ear. She doesn't understand, but her mouth understands his tongue and open lips. The moon stirs under Alice's skin. In partly wet nylon, she is shivery and wants to go indoors, but Max protests about the long walk back to his Quod cell. He doesn't feel like moving. She senses that the beer is keeping him firmly moored to his bench seat.

'Why go, eh? Beautiful Sweetie-pie. Here,' he says, placing his jacket around her shoulders. They shift closer. Floodlights immediately switched on, make an arc of light across the table. It all seems like the right cocktail for a good evening, the ocean, salty breeze, the tick, tick of bike wheels. A sudden thrust of bass and drums crashes through the pub's walls, waking Alice from her dreamy state.

Max waves the waiter over. 'I worked in Mt. Magnet for an iron-ore company as sorter. Done lots of things. Split rocks at a gold mine. Worked for a pommie, James Andrew Osborne as driller's assistant, pulling core samples. Bogger driver. Front-end loader driver. I was a brickie's labourer in Tea Tree Gully. My brother worked me so hard, my hands bled.' He empties his change on the waiter's tray. 'Oh ja, same again, mate.'

'Doesn't sound like a brother to me.'

Max wants to talk about everything. He's off-loading memories, places and people of the past. Alice feels swamped by his details, and is only half listening. She stares at the circles around his eyes, hidden beneath thick lenses. He takes off his glasses, first wiping his eyelids, then the glass. 'I am half blind,' he says, 'like Mr Magoo.'

Alice laughs as they both repeat, *Oh, Magoo you've done it again!*

Max's eyes are still swimming, while he's telling her it's permanent damage. Run over by a British army truck when he turned five. Alice asks him to slow down, he's talking too fast, his English filling again with Hamburg dialect. The family received chocolates, he says. Every week, clothes, stockings, food parcels from the driver. The corporal, feeling so bad, spent a whole year leaving his army supplies with the family. Max continues while a Congo line spills from the hotel's lounge bar, someone up-front has a kazoo, another a bongo drum. 'I was in hospital for six months, na?' he says, raising his voice above the din. 'Lost my sense of smell, one knee crushed in accident.' He points to five places on his legs. 'Later, I show you the scars.'

'So you can't even smell a leg of lamb cooking?'

'Nein, nicht.'

Alice raises her answer higher. 'That's terrible.'

The sudden sympathy in her voice surprises him. He leans closer, looking at the last of the swaying bodies. 'But all my plumbing is *sehr gut*, na?' He watches how she sits back on the bench with ease.

'Oh,' she laughs. 'You know, your English is not bad, but it could be better.'

Then you teach. I listen.'

'Okay!' she says, leading him into phrases for body parts, her tongue wrapping slowly around words. For a moment, Alice thinks her expressions silly, Max not saying anything. His voice is hushed, almost whispering. He talks about his pleurisy, his mother back in Grös Borstel. The long wait, watching out for her face in the hospital. The flowers he couldn't smell overflowing on a cabinet near the next bed. 'It does not matter,' he tells her, 'when there is pretty girl on Rottnest Island. I think your breasts must smell salty as the sea.'

'I guess not being able to smell has certain advantages. You know, toilet smells and all that.'

He laughs, lifting the last of the jug's froth, tentative about pronouncing the next word. 'Hm. There is one unadvant…one problem. I cannot smell things cooking.'

Max waves his wrists in a semi-circle. His elbows settle on the table as if engrossed in a book. He's acting now, in a different caricature, contorting his face into spasms, snorting and coughing, slapping the tabletop, chuckling and sniffing back an overflow of tears and laughter.

Alice is tickled by his quaint expressions, sending her into convulsions before she's even heard the story. Max's mouth, wide open, is steaming words towards her, panting and puffing like the pages of his hot sex novel. He wipes his eyes and winds the chuckle down to a slow guffaw. 'Of course,' he says. 'My sister was cooking the roast must be for two hours. There was a man and woman going at it. Ha! Bodies getting hot. I did not see the smoke coming out, or curling up the ceiling.' He waves his fingers high in the air. 'Then my coughing got stronger and stronger, and I couldn't breathe. He, he.'

Max continues to laugh, slapping the table and rattling the glasses. He could have blown the whole house up. Gas burners still alight, his sister's shrieking finally bringing him to the surface.

Alice's eyes are dry in the night wind. She feels they could flood at any moment. She doesn't want to think about the last few months in the Stanmore flat, the arguments with Irene and Veronica about the Italians next door. Now she's in the company of a proud German. Talk about switching countries! But he fancies her and that's all she needs. They seem to be having a nice time together. She likes the way he sends her into instant mirth. He's sugar and salt. The sugar is the vulnerable Mr Magoo. She imagines him bumping into things, mistaking objects like the comic character. Alice smirks, seeing the pudgy fellow on vacation, Waldo in a raccoon coat, losing his banjo, Magoo mistaking a bear for his nephew. She thinks, shall I tell him about this, it was so bloody funny, Magoo, nonchalant and oblivious to the fact that he was chatting away to a big grizzly, clutching Waldo's banjo.

She smiles to herself. The two are constantly meshing, Magoo and Max. Both have car stories. Max needs a passenger in the car to let him know when the lights change. He can't see the new flash of colour. Her face stretches. She sees radiator smoke, water trickling, cars crossed and re-crossed in the traffic, a Magoo-type Max padding through a mass of bonnets, leaving his sizzling wreck, asking an officer for directions to the bus stop.

She notices at times Max searches for words, snapping his fingers as if raising them from some inner memory. His English is a mish-mush of what he's learnt in the Pilbara; words like 'extremely' and 'most kindly' from James Andrew Osborne, swearing from ocker workmates. At least, he's mastered the TH. It took him two years while working up north, he says, 'so, no more "zis" and "zat"'.

Alice likes his ice-blue eyes, crew-cut, and crooked chin. He's definitely complex. Her heart is sinking under all the facts: mother an alcoholic, his tuberculosis scare at seventeen, not allowed to smoke, only his dad visiting while he lay twelve-months in a hospital. What was life like for her back then, skating at the rink, cuddling in the back seat of Ray's car, sashaying to the samba, neck craned in her debutante waltz at the Masonic ball?

She thinks about his family's hard times during and after the war, his mother washing cars outside in a German winter. Going hungry. Alice remembers her mother's keepsakes in a hatbox, the Victoria Cross and other medals, photos of Pop, parts of Uncle John's uniform. Her family talked about the soup lines, the depression, soldiers and sailors dancing in the streets with beaming young women, the tickertape parade in George Street, Sydney. *The Sun* newspaper, printed when Jimmy was a toddler. The front page splashed with the words, *WAR ENDS*. But to Alice, all this pales when she hears Max's hellish stories. She finds it hard to think about his family eating a St. Bernard dog, like he says, cutting and cooking it after it hung three days in the cellar. She is only half listening to his next exaggeration. Some things seem so far-fetched. He's ordered another jug of beer. She doesn't know where he's putting it. They cuddle close for warmth, but her mood is transient. She's wishing she could join the Congo line. It seemed like fun. Then there's the woman in the yacht anchored off the jetty drinking champagne. She'd like to change places with her.

***

In the night, Max and Alice lie awake in a single bed, the tiny cell of the old Aboriginal prison surrounding them like a cocoon. Max kisses her bare body, pretends to smell her within inches of her sex. He gurgles and splutters as she laughs a little embarrassed. They talk until the early hours of the morning. He has her sighing, taking in deep breaths. He knows she is fascinated. He goes back further in time to his grandfather, stories about tenants, home units and the old fellow's property in a little Dorf called Sprötze. He tells her, Otto Freidrich Klauss was a cunning old eccentric. The best time was when they went through all the units collecting rent money, the old fellow pretending to fix problems. Instead he just chalked the walls and never returned. After, they would sit in the park, Otto unwrapping thick rye bread from re-used paper. Max sitting there, waiting.

Indian Ocean Town

Memo 11:   *'Play with fire and you'll get burnt' is a good sex lesson.*

Outside high on the slope of Mount Street, the river flashes plates of brightness, sails jazz into the wind with their wild jungle colours. Old Gaffers zigzag the river, and bodies stretch along the jetties. This is the time of year when Crawley fills with Macedonians on their yearly pilgrimage from Jaguars and Volvos. Men in black leather tap the ends of cigarettes, exchange each other's mirror image of neck silver. Tubby boys, still thinking of religion, hammer boards, sink their bodies into the shallows for cross and country. Alice and Max, strolling bare feet along the grass-bank, halt at the river's edge amongst families raising themselves from their picnic hampers. In amongst the incessant ethnic clapping, they proudly kiss, pretending it's for them.

It's been three weeks since leaving Rottnest, and Max and Alice are constantly hooked in each other's arms. Today, the city streets are shadows and shapes of girls in tight sweaters, American sailors on R & R, Salvation Army Officers on street corners rattling tins. In Murray Street, they leave the crisp smell of hot chips and street café coffee and head through the musky perfumery counters of Boans. They descend the stairs into the food hall. Strong aromas of Brazilian, Italian and Mocha bean float down the aisle. A uniformed waitress shunts the machine's handle back and forth. The burbling, choking sound of brewed coffee mingles with the clatter of drinkers and shoppers. The espresso drips a white overhang on their cups. Alice and Max choose stools and a bench alcove under the stairs. Already they're loaded with bundles; Max's new shorts, belt and shirt, some postcards. Alice slides a pearl along a gold necklet, straightens the clasp at the back of her neck. They sit and say nothing. She is feeling shaky; something inside is nagging at her bladder.

'Not much coffee in there,' he says, finally.

'I know I shouldn't say, but this store amazes me with all its smells. It's like a European smorgasbord.'

'No use talking to me about smell?'

'Oh, yeah. Sorry.'

Max opens his wallet and fingers the dollar notes. 'I'd like to get some liverwurst later, maybe some Gouda and crusty bread.'

'Do you eat sauerkraut?'

'Nah, not that stuff.'

He tells her he hates boiled cabbage. He will never eat it. It only reminds him of going hungry for three days in Hamburg, gulping a priest's lumpy, lard-encrusted meal down, stolen from his kitchen, then having to deal with being discovered, the old man trying to blackmail him because he needed a friend.

'I shot out of there. But they caught me and put me back in the boy's home.'

They sit amongst bubbly voices, eating, Alice moving her chair in to let a pram and toddler pass.

For the next ten minutes, Alice can't think of anything in her life that matches Max's terrible tales. The brewed coffee reminds him of his mother grinding cheap beans in their Grös Borstel apartment. He remembers the bareness of rooms, windows, a grimy stairwell, front door opening onto steps and balustrade, weeks of a damp sky. Once, he got the strap all the way down the stairs for buying sweets with the gas money. He still sees one or two images of a bombed Hamburg, watching old women picking up stones like squirrels for winter storage, filling metal barrows relaying them to a higher ledge of plaster and concrete. He doesn't have the words or the energy to tell her everything, but it will come later when he has the English. He can never forget his boyhood nightmares, overcrowded tenements with aunts he hated, and the humbling bleary eyes of the British lorry driver. One day, he says, he'll get over the sting of watching his mother drunk and abused, her drunken boyfriend putting a knife to his throat.

Alice watches his changing moods. Some stories seem outrageous, escaping from every boy's home he'd been sent to, wandering the streets for three days without food. He can't piss in a men's urinal if another man is standing next to him. She notices when he's back in his childhood he is morose and cutting.

They climb the ornate-timber stairs to the third level and find the lingerie department. Max lifts out a matching set of pink and black lace. The corset bra sends a slight smirk to his face. While he parts racks of underwear, Alice follows, watching him cast aside petticoats and chemises. The scanty black camisole and undies he swings out will be her evening back at the lodgings. First a shower together, then a sexy saunter to show off her beautiful figure, and later, coming down on her, removing each piece delicately with his teeth.

Their first night together on Rottnest in his room, he had kissed her with a gentle brush of his lips, bouncing awkwardly on the doughy mattress, his hands caressing her with long strokes, circling her buttocks. He was stiff against her, prodding, and then he had slipped into her from behind. She enjoyed the first twinge of heat, then a searing pleasure, until she plateaued and he was fluid, withdrawing on her stomach.

Alice worries about the latest purchase, as if satin and lace are props for his fantasies. He seems to ache for her all day. And if they're not ducking into his bed-sit, they're pressing each other in late night alleyways, in an empty lift, or in a quiet stairwell. She doesn't know what all this means. She feels strangely vulnerable too, each time after making love, letting the semen drain into the bowl. Lately, she is looking for a different colour. She is five days overdue.

Max carries the shopping up the stairs of the Mount Street boarding house. It's quiet, no landlady. Alice pours herself a drink of water. He is already tapping the bed. It seems this piece of furniture is the central ingredient in their relationship. His hands creep inside her t-shirt. While he is kissing and fondling her, he slowly teases out the words, *'Ich Liebe Dich.* I love you!' he repeats.

Alice straightens and sits up. 'Sorry, I've got a stomach cramp. Maybe, it's you know what.'

She is doubled up on the bed. She can't talk or concentrate. The pain is excruciating. 'I'll be back in a minute.' She sits on the bowl. It's only a little trickle and there is a burning sensation. She can't understand this internal pressure. She's never had this before. He's in love with me and I don't know what the bloody hell I'm doing.

Alice leans her elbows on the bathroom sink watching clear water run slowly through the gusset of her undies. She scrunches them into a ball, letting them dribble down the glass under the mirror's light. She's forgotten the time. Her reflection is someone she used to know. She thinks about her old friends. I'm just like Heather, aren't I? The woman in the mirror doesn't answer, but the one in front tells her she is a stupid bitch. The stapler in her body that is attaching her groin to her abdomen forces her to the kitchen. The more water she drinks, the less her stomach and bladder hurt. She guzzles four glasses, refills another and carries it back to the bedroom. In a slurry of shapes and shadows squirming through old venetians, she finds Max asleep, rolled up like a caterpillar in a scrunch of blankets, sheets and bare pillows.

A Proper Diagnosis

Memo 12:   *Love conquers all.*

The next afternoon, Alice enters the gynecologist's surgery. She is anxious and tentative about this appointment, Max choosing one of the most expensive doctors in Perth. She is even more frustrated that he'd waved goodbye at the lift, wanting to view the Tudor clock in London Court. He'd heard stories about its quaint midday performance, the precision of jousting knights on horseback. His body backing away from the closing doors, had said, 'man on a mission'. Pointing to his wrist watch, he'd mouthed the words 'R & I Bank!'

Alice knows the certainty before her. A medical professional judging her as a loose single girl getting herself into trouble. She expects that he won't even ask how she's feeling, thinking or hating the formless thing inside.

White coats greet her in the surgery. After five minutes of waiting, she rests her arms on the counter. The doctor peers over his bifocals, while the receptionist thrusts a form in her direction. Another lady buzzes around, the tread of her nursing shoes mimicking the melodious ripple of her Welsh accent. She opens a curtained screen, addressing Alice as 'Sweetie!'

Alice can't speak. Her heart is under pressure from a rhythm of tender hammers. She can hear the doctor in the next room, the clink of instruments under water. She imagines them being sterilized for her. On a starched linen gurney, she wrestles with the formless smock. Stretching out her legs, she isn't sure whether to kick her shoes off or keep them on. Finally, she slips them from the plastic sheeting. The clock on the wall is the only thing talking; five more minutes and Max's ice-blue eyes might be fixed on that arcade timepiece. Or were they? She rolls onto her side re-positioning the awkward garment. She is harboring a little foreigner inside, building its body art. She closes her eyes, listening for any machinery. Is it an assembly line in there? Plop, the boy-bits. Plop, brown hair. Plop, blue eyes!

The doctor speaks in small "ums", then slaps off his rubber gloves. The women hover, labeling phials and clicking pens. Alice can tell the specialist is suspicious, staring at her finally with both hands flat on the table. She jokes to herself. So, tell me Doc, what's the good news? Six weeks is it. Well, what do you know? This is great! Yeah, the kid's got a father in town looking at a clock. Couldn't be better, could it? And me, well I'm thrilled really, losing my job, the big belly thing, rolling around in nine months' time like Humpty Dumpty. Yep, I'm positively ecstatic about all this!

But real sensations float like a cloud in the room. Her head is full of diagrams, the doctor's wall prints, coat-stand in the corner, a long plastic calendar, an odd-looking dolphin statue scripted with the words *Tweed Heads, NSW*. His red gumball machine, smaller than the supermarket kind, is stacked with colourful balls. She isn't listening to anything. She's twisting the dial, grabbing a handful, crunching into the lolley casing. A large gob of chewy stirring saliva in her mouth. As the gum swells, she imagines blowing like jiggery all over this man's face, laughing long and loud, watching it catch on his plastered sweep of hairs. See it's there, she thinks, caught on your freckled, pocked forehead.

Now he's pushing little packets across the desk. 'For the future', he says, slipping brochures from a rubber band. Alice has heard about the Pill, but it seems all hocus pocus to her. With all those medical details of ovaries, condoms, creams, drugs, the Catholic rhythm method, she didn't know a goddamn thing.

She assumes a different pose when the doctor scribbles out a prescription and hands it to her. He would like to see her in six weeks for a thorough examination. She's to take care of her health, take one antibiotic with every meal. 'The cramping will disappear in two days. The infection is a chill. Best to keep your legs crossed after sex.' He leans back in his chair and folds his arms. Alice nods, pretending that his advice and knowledge is something she has inherited from all the women in her life. She is especially pleased that the Greek goddesses had laid out their eternal plan.

The specialist points to a chart on the wall. He is approximating the birth-date as September. Alice gives out a little laugh. Finally, he reaches across the great divide with his dry, milky hand and says, 'Congratulations!'

She pumps out another breathy cry.

Alice enters the lift annoyed at the doctor's presumption that she's embracing the little thing inside the size of a baked bean. One-point-two centimetres – putting her life on hold. Now she's tense, and can't think of anything beyond this pegging of pregnancy. In the London Court Café she focuses on small details. Does she tell Max the truth? Where is he? How will he take the news? What if she has an abortion? Will he go along with it? Women did it all the time. She can remove one more unwanted human being from the world, right here in Perth. Her hometown folk never knowing. She can leave Max to his Magoo wanderings and continue her own travels. Tonga. Nouméa. New Zealand's hot springs, cow-grazing plains and ice-capped mountains. God, she'd have to tell Irene and Veronica!

Seven Trains

Memo 13:   *Everything in woman has a solution. It is called Pregnancy.*

Early morning. The uneasy feeling again. Her body commands something from her. Alice wants no part of it, or its torture. Worse is the occasional accident. The sudden eruption, having her behind a bush, bent over, spewing into the soft fur of a grevillia. The only thing to wipe her eyes and mouth is the back of her hand. This is a strange beast she cannot wrestle.

She is crumpled. Sweat trickles down her collar. She feels like a saltmarsh. The road outside the boarding house is hot. The taxi hasn't come. The bags are heavy. Max decides they'll walk from Mount Street to the City Square. In Murray Street, she discovers the proximity of two public toilets, now necessary landmarks. If she had time she'd discover more, but the décor of dripping taps, urine stench, tissue-blazed floors, vandal tales, is really no place to linger, especially in her nauseous state. Max is outside, pacing and puffing on cigarettes. When they finally get to the station, Alice surveys the rest rooms at two side entrances of the building, and as the Transcontinental Express sidles, huffs, then fuses into the long platform, she notes with her fingers crossed, there are toilets at either end of the carriage.

Go ahead. Ask Alice how she is feeling as she enters the murky surface of a claustrophobic carriage, hot and tight as a phone booth. Ten-deep in the cubicle, surfies in singlets are juggling their gear. A boy, sliding his duffle bag along the floor on a top step in front of Alice, butts into her. He topples to the side, grappling the straps of her backpack. She stops suddenly, removing his sweaty hand. His impatient flesh staining her blouse. 'Wait, will you? No one's moving!' she says, lifting her backpack higher. He glistens like wet soap, giving her that 'so what' look.

'Dickbreath,' she says, turning out of earshot.

The next person is just as hopeful, trying to pass his surfboard to the brown skin ahead of him. The strong residue of Coppertone makes Alice gag. Between waiting in the queue, and in each exhale and inhale, the sharp aroma of coconut oil has slipped into her lymph nodes and nervous system. The acid rises from her stomach, sharp and toxic. *Fuck*, she says, tasting a dry retch. She has felt this sharp burn in her throat before on Sydney trains, entering crowded carriages that smelt like shit. Body odour and a stench of four-day old socks so bad she often held back a heave.

There's a dry hot wind wandering through the vestibule, encasing the smell of humid bodies. To make matters worse, fans are whirring and there's an air-conditioning notice on the door apologising to passengers. Alice reads it as, "Suntan lotion kills patience". They shuffle in by inches.

Outside a woman in tight leopard-skin pants is screeching. The man next to her, dipping into his open suitcase, yells back over his effusive clothes. An orange caterpillar-like vehicle, weaving in and out of bystanders, narrowly misses the man. Alice dips a hand into her overnight bag looking for the oranges from the station's veggie stand. Where are they? She needs to roll the orange skin over her hot forehead, squeeze the flesh slowly into the dry rope of her mouth. She might use them as weapons, adding more flavour to the surfers' glistening tan, or maybe she should spit the pips like BB shells on the backs of those raucous ladies in white bowler's hats. A sudden heave and resistance to her nausea sends fibre-like splinters into her skin. Where are the fucking oranges? They're not in her backpack. Blast! Maybe Max has them. If only he'd stop ushering every female on board first.

Alice's nausea increases along with the noises around her. Why doesn't that father tell his wailing boy to shut-up? Oh, for heaven's sake woman, pick up your two-year old, his nappy is about to burst. Frigging hell! Did that bloke in the Hawaiian shirt have to bust his pie bag? Here she is on a four-day train trip with a collection of goons, and silver sponge-cakes in ripple-sole shoes, and the only sane thing onboard is hubby in his rickety legs tuning out the cackle with his hearing aid. The rest on the Trans-express are doing the relative thing, hugging or blowing kisses. Oh, please! I've already vomited this morning.

Alice swings her backpack high onto the carrier, places her rattan basket and brown paper bags at her feet. The rustling noises take her back to the souvenir shop, to the owner with a sister in Terrigal, her empathy for seashells, the same little ones that pattered the shores of Orange Bay. Where will she put them? How will they look at home? What do they mean to her? Would they weep and smell like the limpets she collected at Temple Bay? At least the ornaments have taken her mind off the little ball rolling around inside. Funny, she thinks, that doctor, privileged Wednesday golfer, telling her that the baby measures the size of his golf tee. Her mind switches back to Temple Bay, to Everglades, the colonies of crane and ibis. She's thinking about the wildwood and their mating. Did she have the right mate, and now wonders about Max? Has she done the right thing, dropping her guard, allowing all that intimacy? Where will this strange path of motherhood take her?

Max stands in the aisle, flapping his ticket on the back of the seat. 'I need to borrow your fifty dollars. I spent all my money on Rottnest Island. Presents. The specialist was one hundred and sixty, na?'

'Yeah, but it's all the money I've got on me.'

'I need it for something important.'

Alice unzips her purse and folds the note into Max's hand. 'I could have gone to a G.P. It would have been cheaper.'

There's a shout and a loud whistle. Alice watches a guard unfurl a green flag. The train grunts and jerks, gradually easing from the platform. Outside faces stare rigid like wooden dolls. Some move more freely, waving folded newspapers or hats.

Alice listens to the party plan of silver-haired women, all florals and brooches, and feels like thumping them. Their voices scratch at her brain. She's surrounded by their hyena calls, swaying pearls and shuffling panty hose. She pictures them at the club, thick legs under a rickety card table, bending linen, their cacophony rising over the clap of balls and squeaky chalkboard. She can see the train hurtling along a mountain bridge, carriage dangling wildly off the rails, the women oblivious to the thrust and back-draft, still shoulder shuffling in gradations of laughter.

She'd laugh too, except it would hurt.

Everything is working poorly. From her window, her eyes fixate on the rushing countryside, the track continuing like a ladder. Clumps of banksias, grasstrees, and spear grass, flash past like long lost friends. At the rear, the click-clack of her single life disappears into the foothills of Perth like loud hosannas. Rail lines merge over past scenes of Irene boarding a TAA jet, the aqua blue of Thompson Bay under soft cloud, Mrs Featherstone handing menus to Chef Barker and the boys. They're mocking me there under the trees, she thinks. On occasions she has to remind herself to unclench the hard rocks of her fists. She doesn't want to place them anywhere near the danger zone, the little mountain under her belly harbouring unknown lava. At times it seems vitriolic. Maybe she can break this bundle away from her womb before it's too late.

To relieve the boredom, Alice summons Zorro, her favourite TV character, to the scene. He swings through the silver light of the window, swash-buckling his sword into a Z, ridding the carriage of every amateur pianist. He leaves his insignia on the piano, three sections falling apart like cut cake. Bowlers' hats and white cardigans come under his scrutiny. He zigzags them into little pieces, leaving polyester and cotton as tatters on the arms of smoking jackets, the men still drinking their gin and tonics. Alice supplies him with a stack of oranges, watches how much juice they extract. As she throws, he hooks and splices them over the goons sleeping on their surfboards and jackets.

There is nothing else to do but this. Nothing else to think about on this tedious journey, nothing that will ease this involuntary river of vomit, dry retching, chapped lips and iron-heavy teeth. She leaves her little mess in the smoker's lounge and heads for the carriage. A smell emanates from the toilet like a citrus factory. She's eaten several oranges, a whole bag full and doesn't know why. Maybe, they were just cheap and somehow they soothed the desert sand in her throat. Now she's getting worried that she can't take the second string bag across the border. She has to think about where to leave them, maybe at the next stop, maybe in the bloody loo.

'It's all set.' Max pumps his body into the next seat. 'Tonight we are moving down the front of the train. Getting away from this barnyard.'

'How's that?'

'That fifty was for the steward. He found us a first-class sleeper. After dinner, when it is more dark, we look for B56. You'll be more comfortable in there, twin beds, na? We can have a jiggy-jig as well, my little Sweetie-pie.'

Max tussles Alice's hair forward. Her mood is tense, his nagging about wearing her hair up into a beehive, constant. Only old Frau women wear their hair on top. He's already giving her a list of the ways he fancies her other styles, long waves, two ponytails. 'And what about Pippy Longstocking plaits, na?' Alice sinks below the window, watching a ghost town of telegraph poles, tanks and tin sheds. 'I like it hanging loose over your shoulders,' he says. 'Although it is a little greasy.'

Max reaches up for the hand luggage, her brown paper shopping bags, and the backpacks. While he's carrying them to the end of the carriage, he grunts out scenes of their night together, just the two of them, away from the hen house. Alice can only think of the sleeper, while Max focuses on their new life together. They will get married without all the fuss. Later, he'll return to Western Australia, go up north, save more money. She can stay with her parents, and when the baby is born he will bring them back to Perth. Other people might stay with the in-laws, but not Max Klauss. Living in Sydney is out of the question. The big congested city would be like going back to Hamburg.

Alice contemplates lying down in an hour. If she can settle her stomach, she knows she will fall asleep. Everything aches, her back, groin, stomach, chest and throat. As if buzzards have pecked at her intestine and pulled it through her kidneys. Now she's run out of Dispirin and doesn't know if the train will stop before Port Augusta. But tonight, if he wants to make love, she thinks, I'll pretend. I'll fake it.

'I like your idea of settling in Perth. I wouldn't be able to take the small town gossip, Max. I lived in that town for twenty years and everyone knows your business. At least in Perth, they won't know a thing.'

'We'll buy a house, na? I'll work in the Pilbara for a year. Make a lot of money, my Sweetie-pie.'

Alice leans toward the window, the lights of the inside of the carriage glittering back. She traces the patterns of heads and seats with her eyes. She hears Max talking about being a father, buying a car and furniture, but she is only half listening.

In the curtained compartment she slips into the warmth and haze of the early evening. Under a small side lamp, the rocking clatter of the train makes her somnolent. Tonight, Max is eating without her. She can't face food, especially oranges. The warm shower and the fresh sheets against her skin soften the day's war in her belly. Her head nestles into the pillow and then a sharp pain registers itself in her groin. Despite the previous nights of being violently ill, there is something monstrous about this. Her body is leaking from every aperture. She takes a tissue from her bag and blows her nose. No pads, no loose tablets. She slaps the open leather hard against the bed rail. The bag dribbles its contents to the floor. Pulling a pillow and compressing it into her stomach, she tells herself, 'I'm sick. God, so sick!'

'Hi, my little Sweetie-pie.' Max places a paper bag on the bunk, his Blundstones crunching and powdering her shell bracelet on the carpet tiles. 'Here, I smuggled a piece of pie. Wow, you should have seen the menu. I had

Chicken Kiev, asparagus, potatoes with cream cheese. Little chocolates with the coffee. Here look, two for you.'

'Max, I…please don't.'

'Well, no need to eat them now. Perhaps, in the morning. Guess what, we are being served breakfast tomorrow? Wunderbar, ja?'

'Yeah, beaut.'

'Move over my little Sweetie-pie, now that we are alone, eh? Um, your breasts, they are swelling. Ooh, you feel good.'

Alice feels the tips of his fingers circling her nipples. He bundles himself alongside. They're both lying in a foetal position, but she can't move. She feels wet down below. 'Max, I'm having bad stomach pains. I can't think…I… I've run out of painkillers. Can you forgive me? And you've gone to all this trouble. I'm in a mess. I didn't think pregnancy would be so uncomfortable. I've got to go.'

Alice is sitting on the pan again. She feels like putting a sign on the door; this lavatory belongs to ALICE BENNETT. At least, it's no longer like the second-class with the rattling door, someone telling her to hurry, the latch twisting and clicking, door pulled back and forth a centimetre or two and then the noise of shoes receding down the aisle. This is different. This is first class comfort. A toilet all to herself!

On the second day, the train wheezes motionless for several minutes. Alice heads to the tearooms. She angles her belt buckle into the station's hard countertop. She can feel a cramp coming on. They've pulled into some isolated shunting sheds and siding. The man in the Panama from the Express tells her they could be a while, he can see with his x-ray vision that they were changing engines. 'One has broken down,' he boasts.

We're changing tracks, you moron.

Alice can hardly open her mouth. 'You got an orange.' She leans further over the wooden counter, finds its cool grains soothing on her irritated arms. The woman behind the counter points to the drinks' cabinet.

'Oh, no, I meant,' she says, crouching further over, crossing her palms. 'Gimme those Cool Mints, the large ones and some Dispirin.'

The woman places a packet of Aspro beside the Cool Mints, butts out her cigarette in a loaded, smelly ashtray.

Alice grumbles to herself. *Well, how bloody much? Am I a mind-reader?* 'I'll have two packets of Aspro.' She pushes a five-dollar note past the foul ashtray. *You should be paying **me** to eat this stuff.*

'Five-twenty,' says the woman.

'What?' Alice upends her purse. Hears the cool tinkle of the coin rolling on the floorboards, and walks smartly out the back through a large room.

Back in the cabin, Alice finds Max's wallet opened on the bed. She hears his footsteps in the corridor, and quickly lifts a fifty dollar bill. 'Ah,' he says, unhooking his jacket from the back of the door. 'I've had the lunch and now I look around, ja?' he says, smiling, waiting. 'I'm still sick,' she returns.

Alice sits on the top bunk, dangling her legs. She doesn't feel guilty about sneaking back the fifty. Previously, she didn't mind the noisy goods train, the pong of dagged sheep, chickens choreographed like mush in wire ready for market. She's forgotten about the mute in the refreshment rooms, the number of Aspros taken, but it annoys and puzzles her that Max has over three hundred dollars in cash.

She watches her reflection in the window, drops it down with a bang. Max has joined some men outside, drinking beer. Over the intercom, there's an announcement. 'All passengers are to change trains. A guard will direct you to the far end of the platform. There's just a short walk across the lines. The train will depart for Melbourne in precisely twenty minutes.'

Alice humps her backpack over her right shoulder and joins a mumsy lady with a valet and a lap dog. Both lady and dog flounce fur into the air. Alice learns that she's a widow ready to spend the old boy's money. When they reach the end of the platform, the women, digging their heels into metal stones, gape at the Gothic locomotive in front of them.

'It's true,' says the widow.

'It's the Orient Express,' says Alice.

'No!' says the man, walking behind. 'It's the Overland.'

'I don't care what it is', says Alice, picking up the lady's dog and trailing her voice over the rails. 'It's a dream.'

Both women strut through the first carriage, bending and gawping from door to wrought-iron carrier. Alice peers in at the toilets, jiggles and kisses the dog at the sight of the little brass handles and snowy soft toilet paper. They walk through a full-length side corridor. The seating compartments are fitted out with polished timber paneling and chrome fittings. The twin wooden sliding doors to each compartment have ornamental glass. Alice whirls the little Pekinese around and around, and comes full circle in front of Max glaring down his ski nose.

'You didn't tell me we were moving!'

'You were too busy drinking with those men. I did wave, Max. Anyway, how come you didn't you hear the message?'

'Never mind. Come, we are back this way. I've got all your stuff. And get that mutt away from me.'

'Oh, he's a cutesy, wutesy, little thing, aren't you?, she says, feeling lightheaded.

The woman, with her hands on both hips and slightly hidden in fur, grunts at Max's rudeness. 'Young man, Bobby is not *a mutt*!'

'You better take him, Mildred,' says Alice, swaying on her feet. 'Before he's pork chops.'

The widow lifts the dog from Alice's arms, leans in with confidence on her mind. 'You take care, young lady. I'd watch out, if I were you. He's a one, he is.'

The train grates on the tracks, reversing slightly before moving forward. Out of the window, on the other side of marshalling yards, sand and bush; a lone thorn tree signal some hope of nature. Alice moves lethargically back to the first carriage. She loves the polished comfort of timber and leather. It reminds her of Mr Pringle's studded couch and swivel chair at the bank. She likes the ornate work on each mirror above the headrests, and wonders if they're ivy or grape vines trailing the beveled edge. When heads turn, she can't help giggling and waving at their silent voices and stares. At the end, standing in the cubicle, the last glimpse of station, the animals, the sound of running feet. The only thing that attracts Alice to the place is the little valance of scrolled wood outlining the chalet roof of the station. It has old world charm, but the people have died. She thinks she sees a woman crying. For a moment she imagines the image is a lion? That bit of fur around the woman's neck? Has the lady lost someone, leaning there against a timber post amongst a suite of suitcases, wiping her face with a lace hanky?

Alice fumbles in her bag for more Aspro. She swallows a broken tablet, and burps. She floats amongst the seats, cases, coats, books and newspapers that travel in the compartment with her. Leaning out of the window, she counts the railway sleepers, until finally the open jaws of the track gobble them insatiably. She enjoys sitting near the window, facing the way she's going. Max raises his eyebrows at her from the other side. He makes a side-to-side waddle, trying to make more room, watching out for any sign of amusement. Alice only manages to raise one corner of her mouth. What does he expect, laughter? Plus there aren't any females to talk to.

Max is now asking a gentleman at the window to swap seats. But the man coughs and flaps out his newspaper. Max shrugs at Alice and is about to light a cigarette, when the same man points his folded newspaper towards the Non-Smoking sign, sending Max grumpily through the doors, slamming and rattling the panels.

There are two men in the corridor. One is a passing guard, and the other, a young man in a beret, coat and scarf. Alice watches him bumming one of Max's Camels, red embers from their tailor-mades glowing in the semi-dark. Both men lean on the corridor window. The young man coughs violently, bends an arm into his waist. He peers in at Alice over the ivy detailing, his long hair falling over his ears. Max is alongside, nudging him.

Alice thinks about the woman on the platform. Does she belong to this sick fellow? He must be around twenty-five. Has he left her at the station? Did they split? Maybe they are married. Did something go wrong? Alice watches the young man's eyes, droopy and dark. Perhaps, he's a gigolo. Perhaps, *she* has made the decision not to come on the train. She looks so much older than him, a little agitated and tired. There's a laugh, Alice thought. Join the club.

***

Crossing two states, Alice and Max board three more trains. By now, she wants to hear the same voluptuous sounds of another iron and brass beast, the high wind clouting steel, a sweet gnawing of timber joists above the headrests. On the Overland, she relaxes in the slumber of leather, slipping her spine down into the indentations of the buttons, Readers' Digest falling from her lap, the whooshing countryside ferrying her into semi-unconsciousness.

The next train out of Melbourne is uncomfortable; Alice is annoyed stuck to a vinyl, bottom clinging seat, air-nodding fitfully into Albury. At the Victorian border, a sprawling carriage with comfortable blue seats strokes her tiredness. The train fast-tracks them across the countryside, through acres of green farms homing them all the way to

Sydney. Alice is lightheaded, lost in the sensory clacking of the train's idyllic motion. Max is asleep, his lustful groping subsided. Later, at Central, coming out of the illusory world of sleep, Alice gathers her things. She can smell the old mustiness of the station, human beings rushing about. She feels washed out, her nerve endings, shaky. She's thinking about home, wondering if her friends will respond to her marquisé engagement ring.

Alice screws the cluster of stones further down from the middle knuckle. The train's soap helps, moving the tight ring from her right hand to her engagement finger. She isn't getting a diamond, Max states. The Germans don't do that, but she doesn't believe him. Saying the engagement ring is their wedding band moved from right to left. Poppycock, she thinks. He's just getting out of it.

Now she's scuffing her shoes slowly along the platform. They're in a herd of people at the ticket gate. She knows she's spotting again, feeling that wet glue inside her gusset. Something's wrong, it's not supposed to be like this.

Max decides to give Alice the good news. He is going to buy a pipe to save money on cigarettes. He will go back to his favourite tobacco, Cherry-Blend, if he can purchase it in

New South Wales. And there will be less beer drinking, but the coffee will stay. He lights up, stubbing half of the cigarette under his shoe, as he catches Alice's scorn.

At the country end of the station, and beneath a black and white board, Alice points to the Temple Bay line. Huge clocks display the next departure time. Six hours to wait for the train. Max's voice is grating. 'Where is this Green Point, somewhere in Nova Scotia?' He drags the bags to a bench seat near the information office. Lights another cigarette. 'I must have a shower soon. I am so itchy. Wait here with the luggage. I am dying for a bloody cup of coffee, na?'

He's blowing smoke in her direction.

'Well?'

'Don't do that!'

'I just wanted to see if you were still alive.'

Alice glares, telling him to *piss off* with her eyes.

Alice's anger is buoyant. She isn't going to wait around for six hours by herself. She finds the locker room in the far corner of the station, and lifts the heavy bags on the counter. The attendant, closing the metal doors, says, 'There!', and hands her the key.

Alice buys a cup of tea and waits near the clocks. She is too disheveled with rage to look for Max. He should have given her a minute, they could have gone to the restaurant together. She knows her way around. How many times has she been here before? Visits to the Cross, skating at Prince Alfred Park, relief work at the bank, the weirdos she didn't look in the face. Once in a long queue at the information desk, she waited to find out about her trip to Katoomba, watching a man pick his nose and eat it in public. Another time at the age of fourteen, and buying a ticket to visit a school friend in Narrabri, she discovered an old woman sleeping on a toilet bench, a mass of gooey bandages falling loosely from her lesioned legs. Once, when she raced home from the Capitol theatre, an odd fellow in a khaki overcoat had exposed himself on the platform. *Don't look*, the commuters said.

The nagging is beginning again. Bladder full and tight like a coconut. Alice concentrates on the locker key in her cardigan pocket. It wouldn't do to lose it. Max would have a fit if they couldn't get to the bags.

What are these women doing? People don't realise how ugly they look arguing in a public toilet.

Alice hears voices running hot and cold. Foul language and the name Vinny. A woman in a scarf towers over the other. Now she's pulling out handfuls of wiry hair. Alice feels embarrassed, she can't watch, so pretends to be busy at the sink. She slips off her marquisé ring. The soap is thick sludge. She doesn't want the glug to lodge in her stones. She hears the cleaners in the back toilets, swirling water, ignoring these two angry women. A few metres away, thick strands of steel wool and matted hair fall to the checkered floor. The cleaners drag buckets, pushing rag mops through squeeze-clamps. They move around like nuns in penance. The ruckus heightens, the anger more so; the lady with the steel wool hair has her friend pinned to the ground, kicking her in the waist or is it the kidneys? It's too painful to watch. They're crying, screaming. The obscenities hurt Alice's ears. It's disgusting. She runs outside, waves at a station attendant in a blue uniform. He moves more quickly when she tells him someone's being murdered in the ladies toilets. She can't go back in. It's pathetic.

On the Green Point train, Alice relates the incident to Max. He tells her to go slow, stop babbling. He can't understand a word. 'I feel responsible,' Alice says. 'Two policewomen came, clamped handcuffs on the two, then dragged them out still screaming at each other. Max, there was blood everywhere. One woman bit into the other lady's ear.'

'As they say up north, they're on the turps, na?'

'Yeah, I guess. I hate Central Station. It gives me the creeps. I'm so glad we've left that place.'

'Don't think of it anymore. The police will handle it, put them in the lock-up for the night, yeh?'

Max continues to talk. He's telling Alice about a night he spent in the East Perth lock-up. She hears bits and pieces of his conversation as she sinks deeper into her seat. She feels the weight of the carriage's thrust hard against her chest. She hears the words, *magistrate, stupit, bloody cops,* his repetitive question, *Vat is bail?* The train is dragging Alice to the ground, iron girders crushing her chest, heavier and heavier, her mind fraught with metallic screaming as she looks down at her empty left-hand finger, the marquisé ring gone, still sitting somewhere back in Sydney, in that soap sludge, in that God-awful Ladies toilet.

The Reddest Rose Unfolds

Memo 14:   *A cup of tea, a Bex and a good lie down is the best remedy.*

All things pass, and Max and Alice are back in Western Australia. Alice's body has settled, and in her new experience of living in a Scarborough flat, she is fit and happy. Close to the beach, she enjoys swimming, walks along the promenade, looking out to sea, a land's edge facing the opposite direction to home. She's still not used to the sunrise and sunset being contrary to the east coast, but likes the idea of South Africa, India and Madagascar at the other end of the ocean. She's stopped ringing her mother lately, waking her when she's asleep by nine.

Alice likes musing about exotic places, decorating her beach flat with large calendar prints. Behind the toilet door, scenes of canals in Venice; February in brindle shades of the Leaning Tower of Pisa; March the blues of the Archipelagoes. Near kitchen utensils, a hinged calendar features the Tyne Bridge, Castles of Northumberland, Calgary's Larch Trees in variegated green and cloudy backdrops. An arrow swirls under the picture of Little Panache Lake. August is the busiest month: her dentist appointment, doctor on the fourteenth, Max returning on the twenty-fifth. With more dates to think of than space, Alice puts the tenth and seventeenth into her memory bank, not long after her birthday on the eighth. It could be a double celebration; November is texta-marked with three birthdays, including her father's.

Alice is supposed to be asleep by now, but can't drop off. It's the snapping motorbike in the driveway. She can time her first eye-blink by her next-door neighbour. Shift-worker. Late nights, early mornings. His boot leather busy on the pedal, even when he gurgles down the path at five am

Tonight she is painfully bundled on the lounge, aching for conversation. Not even the landlady's dachshund visits to tease the bird. Suddenly she hates this hermetic life. Being pregnant is like having a pillion rider that is unable to talk. She can only give it a tummy rub and say, 'How you going in there, rosebud?' Even the people at work stop ringing once they handed over the monster card and baby bouncer. Alice wonders about Mildred, whether she still lived in Floreat Park. The warmth of her shoulder hugs, hand squeezing, effervescent chitchat has faded like myth. It seems so long ago. Alice wants to talk to her now, but maybe they didn't have anything in common.

She groans at the new collage of photographs and letters from Max. His grey singlet is just as tatty as a front fly-screen door.

'Inside the hut,' he writes, *'it's a Fremantle shipping container, hot and stuffy. Davo is playing cards with Mick and Yorri (a Pole, not a noodle-hoover). That's Derrick in the baseball cap at the side of the truck. We had a job to do last week at Mosquito Creek. We'll have it finished before the rain. One minute it's dry dust, the next it's a wash-away. Floods for days, miles. That's what they tell me. Tomorrow, it's a shooting trip. Derrick has four guns. He lent me a shotgun. Plus bullets. He tells me plenty of stories about Dugites. He says some snakes are like train carriages filled with rats. When anything bangs into the truck, Derrick just shoots. Wild bugger! Last Sunday we went out, about six of us, spotted a big red, told the dog to run, but bloody Coco kept spinning his legs in the dust, even when we yelled to stop, he kept running. Bloody funny, I nearly pissed my pants. There was Coco passing the*

bloody kangaroo like his tail was on fire. We told him to "go" but not that fast.

See that photograph, wiping my mouth, bastards bumped me, beer went everywhere. The toothless clown in the blue singlet with his hairy arms around the dog is Mick. The little white mutt is Coco. Such a good dog. Well, Sweetie-pie, that's it. Some news of what I'm doing. A couple of fun times, the rest is plain hard work, mostly a piss-up, then sleep.

In Max's long letters, he's dictated most of the words to Derrick. He wishes he could write better English, but the postcards, schmaltz, and familiar words are easy to copy. *I miss your warm cuddly breasts, your cooking and kisses. My bank account is growing. Already I saved seven thousand dollars. I need a haircut, the taste of your wunderbar roast chicken. Some clean sheets. This place makes me itch. Some of them are lazy bastards.*

On another postcard, he writes. *We play cards on the bunk beds at night. The only thing of interest on weekends is Davo's metal detector. Outside, there is zilch, further out, desert, but watch out for the big stack of beer cans. The skins on the fence are drying for the blackfellas in town. I forgot to tell you last time, Sweetie-pie. We had kangaroo tail soup. Delicious!*

Alice sits alone with her stack of mail imagining Max slicing into a leg of kangaroo. A vision of steamy juicy meat reminds her of their Sunday roast lamb, the day they arrived from their Nullarbor journey. Her mother's steely silence is something Alice can't get used to. Especially her huffing and puffing, the long drawn-out breaths, her temper thumping to a boil like potatoes. Max, not noticing her mother's moods, keeps on asking how many people are coming to the wedding.

Alice remembers standing there in the cigarette-stained kitchen, finding rooms hard to cross. Her mother ignoring her at the kitchen sink after meals. Her dad left a scraping sound across the lino with his chair, leaving a paper boat napkin floating in gravy.

It annoyed Alice that the conversation was brisk when Kevin came home from work. When Jimmy rang from Walcha they laughed out loud. She thought of all the years they endowed him with everything, golf trophy nights, a twenty-first with over eighty people, rented hall, and a keg.

Her mother's words of wisdom, 'play with fire and you get burnt' had multiple meanings, but never saved her from sex.

Some images leave her eyes moist in the ridges. Propped against a steep of pillows, her grandmother's fallen face chalky and stark against the brassy glint of the headboard, her mum sewing silently on the Singer. Betty Parker, holding her hand after school and settling her on a kitchen stool, serves up plated repetitions of her delicious chocolate cake. Sometimes green Aeroplane jelly wobbles in a bowl towards her, or a fresh Devon sandwich brimmed with tomato sauce.

Heather turns up in the twilight looking like a ghoul, with dark circles under her eyes, still warning Alice about motherhood. Once, in her Morris, they had driven to Wiseman for Mannie's clothes. Heather had started the day calm, until she opened the boot, shoving bottles, bunny rugs, nappies, a Teddy bear and tote bag into the pram. Outside 'Tots and Teens' jostling Mannie through an array of plastic ducks, she held up his soggy nappy. 'You'll be doing this one day, Alice. Carting everything around, making lists.' Then she'd stomped the pavement, swearing loudly about forgetting the effen film.

In the main street, Alice calmed Heather down with an ice cream, but eating a dribbling cone, mixed with a buoyant smell of Johnson's baby powder and a pumpkin nappy leak, hadn't been a good idea. Leaving town, pages of a parking fine flapped under the wipers. Unhinging the paper, Heather began ripping it into tiny squares. It looked similar to the dot-to-dot creases on her silk blouse. Forget the anger of a big kidney stain of mucous on her right shoulder. Forget the trickle that made two wet patches revealing dark nipples. Forget the wet lap. If she'd seen anyone at all resembling the council, she would have killed them instantly with her demonic stare.

***

In the Scarborough flat, Alice can't get warm. She looks down at her hands, reddened now with the rubbing. She wants to rock and rock. The motion reminds her of the wash on Temple Bay beach, the memories of two years ago – all that rocking. Forward and back, forward and back, trying to stop the thud and roll of headaches, the abdomen and bladder clench. Now in her second pregnancy, there are only a few sensations, sometimes a small twinge of anxiety, or a shuddering spasm like déjà vu. But she still prefers to rock.

The telephone sudden and loud on the wall snaps her from her daydream. 'Max? What time is it?'

His voice bursts through the receiver. He's so excited he can't get the words to flow freely. He tells her they found gold today. And he's been waiting in a queue for over two hours. All the construction boys wanting to make a call tonight. It's crazy. One phone box out in the middle of the desert, utes bumping men from the back of the tray, drunk as skunks. 'They piss in the bush, then run back to the line. Plenty of shoving. There's already been a fight. Some of 'em take their time talking to the wife and kids. They just won't hurry up. Bastards,' he laughs. 'Then they tell you to shake a leg. Well, I do that, Sweetie-pie, and they just laugh.'

He's talking again about the North, eating donkey stew, but Alice can't imagine the terrain or working conditions. To her, the northern landscape sounds like a red dust bowl. Something like tons of paprika sprinkled over inland dunes, or their camp like tins of Spam set on wholemeal bread with a few clumps of lettuce leaves. It isn't anything to think about. Not like two streets away. Sounds of a winter surf bombarding sand-ruts and rocks, the smell of salted fish and chips; Scarborough's hamburgers with freshly cooked mincemeat, onions, pickles, and beetroot. She is getting weird cravings. Some days she sits in the park eating chocolate and chips, rugged to the chin in her velour coat, watching the wattlebirds fill their little red sacks. She whistles to the magpies, delighted in teasing the gulls with one remaining chip. She tells Max her stomach is a pumped up ball. She gets a few twinges walking on the foreshore; maybe little 'rosebud' gets excited at the beach.

Max tells her it's a twenty-four hour summer where he is. 'My shirt-sleeves and stubbies are starting to stink so bad that blowies are using chain saws to cut through the screen door. Three more weeks to go, Ally. I can't wait. But I am learning about the country, all right. The Aborigines just sit under a boab tree while we work all day in the hot sun. The other day, a few of us boys went out into the bush and blew up some trees with gelignite. Just for kicks. Whoa! Should have seen that timber skyrocket. There was this enormous rain of leaves and bark like confetti.'

Max's happy voice calms Alice. She can hear he's different tonight, relaxed. His voice isn't slurred. Derrick's influence. She likes the sound of his boss, the way he includes Max in his escapades, fun with his dog; the fact that they have coffee together instead of beer when they meet in his Rivervale home.

For the next few minutes, Alice talks about the baby, the bedroom piling with towels, basinet, nappies and a baby bath. She's bought a book of babies' names. 'I like Jody, Rachel or Mia,' she says, adding Maggie to the list. Max is quiet for a moment. 'Nup,' he says, 'I'm positive it will be a boy. I like Mark. Mark Andrew Klauss will be a great little snagger-dagger.'

'You don't know that,' says Alice. 'What if it's a girl?'

The line goes dead for a moment. 'I've got to go. The bastard behind me just lifted me out by the neck. Wanker. Love you!'

'Yeah, love …'

Even though the late call is promising, Max's language sounding quaintly ocker, it still leaves Alice feeling drained. Now another demand that she has to deal with, not that she has any control over nature. She is holding back an ironic battle cry. But mummy wants a little girl first. *A little girl, Max, damn it!*

Alice lies restless under a velvet rug, the cream blankets and quilt, looking more like uncooked pastry in the lamp's weak light. The whole flat stinks of garlic from a stir-fry. She can't sleep. Her small bedroom is a movie of hometown faces. Betty Parker trailing her silken voice and skirts across the room, Irene disappearing into the expanse of lane. Her dad's exhausted face, as if rolled over at work by drainpipes, Heather honking in the Morris at the front wire gate. She sees the hand patting by Doctor Fox. She wishes her Temple Bay doctor could visit her now. She isn't comfortable with her Innaloo man. He doesn't know her history.

Alice tries to concentrate on her breathing, summoning some form of meditation. It won't do to attack the bed with her body, disturbing baby. In the dove-grey light she picks a point in the room, resting her eyes on a brass frame on the dresser. Her hanging smock reminds her of a svelte woman's dress, a pattern of flowers sewn on the old veranda Singer. Her mother is young and pretty in sporty pumps and socks walking along the Corso.

Like her mother, Alice loved Manly, the carnivals, beaches draped in hessian, muscular men in one-piece bathers and caps flipping sand with their toes; the wash of breakers mingling with the announcement of races. Once, Lois and Jimmy, fingering the wire cage, discussed stealing two shilling pieces from the wishing well's rockery. They had chased her along the promenade, trying to quell her jeering about getting the strap from dad.

Alice still hears the sounds of the old Temple Bay house, bedroom door needing oil. Her mother, leaning on the doorjamb, her voice scratchy like sandpaper. She has strong memories of her in hair rollers and in a high-buttoned flannelette nightgown. Alice is pushing her body back into the wardrobe cornice, trying to say sorry, needing to explain about the soaked mattress and useless pads. She can't bring herself to talk about six-weeks of bleeding, the violence of her body erupting on a three thousand mile journey. Whenever they talk, it's short bursts of *yes* and *no,* or *dinner's ready.* Images still hammer at her heart. Her mother's scowling face, bitter like bicarbonate soda, complaining over and over about the washing, the airing, just when she's going to golf.

She wanted to go with her. Back to seventeen, playing golf at Everglades, the time she lost her ball in the waterhole, rolling up black jeans, trudging in the muddy edge, feeling something slimy. Her mother saying it might have been a water snake and not a frog. Alice flew out of the water at top speed, her mum laughing, holding out the old snake killer just in case. Edna, dressed in sunshine yellow, looked like a gladiolus in full bloom. Alice remembers her laugh, the mischievous chuckle. Was that the last time they had fun together? She couldn't remember.

Alice digs through the compost heap of her mind; the lasting good memories mixed with the bad. Warm days in the sun. Currawongs in the street. The flapping clothesline. A strong stench in the laundry like fishing berley, her nightclothes left to soak in the concrete trough. After her wedding, Betty Parker visited with her usual trilled *yoo hoo!* in the doorway. Holding a fruitcake with almond icing, she swapped over the cake for a towel, as Alice's arms dripped Sunlight soap bubbles. Betty had that look about her like a bride the world forgot. Alice told her she didn't miss anything. The wedding service was in a church that looked more like a Girl Guide hall. Alice couldn't tell her the rest, a Salvation Army Officer straightening a large book, waited for her mother's back to turn. He was more a witness to the chilly atmosphere than the signatures. The photographer fussed and bumbled, looking for a wedding party, the bride's father, anyone! Max later complained about paying him for his wasted film and time.

Maybe it had to be like that. Maybe, the last image of Max in a window seat taking off from Mascot was all Alice could cling to. But she didn't want a kid on her own. She could hear the prattle by the town gossips: 'She's in the family way, got a bun in the oven, in the puddin' club, just got married, just this week. Fancy that, blah, blah, blathering blah.'

***

The Temple Bay house is shabby and cool. Her dad disappears after work to snore loudly in front of the television, mouth wide open, beer dregs in a glass on a smoker's stand.

Alice remakes her bed. Cuddling both arms into a sudden cramp, she's curled up on the dry side of the mattress. The smell lingers in her nostrils. It isn't sweet. It's like meat gone off. She can't understand why she is menstruating. It's not meant to be like this. Her mum's sour face prevents her from any discussion. She's as stinky as a mangrove, damp and muddy. Her body disgusts her. The shedding of this gooey muck has taken all the glamour out of being a happy, pregnant woman. How can she hug a pain?

Her mother trails the broom across the porch boards, raising her voice through the bathroom door. 'Your appointment with Fox is at nine thirty. You'll be all right on your own. He'll probably give you something to settle you down. I'm off soon!'

She hears the clubs rattle on the porch. She's been in the shower for an hour scrubbing her fanny. It won't do for the doctor to find a mess, let alone the smell. Yelling back, Alice asks her to go to the surgery with her. In the sun's tracks on the veranda and toweling wet hair it's begging time. 'Couldn't you go to golf *this afternoon*?'

Her mother continues polishing her clubs. 'I talked to René's friend. She's the nurse up there. Just tell her you've been spotting. She'll look after you. I think her name's Thelma.'

***

In the surgery, the tread of nursing shoes ripples over the squeaky linoleum. Alice stands each time a blue uniform passes. After twenty minutes, she's directed through doorways, through the sharp odour of antiseptic, sanitized bleached curtains, then finally into Thelma's office. Feeling a slow trickle, she squats on the vinyl seat, her thighs pressed tightly together.

She hears the name 'Alice Klauss!' It's hardly recognisable. At the reception desk she wrote Bennett, forgetting her new name. She has ticked the single box, now she has to correct the form to her married status. Thelma sparks a smile, introducing herself. She points towards the end passage. *Take your sample, place it on the tray near the fridge, there's a good girl.* Next, it's the vein prick, a little ruby of blood left under cotton wool.

Doctor Fox greets her, lifting his white coattails at the back of the seat. Alice knows he's a Catholic man, comfortable with eight children in his surgery-home. 'I remember you as a little toddler, Alice,' he says, pushing his chair further in. 'Now look at you, all grown up and having a baby.'

'Yeah.' The words 'double trouble' couple under her breath.

'All you need is plenty of rest, young lady. Your mother tells me you've been travelling?'

'Yes, Perth.' A zillion light years away.

'I want to see you again next week. We don't want any complications. The bleeding is slightly abnormal. It's just a matter of keeping an eye on you and, of course, on the little fellow.'

Outside, Alice bursts into tears behind a black Jaguar in the clinic's driveway. When a pensioner passes her on the steps, she quickly mops her face and hurries down Ridge Street. For the rest of the day, she bundles herself in the cold shed, curling up in her grandmother's crocheted quilt, the sofa's forearm piled with books.

By mid-afternoon Edna returns from golf, parking the red Beetle in the laneway garage. Pushing her buggy into the shed, she stares at Alice huddled in the corner. 'What are you doing in here?'

'Trying to stay out of trouble.'

'What did Fox say?'

'I have to rest.'

'I'm going to the shops later. Best thing for you is good old chicken soup. Oh, by the way, Irene came by. She left a wedding present for you. It's on your bed. Don't go messing things in here, will you?'

'No, Mum. Can you get this at the chemist for me?' Alice hands her a prescription with the edges grinded sharp as tin foil.

Alice hates the solitary confinement. Max working in the Pilbara, her old friends not wanting to face her. She wishes Heather lived closer than the woop-woops. A good heart to heart would help. Why is she shivering? Even the crocheted woollen poncho matted at the holes is cool. The shed has some warmth, an old hooked rug in the corner, bare rafters loaded with junk, the tiny window glowing silver in the sun. It's cozy enough, but she can't stop shaking. What did Mildred give her? She could do with some of it now.

When Alice returns to the kitchen for a drink, her mother hands her a package from the chemist. 'They're only iron tablets. Not much they'll do.'

'Irene gave me a set of towels. Did she say anything?'

'Just that she was getting engaged to a Dutch boy. Thought you'd want to know.'

'Well, I'll be...'

'There's a letter from Max on the glass cabinet.'

Alice crosses her legs on the bed looking at the one page and two paragraphs. She's hesitant to read it, crumbling into a cry. Instead, she places a notepad on her lap, and writes to Max that she's been being poked about like a leg of pork. Other than that everything is 'cooking apples'.

Late evening and Alice's mother calls her to the phone. It's Max in his usual breezy self. 'I'm in Perth for a week. God, the job up north is bloody hot, but the money's great. I'm saving hard. How's the baby?'

'It's a barbarian,' says Alice.

'What?'

'I can't wait to get it all over and done with, Max. Mum says dad is disappointed by the way I got married. I hate it here.'

'Maybe I should get you on a plane, right now?'

'I can't. I'm too sick. I've lost a lot of blood. I've been sent to bed, Max.'

At night, Alice sinks down into the gloom of the old sleep-out. Some of the louvres are chipped and an opaque funnel grows in a corner, the black body of a spider inside. Alice smothers the web with a tea-towel, throwing it out. She has no fear of the spider now, just the fear of what her body will do, bloated and bloody.

In a blink she's gone to sleep, abandoning any thought of a last trip to the toilet. Later, in the dark humid air, she wakes feeling her matted hair sweaty, her bladder pressing its contents of chicken soup. She can't sleep here anymore with night noises filling her head, a tap blip, blip, blipping in the bathroom. She stares at the fibro ceiling, remembering her dream. Men in an iron-ore town climbing girdered steel. Max scratching his red dusty jocks, walking in a gully between high cliffs of a canyon. Gunfire flashes and bullet casings on the ground look like the sign of the Trinity cross. Stockmen are waving like hooligans, bumping a Ford station-wagon over corrugations of chilli-coloured earth. A boat floats on a shimmering river, on a dry creek bed. White skulls. Everything's white, the white skeletons of trees, except a crow flapping black wings in the dead heat of sun.

***

Alice's next dream floats an embryo, an umbilicus connection of flesh to brackish water. The tenant rises, falls, lifts momentarily until it is no longer in the lap of Freud, just unformed debris floating. This wet and wrinkled being cannot construct home in a landslide of cells and tissue. A tide of blood washes through her body. But the young body can't hold the bundle, can't rock the cradle, can't reach inside with nursery hands to plant the nappy pin into the walls of its intention; walls so thick with mucous and vessels and blood, it wants to drop its lifeline back into the bottomless swirl of a blood-red river.

The implosion inside her womb wakes her. Then, the sharp gouges like barbed roses scores through and through. Cut flesh. Alice has to sit upright and yell. Soon her cry doubles, then fades into exhaustion. Prickly and wet, the hot liquid has no other escape, except to push through a tender vaginal tunnel; black oval pools, small bulbous clots. The final surge, and only a soft mattress, a kapok density, can swaddle and soak up the last remains of "baby".

Flooding sideways, down the sheets to the floor, the blood seeps into a shag-pile rug. Her mother, listening to Alice's final whimper, leans against the bedroom door, holding a hand to her gulping mouth.

Soon the ambulance siren peals down the street: white uniforms, a hospital bed, her head and the walls cracking around her as she wakes up screaming, screaming for the lost body of a child she will never know.

Helen Hagemann

Scamp Baby

Memo 15: *Remember to have a watch handy to count the minutes between each contraction.*

Alice has a two-year-old. Mark Andrew Klauss born on 30th November, weighing eight pounds, ten ounces. Her body has taken a beating, but he's grown into a gorgeous, affectionate lump. Bright and wide-eyed, he's showing early signs of intelligence by putting all the right plastic shapes into his Tupperware Toy, first pop!

With her breasts as weighty domes, Alice thinks about her condition after the miscarriage. Days of silence. No visitors. Parents nursing their disappointment, learning that she would take off again to Perth. Perhaps, they were pleased. Alice didn't know. They weren't talking. They were just silent and downcast. Then the marvelous change of state, settling her into a new life, making the pain of loss, no matter what sex the baby was, a mere blur. And inside

192

the strings of her body, the vulnerable bits and enormous heart-bones, Alice knew that on that first night together on Rottnest Island, Max was going to be her future.

Now she is pregnant again and Max is still forecasting the baby's sex.

'It won't be a girl, Max. You can't be right both times.'

*　*　*

'Aw, fuck! We're bloody lost.'

A thick cloudbank fills the night sky, a rooftop haze from summer bushfires. In the dark, a dog barks a half-mile off beyond the field. Something glints in the moonlight. Are they near the trees that butt the back entrance to the hospital? It appears they've stopped near a football oval, a limestone road cutting an entrance to double wire gates. Where in the hell are they? The contractions are becoming violent. With each pain, she seizes the seat belt pushing her body forward, straightening her arms and buttocks on the seat. Leaning on the open car door, Max rests his hand on the roof. 'Pass me the street directory, will you?'

'We did two dry runs. You should bloody-well know the way by now.'

'That was during the day. I thought I turned into Cedric. Anyway, I can't bloody see, remember?'

Alice watches Max's shadow disappear then brighten, silhouetted in the car's high-beam. He holds the book to his glasses, shaking nervously with laughter, raising it now and again to get a sideways glance.

But Alice can no longer talk. Her mind is lost in the breathing patterns of quick successive puffs. Her clothing hampers her comfort. She kicks off her shoes. The weight of the baby bears down into her skin, her emotions, skeletal and nervous systems. Another surge and she doubles over, tightening her pelvis and knees. She feels permanently contracted, her muscles stubborn and tense. She presses her legs together; the back of her dress wet now, the humid night staining her skin. She can't let this happen in a Honda Scamp. Perhaps she might walk barefoot somewhere, squat like the Indians? She is that close. Howling with the pressure, Alice rises, jerks back, and strokes her belly as if this could sedate the attacks. Her breath pants in successions.

Max jiggles on the spot. 'I won't be a moment,' he says, holding his crotch.

She hears the ribbon of Max's urine splash the ground at the end of the lights. Mark at home snuggled in bed with his GI Joe momentarily replaces her panting and puffing. She recalls the day he was born at Saint John of God's, her son refusing to come into the world on time. Eighteen hours or was it longer? She couldn't remember exactly. All that gas. Coursing the drip through the corridors in order to pee. Then he arrived like a bright orbit, his tiny peach face glistening with eyes shut tight, until they trundled him down to the nursery. Chucking his new lungs into overdrive, he let the whole world know he was a feisty child. Still is, thinks Alice. But this one is going to be 'au naturel'.

'OW, OW! 'Oh, Max.' Alice gulps and moans again. 'They're getting longer.'

Max is tucking in his shirt. 'I know where to go now. It's in Osborne Place.'

'BLOODY HELL! Alice yells, reeling back. 'I think the baby's coming…NOW!'

'You shouldn't wail like that, someone will think I'm murdering you out here in this field.'

In the December dark with a cloudy moon cover, Alice is bracing herself for the next spasm, and the drive to the hospital. With her belly still for a moment, she is breathing, thinking about their wrong turn, Max comically pivoting the street directory around in his hands, memorizing a pinwheel of turns. Alice wipes her silent tears. She has a strong urge to cuddle and kiss him, admiring his calm and now sudden surety of her. He could be nice if he wanted. She inhales a strong gulp of air, her taut belly rising in the sudden skid of turning wheels on limestone; Max wildly reversing the Honda Scamp from the underbrush, grinding the car back through moist oval dirt. They head along the bitumen. Any minute, Alice expects an emotional flare-up, but he's assuring her that he knows the way. The bloody lights are blaring into his eyes like sparklers.

'Do you know where the entrance is?' she says, finally.

'Yes, hold on Sweetie-pie. I've got it. We have to go back along Cedric, then into Dennis.'

The car hums in second gear, moving through the avenues of hospital trees. They are both tired from their long night drive. Small outside lights of the maternity wing come into view. Max is in conversation with himself. 'I got the wife to the hospital, even though I couldn't…' He grins, turning to Alice as if she is part of his imaginary audience. 'Ve have vays of *not* having ze baby in ze Honda!'

The maternity ward is a jubilant relief. Max sighs at the desk, reaching for a pen. The admittance nurse moves through her casual night shift, directing the incoming pair. With Mark home alone, and daylight approaching, Max insists on going home to bed.

Alice slithers into a hospital gown. Is it her tiredness that is making the room sway? A nurse draws a curtain around the linen gurney. Alice feels weightless, lying back on the bed, the room swirling as if she is drunk. Was this floating flourish the first sign of baby?

The nurse quickly unwraps the blood pressure pump and flings it into a tray.

'Have I arrived on time?' asks Alice, resting on both elbows.

'I'd say so. Your water's just broke.'

Part IV

A Smoking Disaster

Memo 16*:   It is much too complicated for a woman to know the mechanics of a motor vehicle. When broken down, point a curvaceous leg out towards the road and thumb a ride home.*

Maggie is home again from Melbourne, partly due to an ill-fated scene involving a guy. This time she put her fist through a boyfriend's bedroom window just when *he* thought it safe to tumble in the cot with an old flame in his North Carlton flat. Melbourne, too, is a lack-lustre city for Maggie, especially the music scene, her band Spokaine splitting up just three weeks before moving into new digs in North Fitzroy. Alice's not sure how all these dramas happen, but she knows it's not Maggie's fault, nothing ever is. She blames the freaks she hangs out with, musos living up to their own song lyrics, 'money for nothing and the chicks are free'. Anyway, she's back for six months and it's no bother. Maggie says, 'It may be longer, Mum. It all depends on a certain band member getting off his high horse.'

Music and television suddenly gate crash the silence. Tim from the old band and Maggie's friends call by at all hours. Alice is restless. Hearing *Rage* at midnight, she reaches for the earplugs. In fact, the house around her seems to be pumping. The noise, keeping Max away.

During the week Alice escapes. Her hours at the library have increased from sixteen to twenty, and for the rest of the week Monday is an important tutorial on paper-maché and models. Tuesday is photography and Friday is mission day in the canteen. Two middle-age women trying to get a young guy with spiked hair to talk. She's learnt how to juggle time and a new credit card. She tells Maggie her latest fashion, hours at the gym, vegetarian diet, are all to blend in at university. She says, 'Yeah, right Mum. It's some guy.'

How about that!

Now that Alice has bought everything in black, she's wearing Toshi's white fur again.

Ten days into Maggie's home-stay and the whole world erupts. She calls from the lounge room. 'Mum! Look at this. Hurry!' Tim has stopped strumming his guitar and watches the TV. 'They've attacked America.' Maggie stands upright, almost blocking the screen. 'This is surreal.'

Alice watches smoke pour from twin buildings and suddenly she's caught up in the horror. Another plane crashes into the side of a burning tower. At first, she thinks it's a film, the World Trade Centre collapsing on its foundations. In amateur video footage, New Yorkers flee down Broadway, closely followed by a cloud of smoke the size of buildings. Thick dust billows around shouting people in the streets, barely visible.

Maggie goes quiet, just stares at the box. Tim is adamant that he's not going to war. He's about to get married. Before Alice has a chance to say something, Max is at the door, peering through the screen. He's forcing a smile, reminding her about the car service. Spotting Maggie he says, 'I thought I heard my daughter.'

'You guessed it,' she says, passing the relay of car keys. 'Sorry I haven't been over, Dad. Been busy.' She steps outside and the conversation is brisk and chilly. They're talking about America.

At eight each night Maggie visits her father, strumming the music of the day for him. After three visits, she stops. The pungent smell of his breath sending her out the front door, Max striding behind, swearing.

'There was nothing to talk about,' she says. 'After a few ports, he just ignored me.'

Alice watches the coverage of the horrific scenes in the Big Apple for almost a fortnight. The only way to stop herself from feeling miserable is to re-organise her new collection of old library books. In the evenings she reads the books: one on gardening, a history book by Manning Clark. She can't contain all the worries in her muddled head. Three paintings in the shed need framing, her last uni assignment is overdue, and she's supposed to attend a weekend gig at the Fremantle Arts Centre. Spike visits her dreams, taking her on a journey through ruined houses. In a Kombi, with peace signs hand-painted on the sides, dust plumes as they pass a bizarre safari hunt. Somehow the dream brightens her spirits.

***

Sylvia is trying her best to make Alice laugh. They've been friends since the beginning of their art course, and despite the gaps in family history she knows why Alice needs to paint. There, in Sylvia's house everyone is watching television. To lighten the terrible news, both women talk about a future exhibition. Sylvia hassles her for more gossip. 'Well, is there anything?'

'Not much. Anyway Sylvia, he's too young. I'd be called a cradle snatcher.'

'Get with the times, Alice. You can do what you like. Young people I know at work swing both ways. So, you'd be normal.'

'Really?'

But you'll have to go gentle. He's been hurt by some girl.'

How do you know?'

'I know everything, Lovey.'

'Hm.' Alice contemplates Sylvia's surety for a moment, and doesn't go any further. 'What time does this thing start?'

'Two.'

'Better shake a leg.'

***

The girls motor along the freeway. Earlier in the day, the lanes were spread thin of vehicles. Now at five o'clock, cars duplicate themselves at each side. Alice rakes her eyes over the scene, the latest Commodores to the left, Skylines, Fords and WRXs to the right torturing up the afternoon with their manic road speed. Sylvia is wide-eyed. Laughing. Since leaving the Arts Centre, the car is a continual trail of tail-pipe smoke, whacking great plumes in all directions. The drivers alongside on the Mitchell Freeway near Lake Monger are loud and abusive. A woman in the middle lane spitfires words, leaning from the steering wheel.

'Oh, get lost,' says Sylvia.

'What's she doing?'

'Giving you the finger,' she says, leaning from the window and holding up her own middle finger.

'Bloody hell. I can't help it if the car's smoking. What does she expect me to do?'

'I reckon it's fun. I always wanted to drive in a hoon's car.'

'It's just had a service.'

Alice thought back to the man across the courtyard, clanking spanners, a little stagger-footed, but she knew Max wasn't drunk. When he turned the ignition key, the motor hummed. She remembered sniffing near him, but he had stepped away from the car, thumping the bonnet lid down hard. In a full breath, he told her he'd changed the oil, checked the spark plugs and topped up the windscreen-wiper water. Wiping his hands on a cloth, he silenced the engine, pushing the car three or so metres across the courtyard. This time his breath came back to her, smelling of port. He'd checked the points, drained the oil, road-tested the car along Butternut, and around the golf course. Being divorced, she could no longer protest about his cocktail hour, or remind him of the drink-driving laws. She also didn't want to appear ungrateful getting a free service, so she kept her rage quiet. What bugged the most was the fact that the Toyota had cruised easily on the way to Tomas Hayden's exhibition with not one spark of trouble.

'He's a rotten son of a bitch.'

'Who?'

'My ex. He's done something to the car. I know it.'

'Don't worry! Dave will look at it when we get to my place.

The day washes over from grey to phantom pink dusk. Alice stares at the shapes of cars cutting in and out of the lanes. Sylvia, tipsy from the exhibition, giggles continuously about a couple of radicals, cruising the freeway. She's enthused by her left-wing sensibilities; two women smoking the night sky, while others hover behind their smoky cloud.

A Toyota Landcruiser pipes up once, then blasts the horn in long bursts. Sylvia chuckles. 'I've never had this much attention on the road before, have you?'

'No,' says Alice. 'No, never, never!'

***

From the front door, Dave watches the black shimmer of emissions waft beside his Holden Astra parked in the driveway. 'Jesus,' he says, scratching his cheek. 'I could smell that car for miles. What have you been up to.'

'We're a couple of drunken hoons, that's what!' Sylvia swings into Dave, kissing him on the cheek and arm-locking him against the roller door.

'Good exhibition was it?'

'Absolutely, fabulous crap, darling,' says Sylvia, slowly. 'Alice's work is more esoteric. Just wait until *her* exhibition. She'll make a mint.'

'Tomas is good, but he's quantity rather than quality.'

'So what's wrong with the car, Alice?'

'Oh, you know Dave, it's just getting old. We were doing okay to Freo, but coming home, well, big tepee smoke.'

'Yeah, should have seen us hoon babes.' Sylvia bends herself into the car, collecting her briefcase and jacket. 'Stay for a cuppa, Lovey?'

'No, I'll get going, Sylvia.'

'I've got the steak and kidney on,' says Dave, ushering Sylvia through the screen door. 'Your son rang. He wants you to pick him up at Lakeside at seven.' They both disappear inside, leaving the silence and the cold circling at Alice's feet.

She plans on kicking the car like Basil Fawlty if it doesn't start. 'Shut up,' she says, to a butcherbird, happy on a light pole.

Suddenly Dave is back, tapping the glass, motioning her to wind down the window. 'The smoke is pretty serious, Alice. Better get the car checked out in the morning. It's probably the pistons or the rings. Sorry I can't help.'

On the way home, the car belches airborne dust like a vacuum cleaner bag emptying at every corner. Finally, she pulls into the carport, wisps of smoke dissipating. Alice has ides of stomping over to Max's unit, giving him a piece of her mind, but the long day has taken a toll on her spirits. It's already six o'clock and no use arguing with someone completely frazzled on a half dozen stubbies. She'll speak to him in the morning when her energy is strong. Maybe when Maggie comes home, they can both front up to Max, give him a sample of toxic tongue, say something like they have learnt from him, the art of being mean.

***

At seven am, Alice pounds on Max's door. 'What the fucking-hell have you done to my car, you wanker?' While talking, she paces back and forth beside his van, then mounting the front porch steps, and staring at him through the flywire. 'There's something wrong with it.'

'Come inside. I'm having my coffee,' he says, placidly.

Alice doesn't want to go inside. In the house, she has to let her anger subside. She has to disguise the tremor in her voice in front of a man moody or violent. 'You come out here. That was some service. You've buggered up my car. I had a nice old time yesterday, car smoking along the freeway. People giving me the finger because I was polluting.'

'Let me have a look.' He shoves past her, flicking out the bonnet switch and studies the black ooze that has slicked every nut and bolt, every engine mounting under the lid, rivulets of oil sliming onto the concrete below.

In the early light with the shades of brick and garden not quite crisp, Alice can't believe what she's seeing. 'Fuck! What in the hell?' She watches his face, raising its bland serenity as if nothing will ruffle the news of this wreckage before him.

'You've got an oil leak,' he says, and marches off.

'Hang on,' says Alice, striding fast and pulling him back by the shirtsleeves. 'What have you done to the engine?'

'I haven't done anything. I did a service. Changed the oil. It was fine. Someone's tampered with it.'

'No one's bloody tampered with it. *You* were the last one to touch it.'

'Talk to the guys at K-Mart Autos. They'll fix it.'

'I can't drive it like this,' Alice yells, across the driveway. 'Wanker!'

Alice is at the front entrance of the carport, wiping her hands on a greasy rag. She tilts her shoulder against the brick column, and pushes her hair back from her face. Patches of the black mire track down her overall jeans like animal prints.

As the RAC van swings away from the road verge, flashing yellow along the street, a car pulls into the second car bay. Maggie climbs out of the car, lifting an overnight bag from the back seat. She shakes her head and laughs. 'Did he make you do all the work, Mum?'

'Come and have a look at this.'

Maggie walks through the pollen-laded salvias, and with her mouth agape stares at the sight of the car. 'What the…?'

'The RAC man found the oil cap still sitting snugly on its little lonesome over there,' says Alice, pointing to one of the black metal struts inside the engine. 'Your father forgot to tighten the oil cap, didn't he? So, the motor shat oil all over the place. Sylvia and I were so late getting home, I never checked under the bonnet. Bloody thing was smoking all the way to Joondalup. Beats me how we're still alive and not a couple of corpses.'

Maggie flares red. 'Is he home?'

'Yeah.'

'The pig. I'm going over there.'

'Maggie, no don't. I'm just going to get it steam-cleaned.'

'Hell, Mum! He could have killed you. And someone else.'

'He was drinking when he did the service.'

'He's done it this time, drunken cunt.'

Maggie rockets her way across the driveway. When her father doesn't answer her pummeling fist on the roller door, she climbs over the porch's balustrade and thumps her palm on the front door. She screeches into the flywire. 'Come out Dad. What kind of game do you think you're playing? Idiot!'

Minutes pass in silence from the house, the day suspending itself into birdsong, the lonesome howling of a dog in the distance, until the slow spitting reticulation breaks through mounded woodchips, firing its iron spray on garden beds.

Max comes out wiping his mouth, a stubby of beer in his hand. Finally, he raises the roller door, cursing Maggie, pushing her backwards with the palm of his hand. She teeters for a second before straightening, until she finally steadies her high heels on the brick paving.

'Bastard!' she says.

'Don't talk to me like that, young lady.'

'I'll talk to you how I like. I'm not fourteen anymore. Did you see it? You didn't tighten the oil cap, did you?'

'Get out of here and leave me alone. I told your mother I checked everything. Ungrateful bitch.'

With Maggie's screaming reduced to nervous energy, she thumps the corner of his shoulder. 'You didn't,' she says, her eyes breaking into wounded tears. 'Don't deny it, Dad. And that's the last time Mum's going have anything to do with you. I'll make damn sure of it.'

***

Alice and Maggie shade themselves under the backyard umbrella, shaking their heads, struck silent by Max's senseless and careless act. Or was it revenge? She just didn't know. After a time, Maggie rises slowly kissing Alice on the forehead, telling her if was a great party, but now it's time for some shuteye. 'I didn't get to bed until four,' she says, rubbing her eyes from the sun's glare. 'Wake me at eleven will you, Mum. Jake's coming over.'

Alice leans back on the white plastic outdoor chair, rocking it towards the edge of sun. Among the flowers and perfumed roses, she chokes back the tears. There would be no more gestures to make friends. No more so-called favours. In her garden, the newly formed water drops balance precariously on her rose petals. Alice is hesitant to go indoors, thinking now that she would never see anything as beautiful as those perfectly diamond studded Icebergs.

Perth to Adelaide

Memo 17:   *The noblest attitude towards any person should be the easiest.*

With the highway finally sealed along the Nullarbor, Alice and Max prepare to cross the country in a Holden panel van. It's a new sensation, a new horizon with quaint place names like Balladonia, Caiguna, Cocklebiddy, Madura, and Eucla. Alice looks forward to seeing the headlands and bays of Temple Bay, the old wire gate of home. Adelaide is first. In Max's sister's words, *You must come for ze Ocktoberfest in Hahndorf, jazz music, restaurants, ze wine tasting in Barossa Valley.* It's part of the country she wanted to see, the semi-rural hills of Adelaide lush again after bushfires, paddle-steamers along the Murray River. Alice remembers The Great Australian Bight, looking inward from the ocean. How those gnarled bitten cliffs looked almost prehistoric.

Out of Perth, high branches of gums swoop by. Max keeps the speedometer on ninety to gauge fuel consumption. Between Southern Cross and Kalgoorlie, houses dwindle. Max and Alice talk freely about the uninviting land, not wanting to live in the bush. After the border-stop at Eucla and salty showers, the country is dry. The long, straight highway. The car, a solid white mass looming towards an opaque shimmy ahead. Inside, the temperature rises to forty eight degrees. Alice pulls the curtains, while the kids douse Max's shirt. They have plenty of water, iced bottles, two plastic jerry cans on the roof-rack, enough for tea, and a quick splash. Even though it's uncomfortable, Alice finds the journey soothing. The hum of the car, squadrons of rabbits and kangaroos, and the peaceful words Max and Alice have between them. Mark and Maggie have their school cases packed with pencils, books and games. They stretch their limbs the full length of the panel van, lost in the sounds of Piaf on the tape deck.

After the first two days, the bitumen is too hot to pee beside the van. With no trees they squat behind clumps of saltbush. Standing at the gravel edges of the road, Alice is amazed by drivers checking for any signs of trouble. *Have you got water, mate?* they ask. Max signals with his thumb.

Holden! One man yells, waving from his Commodore. Metal disappears downhill, then nothing to ripple the surface.

The heat clamps them in. Max swears he'll get air-conditioning installed in Adelaide. It's oppressive in the length of the Eyre Highway, until they reach the Nullarbor Roadhouse to re-fuel. The shop flourishes with hands reaching for orders over display counters. Truck drivers, roadies and tourists pack its surface. Outside, perched on a copper's log, they eat the best hamburgers in town.

Alice thinks about buying hamburgers at the West Perth football game. The whirligig of trips through streets as 'mum's taxi' getting Mark to training and his footy game. He'll miss his end-of-year sports carnival, but the road trip offers a scarpland he'll never forget. The countryside appears more familiar to Alice, than she first realizes. The red earth like a grave. It unnerves her, thinking about her small disaster; fragments of a train journey, a dry painful landscape. Now, the same hills, abandoned metal, semis, intermittent cars and the odd road-kill. What is that flickering inside her stomach? Excitement or worry about meeting a German family waiting in Adelaide? Rainer and Norbert crossing the seas from Europe to Australia. Max not knowing. His letters sent to

Germany, re-directed to South Australia. After five years of catching up on the telephone, it's time to go east.

***

After the long exploration of the wide arid land, thoughts of showers washing away desert grit, they finally reach Tea Tree Gully. Not answering at the Red Cross, they pick up the key from Rainer at her Deli job. Alice and Max sleep soundly for two hours in a comfy room. By five pm, the house is crowded with nephews, nieces and visitors who sit around drinking beer under patio shade. Alice and her brother-in-law Steban do not speak to each other. Instead, she watches him pace the kitchen, circling the lounge, pumping his fists inside his cardigan pockets. She hears familiar words like *Dummkopf* and *Schweinhund*. She listens, fearing his temperament unfurling. Why be in a bad mood, today of all days, especially with the spring carnivals and festivals starting in Adelaide?

Alice is acutely aware that she can't understand a word. 'What's he on about?'

'He's upset with the deli around the corner,' says Max.

'The deli?'

'He's mad with the owner because he only got three cents on each soft drink bottle instead of five.'

'You're kidding me! All that hullabaloo over that?'

'I told you he was like that.'

'I thought he was going to have a heart attack.'

'He's always been the same,' says Max. 'Likes to show off in front of a woman. Knows you can't understand German.'

Alice doesn't say anything, feeling uneasy about Steban. First he's hostile, then stupid. She has seen this kind of man in a video before, a border guard in a signal box on a lonely gravel road, sitting at a table under a bare light globe playing cards, while the enemy motors through. He needs to watch the same film, Alice thinks, to understand that any cursing and hollering after an event is a bit too late.

***

The next day at a camping ground in the outskirts of Adelaide, Alice meets the rest of the group from Canberra, factory workers dry-mouthed for the Oktoberfest. Huddled around the campfire, they drink heavily, hardly speaking a word of English. Two weeks into her holiday and she is forced to join these people, their old nana's cheeks flapping on about bad service, dirty tablecloths, and overflowing coffee in their saucers. She only has to watch their mouths opening and closing like cuckoo clocks to understand that they add further modicums of poison to an out-of-date story about a car crash. When their limited English slips out, they claim a South Australian caused the accident. They're apparently bastards on and off the road, and the corner store thief, a *Deli arshloch*.

In the sixties people used to say, 'If you don't like it here, why don't you go back home?' Alice has always thought this lacked sensitivity. Her good old-time religion has taught her that people are basically all the same. She remembers a few of the old mottos, 'turn the other cheek' – 'do unto others, as you would have them do unto you', and so on. Even back in Temple Bay, the small ethnic community mixed in fairly well over the years. Coz's father owned the Greek milk-bar, Heather's grandmother came from Ukraine, and Pastor Pendlebury was born in Leeds. They weren't bitter about Australians.

As the weather grumbles, so do the Germans around her. They appear not to care if Alice is in earshot or if Max is translating their conversations. Some men and even the young boys listen intently to Steb's vainglorious story of deli corruption. He had carted everyone's bottles from the caravan park, loaded the car, promised a good return, and as a result thanks to that son-of-a-bitch not paying the agreed price had failed to impress his group.

At first, Alice hopes that it might be an off day. Perhaps, in the Barossa Valley with everyone getting ruined on good wine, he will be more pleasant.

***

On the Saturday, the family leaves Bridgewater and heads southwest along the M1. Norbert tells Max they're on roster together in the beer tent for most of the morning. Alice doesn't mind. She'll take in the atmosphere, visit the cake-stalls, ticket the kids on the Ferris wheel, bouncy castle, or dodgem cars. Her heart flutters; all these years she's been married to a German, and now a small country village looms in the distance that could belong anywhere in Germany. Maggie sways side to side on her lap, while the rest are squashed in the back seat of Norbert's station-wagon.

Rainer fills her in on the history. She loves Hahndorf and rolls her eyes and r's. 'I love ze restaurants and *roggenbrot,* fresh and tasty. Makes me hungry already. I think it's one of Australia's only German towns, is that not right, Norbert? Oh, and ze shopping! It's how you say? — really quaint.'

Rainer continues to mouth delicious words in her rich hybrid accent like *Apfelstrüdel* and *Schwarzwaldertorte.* 'We must try some pumpernickel, and ah, the *Schokoladen.*
'

Alice, Maggie and Mark enter the trinket shop. 'So,' says Alice, 'how many times have you been up here, Rainer?'

'Three, no, maybe four. I don't always come to ze festival. Too many people. It drives me crazy. I want to stroll peacefully. Oh, look at zis work. It's perfect, so delicate zis lace, na?'

Alice is fascinated with the town and fascinated with Rainer who buys everything she can afford. She wishes she owned more cash on her so she could buy three or four souvenirs, but Max always held the wallet. By now, he would be shifting coasters under a jug of beer with Norbert in the German Arms Hotel. As she wanders through the store, she picks ups little dolls and looks at the price. She likes the pearl studded china doll for Maggie, and for herself the knitted tea-cosy or the flower-ceramic picture frame. Alice rattles her purse, only enough money to buy a sausage roll each.

'We have coffee. I shout,' says Rainer. 'You look down in ze dumps. Are you cold, na? Here Maggie and Marky, you go back to ze souvenir shop, it's a present from Aunty Rainer.'

They sit and wait for coffee and cake, and for the children to return. Alice can feel a little warmth returning to her bones. She reads one of the brochures scattered on the table. 'This is really interesting. Hahndorf's first settlement took place in 1839 when Prussian Lutheran families arrived. I thought they were Germans?'

'Plenty of Germans came. See zis and zat, beautiful stencils in ze wood and candy shutters. German architecture. This church, old Germany and the bell, imported from Germany. What does it say here? Ah, Hans Heysen. We have a look later at his paintings. He has a cottage studio. We see the museum too. But first, let's eat.'

'We're seeing the Barossa Valley, too, this weekend aren't we Rainer?

Rainer nods and stares across the room, distracted by noisy customers. Alice looks vacantly beyond the red and pink geraniums in timber barrels on the pavement. She parts the lace on a streaky sky splashed intermittently with ivy courtyards and Dutch-gabled roofs. It appears overdone with its wrought iron work and ornamental friezes. Touristy. But Alice knows that Hahndorf needs to mingle the past with the present for economic reasons. It occurs to her how easily the landscape accepts other worlds. That tall grey gums, jacarandas, trellised bougainvilleas, an old windmill, and vine-clad Lutheran churches appear to intertwine pathways to each other.

People are different. They guard their heritage, upbringing, language, goods and services of their own kingdom, as if their country is more superior and worthy. The Canberra group has been stubborn on that count. But Rainer loves Adelaide. She is emphatic about her wonderful city of churches. Although a little sudden with the fly swatter, she is loveable, warm, and effervescent. Her large mascara-eyes under spectacles communicate her sincerity and richness of character. Everything about her matches her beautiful burgundy hair. She switches from one role to another. English to German in a matter of seconds. She works as a volunteer for the Red Cross, likes a good cognac and speaks highly of her friends and co-workers. 'Australia has located me', she says, finally. 'Of course, the Germans had a hard time during the War. Not good. Many persecuted and what for? They were Australians already, long time ago.'

They walk back along the main road and head towards the parking lot. The village is crowded with patrons spilling from fire-lit cafés and restaurants. The streets bustle and the sky turns dirty with rain. Alice and Rainer browse in every shop, Rainer filling her bag with presents for employees at the prison. Hahndorf is a fairytale town with shop-fronts decked in Teutonic script, balustrades thickly spooled and ornate. Inside a mall, dried sausages, salamis, *teewurst* and *blutwurst,* hang in various lengths from plump to middle-size. Clocks tick out the mechanics of a cottage industry and cars and buses spill new arrivals on the hour. Sauerkraut, thick aromatic coffee and fresh *Brötchen* and Papa's best mingle in the air with a variety of smells. Alice likes running her fingers over an interesting array of postcards and jars of boiled lollies.

'I guess the Germans had it hard, especially in the early days,' says Alice.

'We pull the boys from ze pub, na?'

'Yep, if we're lucky. I'd like to get to know Steb, while I'm here.'

'You already know him, na? Don't be too surprised,' adds Rainer, 'if he ignores you completely.'

Rainer's words cut through the fabric. Why is her brother-in-law like this? What has she done to make Steb so nasty? Most of the men she knows like her easy-going nature. She can strike up a conversation with a stranger, or even with a telegraph pole, so her brother keeps telling her.

They drag the men from the pub, while the children wait outside munching on bags of lollies. At the caravan park, Rainer's friends peel vegetables over a large pot on a camp table. Four vans and several tents are pitched in lines along an alleyway of grass. Over the fence, the banging of tent pegs and carnival music resounds, the oval filling gradually with the sounds of trucks offloading festival equipment. In an old corrugated double garage, a young man wiping his hands on a rag passes a few beers over the hood of an old Buick. Steb and the familiar Canberra voices drink beer and overtly watch her and the children unload the car. One man, unpinning the bonnet strut, lets it crash down as if he's showing some sort of male grit. No one waves or says hello. Steban stares defiantly in Alice's direction, sculling back his can. She is both conspicuous and excluded in this four square metres of land. Their rudeness sniggering

around her. She shivers and locks the caravan door in order to prepare tea. Later, when Max and the children
are asleep, she reads until late, the Canberra hecklers and Steban's weird behaviour crowding her tired head.

***

Three months later, Max and Alice return to Perth. They have travelled back via Broken Hill, enjoying the red sunsets, the inland acres of Dubbo's wheat and sheep. Having bought a tent, and fitted out the van with air-conditioning and a Primus cooker, they experience a comfortable time. Taking seven days, instead of four, they relax at dusk drinking tea.

By the roadside, they witness the strangest thing; an elderly man travelling along the road with a wheelbarrow, shotgun over his shoulder, black kelpie tracking alongside. Max believes the vastness of the plains appears to be playing tricks. They turn their vehicle around, and drive slowly next to the man, pacing, head down like an old Digger.

'You all right, mate,' Max calls, winding down the window. The man just trudges on, waving his gun in acknowledgement. The dog scuffing his paws in the sandy edges.

They recognise the man's determination, a lone traveller with a dog, bullets and a swag on wheels. Nothing but the bush, rabbits and billy tea keeping him alive.

***

The front door sticks a little when they arrive home. A fist of mail sits under the back patio wrapped in string. Max is calm enough, downing his first bottle of beer. He opens the first letter, and clearing his throat, almost weeps. His father Erich Otto Klauss will visit him in Australia. He'll take turns staying with each sibling. First Steban in Canberra, then Rainer in Adelaide and finally Western Australia for two weeks. Another reconnection with Germany. Alice hopes that the old man will accept her more than Steban did. What a waste of time meeting that dickhead; his Canberra friends nearly turning her into a shrinking violet.

Alice recounts Adelaide as the worst part of the trip, except for Rainer and Norbert. She can't forget the festival, the sudden change of heart by Yvette, Steban's wife, inviting her for a drink in the beer tent. Until *he* arrived, blustering his cold abusive tongue again for most of the morning. He upset her, hell-bent on reminding her of every Australian fault she exhibited or possibly could possess.

She thinks about those weeks, that wonderful young Sir Galahad, one of her Aussie compatriots, telling him to zip his mouth, 'cause you might be hurting the lady's feelings'.

The Riverbank

Memo 18:   *Freud describes woman as lack, limited and having little sense of justice*

High on the King's Park riverbank and bluff, Alice, Mae and Erich look down to the city. A group of Japanese tourists huddle close to the railing, the strong wind flapping their clothes. Alice is surrounded by different languages, German, Japanese and two Italians. She swings the telescope around for Erich, pointing, looking past its edge at the Bond Tower. She hears herself speaking. *There is no way I can tell him it's the tallest building in Perth.* He pivots the viewer forty-five degrees to his right, at the parachute hovering above the water. He slaps the side of the pole, as if this is the detail he wants to see. *Yeah, they're in Bali, too*, she says to herself. Alice squints into the low winter sun. She feels cold and vague, trying hard to concentrate on the scene before her, on any German word for boat, sail or yacht.

Two days earlier, Erich had asked questions about the museum's stuffed marsupials. Their leisurely stroll had been as painful as today, Alice frantically searching the little phrase book. It annoys her that the pamphlet only contains sentences like, 'Please direct me to the station'. And when she attaches some incorrect word to her German, she hates their long bouts of silence. On the first morning, the icy atmosphere at breakfast had been excruciating, Erich staring at Mae, while the woman bowed her head. Walking through the house they smiled without a word. Later, on the way to school, the children told her their visitors were creepy.

Now this tour-guide gig needs one thing, an interpreter.

The wind strengthens. Mae and Erich turn from looking at the river, and walk towards the flower beds. Alice gathers her coat around her, and moves the telescope in stages through a postcard horizon. For a moment, she immerses herself in its paper sheen, glossy bridges, apartments and skyscrapers. The traffic howling below splashes through puddles of reticulation. She enjoys the silence, until the sunlight darkens, the shutter closing. Alice hears Erich's voice and responds, 'schön, yeah?'

The bluish clouds and crisp air has brought pleasantries and laughter and at noon they enjoy a delicious lunch in the King's Park restaurant. Walking past the flowered clock, her father-in-law's little grunts at Mae begin to irritate. His questions in Perfect Oxford grammar gnaw. It feels like he's trying to trap her. And despite his corrections of her mistakes, Alice notices he's simply repeating certain phrases. Soon he may run out, but when will that be? Will he startle with something fresh? It irks her that he's matching phrase for phrase, pursuing, she thinks, the idea that she didn't really prepare for his visit.

They sit on a bench staring out over the water. Mae is a haunting creature with something missing in her brain. After a stroke in Germany, flashes of recognition surface only occasionally, and Alice can't find any real bridge to cross over and communicate. On certain mornings, she hears them arguing in the bedroom. Mae often forgets her purse or her hat before a walk, while Erich Klauss calls her a *Dummkopf*. Alice hears her sobbing in bed and wonders why Erich needs a bucket of water, towel and sponges.

Mae points at something beyond the spray of rotating sprinklers. Inquisitive black birds hopping under the trees seem to enchant her. Mae walks along the path, throwing biscuit crumbs. The white shapes of gulls hover above the grass slope, their squealing filling the park. They fly in above the grass tips, scoring most of the crumbs. Mae raises her head, laughing, as one bird flaps above her straw hat. Alice realizes the air is singing for Mae, her right hand moving in spirals. More seagulls skate in. She shrieks as Alice claps them away. She's not sure whether Mae has seen this white physical rage of gulls before, the tussle over a fish head or one chip.

The courtyard empties, gulls, magpies and a few crows moving some distance further on. Finding a patch of ground not littered by bird bullets, Alice takes Mae's hand. They sit for a long time near a yellowed sheoak, forgetting about language, not needing the impulse to make sound at the throat.

Finding some sort of communication without words can be amazingly therapeutic. A person's face shifts. Eyes, once expressionless, open out, and the lips shine. A deep pinkness ripples across the skin. The face stretches like an entrance. A gesture. A gaze into a long deep silence that is utterly vacant. Alice notices the small pool of white tears Mae wipes away.

Examining her straw hat and shaking her head, Mae shows Alice seagull poop on the rim. For a brief moment, she senses that Mae is aware, waking out of some dark cloister.

So, she responds to birds! Maybe they could go to the zoo tomorrow. Tomorrow, and that stifling breakfast scene again. Her visitors have her surrounded. Rising at six each morning, Erich and Mae spend half-an-hour decorating the front room with flowers, serviettes and a fresh tablecloth. Walking a straight line from kitchen to dining room is almost a comic ritual, a black and white movie of two old biddies fussing over percolated coffee, bread rolls and honey. Not making a sound, the children stare blankly into their cornflakes like two cutout drawings. Alice has set aside two weeks, her work piling in the office. She prefers to lie in with a cup of tea, instead of this routine tension. Close to tax time, she is expected to turn out figures at the end of the month. Max hasn't considered her work on the cash books, the housework of extra guests, helping out at the tuck shop. She is thinking of telling him to get another slave.

Pinned to the bench seat, Alice's shoulders and lower back ache. In her mind she's praying, *God get me out of this.* She stares at Mae whose messy ice-cream dribbles down her dress. On the concourse, the old man strolls towards the stone steps, his hands clasped behind his back. She's reluctant to join him at the war memorial, just wanting to follow his movements around its perimeter. She wonders how he can look at all the names, some of them killed in Hitler's war. Doesn't the monument to Australian soldiers and airmen disturb him? A man supposedly burning his SS uniform when the war was over. Maybe it's a myth. Max told her that her father-in-law had engineered the cliff guns on the island of Helgoland. True or false? She would like to question him about it, but again her meagre German fails.

By the time he returns to the women, Alice points at her watch. 'Kinder. Schule.'

'You must pick the children up from school,' he says, perfectly, buttoning his cardigan.

'Ja.'

She feels her face burning saying the German word 'right'. Did she pronounce it correctly? Certainly, not much of the day had felt right.

Alice walks up the path, picking pine needles from her coat. She is slightly elated, the choppy river behind, school and home in front. The old man paces, clucking his tongue. She doesn't want to look back for the second time, Mae still sitting on the grassbank, buckling her sandals, oblivious to Erich's impatient scowl.

Helen Hagemann

Last Stop, Tostedt

Memo 19:   *The world does not need ill-prepared tourists, but well organized souls with phrase books, maps and time.*

With the Klauss family's re-connection it comes as no surprise that Erich has invited them to Germany. Alice isn't knocking it. Max's father has sent money for the fare. She wants to travel overseas, London, Paris, Berlin, Hamburg, these places have always intrigued. She admits the old boy's wealth is making their travel plans less complicated. At the travel agent's they punch each other's arm. It's crazy, thinking about flying half-way round the world on British Airways, stopping over in Bahrain; then on to Heathrow before a connecting flight to Hamburg. In the six-hour layover, the whole family can travel to London on the tube.

After eighteen hours of flight, Max makes the mistake of hailing a London cab which circles the airport for over an hour. Giving up, the family head for the underground trains, until Max sees the long ticket queues, and decides that there is no point seeing London. She's not unhappy, looking forward to the sights in Germany, a little heady, still experiencing that weird feeling of sailing through air. Maggie christens every toilet. Mark spends his money buying trinkets in every airport shop. People everywhere, hippies, backpackers, Jewish men and boys in long black coats, big hats and embroidered Kippahs. A united nations of different tongues.

Alice is overwhelmed and excited on the last leg of the journey. The view over the Boeing wing spans old-century architecture and low-rise city blocks of Hamburg. Buildings no taller than three-stories brown the entire landscape. It's late July and the sky is a postcard blue with not a dot of rain in sight.

At the exit gate, Erich Klauss leans with his back against a rail. He's holding his hat, turning it loosely in his hand. He seems a little agitated, but it's mainly because he's organised Aunty Gerda to drive the family to her country cottage in Sprötze. Alice finds this out later in the car. She had him pegged wrong. That crimped forehead was actually a worry groove, and not a sign that he was brushing them off quickly. In fact he had considered the long trip, the convenience of Gerda's empty house, and a hushed landscape that would entice three days' rest.

It's twenty-seven degrees and the house is a children's picture-book of colour, framed amongst hills of heather. Alice can't sleep, wanting to explore the hedged laneways: a pine forest, birds, vineyards, a seven-minute walk to the little shops. She bounces out of bed, picks blossoms and juicy peaches from a backyard orchard. A large valley with low scrub stretches for miles.

On the second day, Max heads to the pub for some male talk, while Aunty Gerda leaves for an important business meeting in Hamburg. Alice plans a shopping trip, catching the train into the next biggest dorf. Spelt like the actor's name Horst Buchholz, Gerda says the market town is two stations south with plenty of shops and supermarkets. Alice writes out a long list, empties a large backpack for her purchases.

The town bubbles in weekend theatrics. Town-folk dance to a squeezebox, and a little chimp somersaults on a camphorwood organ. Stall owners, loud and cheeky, dressed in traditional costumes draw the crowd. Everything is perfect.

Except on their return journey, Alice has a sudden rush of panic. The previous stops and starts of the country train passing dorfs with backyards of strung washing, oak pubs decorated with geranium barrels, have innocently disguised the intensity of the next ten minutes. So far the holiday has been predictable, but now hard steel and glass whisk her to unknown destinations. She watches Sprötze being pulled back and back as if into its own little laneways and hills. The words *dummes Mädchen* clicks in her brain. Her head aches with exasperation, dark pools of emotion rising over that lofty air she has previously assumed as a tourist. Mark passes black looks. Maggie springs up and down, saying 'Mum. Look what you've gone and done?'

Alice is astounded that the bloody train doors didn't open, especially with all her jumping, clicking and pulling of handles. The situation is dire. No one stirs, all except a rubberneck commuter at the back of the crowd, clicking his tongue and raising his hands in the air, like he is pissed about missing his stop. Alice yearns for an Australian to bounce up, push a magic button somewhere near the door, solve the problem, let them out of this tight capsule. Well, she doesn't usually catch trains, and now they're heading for the Black Forest, or further south beyond the Lüneburger Heide. Maybe they're approaching Berlin, or somewhere in Norway? She didn't have a clue. The metal jaws clamp tight, jamming them in. No matter how many times she steps on the control-pad, the train rattles on and on, away from Max, Aunty Gerda and the little Hänsel and Gretel cottage.

'Mum,' says Mark, 'we'll just have to pull the emergency cord.'

'Well, where the hell's that?'

'This is a stupid train.' Maggie tugs on Alice's shirtsleeves, swaying side to side as the engine gathers speed. 'Mum ask someone where we're going.'

'I don't know the German for it.'

'Oh, we want to get out,' calls Maggie.

The train skitters through the countryside, rocking them side to side. At top speed, Alice is panic stricken. Mark glares, mouthing the word MUM! They're in a loud dodgem car, thrusting forward with no voice, no way to turn.

Alice smells the dampness in her clothes. The horse sausage she ate in Buchholz and the sweet smell of her perfume seem to coalesce, making her nauseous. This is far worse that being stranded on a reef at Quinns Rocks in a damaged surfcat, more frustrating than the time she got lost in Phuket. Even worse than the broken axle on their Monkey Mia trip. Here, she's without language. She knows nothing more beyond *Guten Morgen* or *Habe sie gut geschlafen*. 'Oh, piss,' she mumbles, in her dented pride.

The hand waving catches her eye. In the crowded carriage amongst a sway of bodies, a young girl pursues a path through the passengers excusing herself as she goes. She arrives flustered, her acned face a poppy pink. Placing her bag between her feet she looks up, catching Alice's eye. 'Excuse, please. I am student of English. Please, how you say. It is not so worse. You can go back. You must wait on ze train. Ze next stop is terminus.'

'Oh, thank you, so much.' Alice's stomach unravels its ampersand knot.

'Ze train,' says the young girl, 'will arrive in Tostedt in fifteen minutes. All people get out there.'

'How long...?'

The young student, giving Maggie a friendly glance, anticipates Alice's next few questions. 'Every ten minutes. Cross over railway line. Train to Buchholz, platform three. Okay?' She turns back to Maggie, and lifting a bottle of water from her bag chuckles in front of the two siblings, 'Silly German trains, na?'

'Oh, what a relief. So, I can… get to Sprötze?' Alice asks, slowing down on the last three words.

'Ja, yes.'

Alice watches the young girl move closer to the workman. She hears the word English and notices the man twisting his watch. The young girl looks towards Alice's direction, and rucks up her lips, shrugging her shoulders.

'Phew! That was a close call, Mum.'

'Yeah, I know Mark. But we'll laugh about this later. Right now, I just want to get back to the house and go to bed.'

'We can tell people back home how we visited the famous Tostedt.' Mark lifts his packages and sneers. 'And Mum, make sure that man opens the door this time.'

'I won't go near him, he might thump me one.'

They laugh about it at tea, Aunty Gerda telling Alice that the trains are new. 'Everyone must learn *not* to pull ze handles,' she says, in her broken English.

'Next time, I'll get the bus,' says Alice, hardly opening her mouth.

Something about the train drama has made her feel sick. She isn't in any mood to think about Max's grumbling about being alone all day. She couldn't care less about the children fighting over a biscuit. She won't cook or wash their undies. She is going to stay as far away from them as possible.

'Father is coming on the weekend to mow the lawn,' says Max. 'I think you'd better go shopping.' His voice falters for a moment, realizing he can add, 'but not in Buchholz.'

'Ha, ha, very funny.' She certainly doesn't want to get her head around tomorrow. What good would that do?

'He also wants to have a discussion with us after lunch. Try to be nice this time, will you?'

'Hey, I'm always nice. But right now I don't give a fig about anything. I'm going upstairs,' yawns Alice. 'I'm having *gut geschlafen*.'

The VW Golf pulls into the driveway. Alice remains still for several seconds. She hears the tyres scrunching on the pebbles outside. She has slept twelve hours and doesn't want to think about the previous day, especially that stupid train. But the idea of mastering those vice-like security doors on future trips challenges her. She'll show that wristtwitcher next time, turning half-way round on the platform bridge, pointing to his watch and shouting, 'Damn English!' How rude! Just come to Australia mate, I'll sic a big bounding rat onto ya.

It annoys her now that she couldn't think of any German swearword to yell back to the man. She knows one, but she has to avoid it at all cost. Max has previously told her. 'Whatever you do, don't call anyone a *Schweinhund*.'

It really peeves Alice that she hasn't learnt <u>Deutsche</u> and that she can't <u>match</u> up her known words in conversation. While she owns a phrase book, she finds it hard in these three weeks of their trip to learn the language, much less the sentence structure. She knows if she stays in Hamburg for six months, she'd quickly have a repertoire spring-loaded with new words. Already the little dorf's shops like the bank and post office help her understand the exchange rate of *Deutsche Mark*. She has fun in the supermarket gathering up coins from her purse, matching the register's green glow, the women calling *Schuss* after her in their sing-song dialect, especially when they call her 'Austrian'. Into one week of her holiday, she conquers the bakery, learning to ask for a dozen *Brötchen*. The fruit and vegetable shop help her with numbers and weight. And with such a degree of confidence she figures she will get past, *Ein Kilo Tomaten? Bitte!*

Alice opens her bag and pulls out the shopping from Buchholz. So far, it's the best part of the trip, buying little wooden figurines, their tiny heads, arms and legs rotating on a movable axis. She wants as many souvenirs as she can find, especially knowing that Max only wants one souvenir. Money.

Alice whips open her scrunched eiderdown. Dangling her left leg over the side, she touches the wooden boards. Cold again. And only the first day of August. She hears a chorus of voices below, dry sticks cracking, and a rattling, whining sound of a lawnmower. She totters over to the window. A man inches his way under the trees, pushing the machine in and out. She talks out loud to herself, 'the old boy, Erich. I just can't relax near this man.' Alice stays in bed, propping herself against the pillows; her eyes somnolent and sore.

She stares at the walls. For a moment she's back in the town markets, the air sharp with the pluck of freshly offered salami, Jarlsberg cheese, and smoked ham. She sees herself stretching her hand up to the happy couple in the end caravan, clutching a paper-wrapped bratwurst seasoned in mustard. She is dragging the children through the streets of

Buchholz, watching old-timers playing board games in the park, enjoying the atmosphere of their watchful faces, the men feathering fingers over moustaches and potato noses. She re-enters the quaint store with the small-framed windows. This time the storekeeper passes her a stand of wooden dolls all traditionally dressed, a little man holding an Alpen horn, and the ladies clutching a pink tulip.

Stones spattering against the wall rock her forward from the doze. She hears the lawnmower just below the window groaning into the long grass. A ping of rock hits the spiralled-brick portico. Dressing quickly, Alice closes the attic door, climbs down the stairs and sneaks into the kitchen. The weathervane clock on the mantle has moved a further increment to the Lady-in-Winter. She rinses a plate in the sink-water. The toaster clatters, sending coils of smoke in the air. Spreading jam on the oily butter and burnt crumbs, she shoves the whole piece into her mouth, letting the strawberry jelly dribble down her chin. She inspects the cupboards, opening kitchenette doors and canisters. The pantry is shy of real food. There are several jars of gherkins, peach preserves, organic tea, something that looks like bottled cabbage hearts. At least, she has brought the Vegemite.

Alice hears Max yelling from the disused sheep pen, now a woodpile. Erich and Gerda are in the back woods. The edge of the property lacks fences, and for some time Alice ponders the netted peach trees that are in rows to the right of the property. They appear to belong to the neighbour's side and not Gerda's. She hangs back behind the curtains, spying on Mark making a cubby house in a large pine. Somehow he's secured blanket ends, anchoring them to the ground. She watches him lift heavy rocks. Maggie has propped herself on a low peach limb forking her legs over each side, dangling her Barbie doll upside down. They fit in, no matter where they are.

When the old man finishes cutting, he scrapes the blades of the mower with a knife. The kitchen door squeaks and opens.

'So you're up.'

'Yeah, well I had a pretty terrible day, yesterday.'

Max points to Alice's mouth. 'You've got jam all over the side of your cheek. Mouth not big enough?'

'What's wrong with the trees? I saw you up there, lopping the branches.'

'They're suffering from acid rain. It's covering all the trees, according to Gerda. It's the Airforce base and the pollution causing it all. She's worried they might all die.'

'The grass looks good now. Does Aunty Gerda want a hand with the dinner?'

'It's all done. While you were sleeping, na?'

The day turns grey and misty. Alice notices the drop in temperature. There's silence and sadness now, the loud music of the mower laid to rest. It's a nice house but certain parts are creepy. In her dreams, she sees people huddled and frightened behind sealed doors. Perhaps, the story Max has spun about the War has spooked her. Maybe at the table Gerda might tell the story about eating a dog during the war.

One thing, the cellar unnerves her. The first time, going down there, feeling her way in the dark, she'd knocked her shoulders on several framed aisles made with tall timbers, all seemingly rigid like ceramic soldiers.

The racks are full of wine bottles coated in a thirty-year dust, and cobwebs curtained like fairy wings from glass to ceiling. Eventually she fumbles on the light switch on a timber joist, and a potbelly stove further in the corner coruscates yellow to crimson flames between each grill. A damp rush of air flirts at her nostrils, bringing a tang of shallots, garlic, parsley and other herbs amongst tins of oil. Large preserving pans and pots hang like lanterns on hooks.

A strong odour of treacle follows her through the wine-racked partitions. It stops short under a point of light, revealing a case of soft peaches split to the stone. Tall preserving bottles line the shelves above the bench top. The wood is grooved and gnarled. Maybe that's where they killed the St. Bernard?

Alice watches Max pour a glass of red. 'Is that your first, today?' she asks

'Yes. I'll have another for lunch. So you can get me that. Oh, and a good white.'

'No way, I'm not going down there. It's full of evil spirits.'

'You do get carried away sometimes, Alice.'

The seven sit together in the dining room. Mae and Erich on the bench seat under the window, the children together and Max and Alice at opposite ends. Gerda fills the table with malodorous herb salads, bowls of potato and sweet vegetables. The burnt onions cooked on the barbecue outside twist on top of the blood-red meat. Gerda has thought of everything, an elegant table, roses from the garden, cloth napkins and a large box of bon-bons.

'We are celebrating,' she says, rolling out the Chinese crackers.

Alice suspects her high-jinks are for the children. This brings the giggles, the hollow snap of the cracker inside, Maggie and Mark reading out the proverbs printed in English, while Max translates them into German.

When the sweets are finished, Erich Klauss turns to Max. 'Bitte! Here,' he says. He is holding out an envelope.

Alice watches shadows of dark cloud at the window drift into the room. Their union has now turned from family fun to business. She doesn't remain at the table, with all the talk now in German, her father-in-law lighting up a small cigarillo, rolling it between his teeth. He's like a gangster, a birthmark on his face near his receding hairline making him look like one of Al Capone's men. She clears the dishes away, resting her hands on Gerda's shoulders to stay seated.

The very act of opening the kitchen door brings relief, the hard wooden seat giving her a backache. In the room she bends each knee up behind her, and alternately leans each leg out into a yoga calf stretch. She hears the familiar words *Geld* and *Bank* and Max's blustering thank-yous. He seems so melodramatic. Clasping his father's arm on the side, giving his hand a hearty shake, tears like a water-faucet dripping as he rubs them away with his fingers.

Alice looks out at the great expanse of pine trees and further out to the fields. She likes strolling through the pink mat of heather that lines the walk-trails. After the weekend with the visitors gone, there's time to explore the hamlets along the railway line. Even with the previous day's fiasco, Alice has a sense that the railway juncture might be a lively and interesting town, brimming with souvenirs, boutiques filled with coats and scarves, leather boots for the children. On the return journey, she'll leave those stupid doors to Maggie and Mark. At least, they're getting a quick education on how trains lock you in like a bull terrier. And this time, she thinks, arriving in Tostedt wouldn't be a problem. After all, it is the last stop.

Helen Hagemann

After Germany

Memo 20*:*   *Never a lender or borrower be.*

Young men think that older women who make small advances of friendship are just being motherly. It's the Freudian thing. Women the nurturers, soft and mumsie, where boys go for cuddles and comfort. So in this twenty-first century, Alice can't understand why young Spike is so embarrassed when she pays the cashier a shortfall of fifty cents for his lunch. 'You owe me,' she says, smirking slightly.

Alice watches him quickly pick up his paper bag, Coke and snack, and with his back turned, he quietly says, 'thank-you.' He wends his way through the crowd, bumps into several chairs. It's difficult to gauge, but she thinks her action has upset him. Perhaps, he is quietly snarling or chuckling inside. She's not sure. But she feels sorry for him; quietly slumped now in a corner bench, on his own, eating a sausage roll behind a raised book.

In a lounge corner, Alice joins in with her group of chatty classmates. Sylvia gently nudges her with her shoe, 'I saw that,' she says.

'It was nothing.'

'It was a start.'

'Golly he's hard to talk to. I was going to invite him to join us, so I could stop calling him Spike.'

While the others prattle on about HECS and the rising cost of canteen food, Sylvia moves in close. 'Guess what? I went up to Mr Sampson early this morning and asked him, 'So who's the new guy?''

Sylvia muffles her voice with her hand pressed to her face. 'It's Ryan, like the tennis player. Ryan Bannister.'

'Bannister, like Roger.'

'Yeah, and guess what Sampson said? He said, 'If anyone can get that boy to talk, it will be you, Sylvia.' Well, didn't I laugh.' Sylvia knocks Alice's arm with her elbow. 'Little does he know, hey? Nudge, nudge, wink, wink, say no more.'

'It just makes me more determined. It's such a shame that he's too scared to join us.'

'Maybe, he's going to that camp this weekend.'

Helen Hagemann

'What camp?'

'Julie what's-a-name is running it, all about welding metal. You know, using a kind of Ned Kelly type helmet. I've got an extra brochure somewhere. I'm thinking of going, if Dave lets me.' Sylvia leans down into her bag and hands Alice the flyer. 'Just think, dorms, boys in showers, towel flicking. Sparks might fly.'

'Phew! Is it hot in here, or is it just me?'

***

Alice remembers back to the days in Temple Bay. Sunday school camps for teenagers were never as exciting as what has just stirred in her bones. Sitting around in magnificent weather reading the Bible, while she could've been diving off the end of a jetty. The young men were never very interesting or good looking, so devout, listening to the scriptures. At the age of eight, the South Sydney camps were more exciting, playing 'who dares' late at night by torchlight, or drumming knives and forks on tables.

Later with her own children, she made sure camping was fun, exploring coastal attractions and cheap tent sites. They went everywhere during the school Christmas breaks: Walpole, Bunbury, Bussleton, Dunsborough, Yallingup,

Hopetoun. At Dongara, Mark caught scores of tailor schooled off the groin. An overnight storm and swell exciting a feeding frenzy. Alice and Maggie went crabbing near the breakwater. After a swim and lunch, everyone pulled nets, the weighted drag of one revealing a lumpy octopus inking the water.

Life in the seventies was carefree and uncomplicated. The Cold War brought worries of nuclear bombs and fallout, but Alice only knew one lot of Macedonians who had built a concrete bunker in their backyard, stockpiling umpteen bottles of water, a years' supply of oil, Borlotti beans and chick peas. Vietnam was a million miles away. The war never really touched them.

***

Max is building lift shafts, working on hospitals and apartments. He builds new houses, moving the family around in the same neighbourhood. Alice leaves wonderful memories of children growing up, tended gardens, favourite rooms, little plots of ground where a cat or a pet mouse lies buried.

Swan Road is Alice's last hope for stability and her final dream project. A large four-bedroom, two bathrooms, ceramic floor tiles in most rooms, sandstone brickwork in archways and feature walls. By West Australian standards she is comfortable, and by a natural progression the children have grown into feisty young adults, leaving home.

At first, everything is kosher. Then she gets tetanus, tripping over a rusty utensil hook on a Webber kettle. It is part of her life she wants to forget. Firstly, because René Randall in Temple Bay all those years ago has taught her that sickness is the most boring subject between disinterested parties. Secondly, surviving forty-five days in intensive care appears as a miracle. Not like some poor buggers. People suffering all over the world everyday with pain, loss, heartache, disease, malnutrition, female circumcision, disablement, natural disasters, torture and death. Alice wants only to reveal to all and sundry that in the Western World each year one in four die from Tetanus.

Meet the Happy Couple

Memo 21:   *The way to a man's heart is through his stomach.*

It's thirty-two degrees; the sea breeze is a soft south-westerly, and the sky an unflappable blue sheet. Red and purple fuchsias blossom amongst the lavender, perfuming beds with their essential oils. All the bushes have spread and plumped after a good winter soak. Caterpillars chomp and snails trail their hermaphrodite silver across every path. While the temperature climbs, Alice's bones grow stronger. She has put weight on her previous undersized fifty-four kilos, exercising, taking short walks. The garden is her refuge. She fills the air with a light spray of water, the finery of spider-lines dripping beads of colour. She has enough strength to pinch spent leaves, propagate seedlings. Jonquil and daffodil bulbs are poised and composed under the earth. Even in the wildest parts, the tangle of wisteria gives her pleasure.

***

Today, Max is cutting back the bottlebrush and oleanders, stacking an assortment of clippings near the shed. Earlier in the day, his face cringed with the task of dressing her wound, preferring to be out working on his project, or collecting rent. That Mark and Maggie never called or lent a hand annoyed him. He kept on reminding Alice that she was part of the reason why the units were temporarily shelved. Four separate houses needing a lot of energy and her time. It peeved Alice that once he'd offloaded his problems how quickly he headed for the sofa. For the rest of the day, slouched, unwashed, several beers morphing him into a dream-state.

Now the fence, once barely visible, streaks grey bony lines. In a far corner, he's climbed the pines, sawing vigorously. As branches tumble, he yells, 'This is driving me crazy. I don't know why we ever planted these.'

The noise of parrots wakes her. Previously, the golden sun splintered through the roofing timbers, spidering its way under the patio, nodding her to sleep. Wide awake, she catches sight of two twenty-eights waddling their green bodies on next door's pergola. Four doves bounce and flush like quail from underneath the hibiscus. Alice can see an organic sprawl across the lawn, Max aimlessly tossing scraps into the compost. 'I've had enough of this!'

She can't understand why he reduces the trees and bushes to stumps. He is ruining the melody of her garden by carelessly traipsing through the petunias with his steel-capped boots, splitting mauve petals on the path. She hates his *blitzkrieg* pruning, and his unpleasantness.

'Don't cut them back so far, there's no need.' Alice lets the flywire slam. She likes the trees, Geraldton wax, pink myrtle and Spider Net Grevilleas. Since her illness, planting colour and potting earth has brightened the courtyard and patio where she sleeps. If she looks back at her convalescence, her thin breath picking up weeds, or twisting a lemon for ten minutes, then this bee-humming place is important. Didn't he see that? The garden soothes like a balm for good health. She shivers her hands over the double parsley for the aroma, digs up the garlic, and picks the thyme and basil for cooking. Several times, Alice has explained that the potting-mix bags, Thrive, plastic pots, and garden tools need to be under the patio for convenience. She also doesn't like him talking about feral parrots, and getting the gun out.

'I like the birds. They're not doing any harm.'

'I'm going to get rid of those bushes.'

'Yeah. Sure. Rather have a bottlebrush than a hundred of your bottles. Bastard!' A squeaky wheelbarrow drowns out her words.

Alice bunches her feet up into the cane lounge and picks up the phone. Since staying alive in this sweet old world, she rings her mother more often. They share tears in kitchens three thousand miles apart. She adds more calls to the list ringing each other previously on her birthday, during Christmas, her father's birthday, so her mother's added concern is endearing. The calls are brief, but just enough to say, 'Hello, we're coming over next year in November for a holiday.' Her brothers, too, have an edge of wakefulness in their voices. During her illness they rang the hospital every day. They told her over the phone. 'We've had our shots.'

Max doesn't seem to notice, but Alice fears a certain frost gripping their lives. They don't talk at dinner, and by late evening he's back smacking his lips on a beer glass, catching only half of the conversation. In the morning, when some bill isn't paid, or the breadbox is empty, it's a jumble of, *you said, no you didn't. You said you'd do it.* Her bones shake and the calcium grows back thickening her hair and nails. On days when she's breathy, something is kicking the old ghost out of her body.

Life reinvents itself. She walks to the golf course, to the new Coles shops, rides her bike and colours her hair. It is still too depressing to think about their marriage, an abacus of assets, shares, houses, profits, and new units. They discuss moving into one of the units, downsizing, making use of the excess capital in Swan Road. She envisages Max's new quadplex estate: brick walls, shared paved driveway, little grass, treeless and bland. She imagines the close proximity of tenants, the acoustics of their laughter floating to her front door while she lives with a monster. What does any of it mean? What does home mean? She can't re-plant her humming garden in an earth-covered brick yard. The change of moving irritates her; scratches away like an old gramophone hobbled at its centre. She can't get the latest problem out of her head. Her whole body tenses while Max opens her speeding fine.

When Alice returns to full health, the toxicity of her marriage leaves a bad odour; like a chemistry experiment gone wrong, a pouring of acid on dry ice with just a foul smell remaining. Max harasses her about the cashbooks. When is she going to work on the business? When is she going to stop being a lead-foot? She's costing him money, not bringing in any work. Does he have to do everything? Pay for everything?

She is still weak, but as her body begins to fill she decides that the duties of wife and house are dead, buried somewhere in the crevices and corridors of a hospital ward in Thomas Street overlooking Kings Park. She is a middle-aged woman, but a different Alice.

'I'm going back to school,' she says, holding out a carbon form in her hand.

He is unshaven, and slouches in his chair, shorts and checkered shirt wimpled with black dirt. Max grabs the paper, flicking the TV remote. 'What am I supposed to do with this?' he says, smacking out the notice.

'It's my enrolment at Tuart College. I'm doing English and Accounting. Great, hey?'

'So I have to pay for everything, eh?'

'No. It's all taken care of.'

'That's the postman. Do you think you could go and get it? And when you go to the shop, get me a six-pack of Gold.'

'Can't you go to the shops?'

'No, I'm buggered. I've been working all day at the block.'

Amongst the bills, Alice finds her cousin's familiar envelope. Lois has written before, especially knowing that Alice has survived a death-threatening illness. She writes on a regular basis, talking about her research, the family's interesting lineage, their grandmother's side going all the way back to the Norman Conquest. Lois's information ranges from scant to copious, fascinating to bizarre. She is thrilled to discover that an Elizabeth Sydenham was married to Sir Francis Drake.

Another letter in her hand she can't put down. Twisting the verticals for extra light, Alice settles quietly against the bedhead.

Dear Alice

Hope this letter finds you well. An explanation of what I have enclosed. Robert James was your great, great, great, great grandfather. He was a convict, sentenced to fourteen years and transported to Australia in 1826. Catherine came to Australia in 1831 (free) with four of their eleven children. Another one of their g,g,g,g granddaughters is trying to track down all of their descendants. She sent to Scotland and got a copy of his trial papers.

I'm trying to get a copy of the papers as well, so I'll send you and Jimmy one when I have them. John Garbutt was born in Yorkshire in 1833. I'm not going down that track as the descendants of the Garbutt family are writing a book so they want to search out the family for themselves.

Love to all

Lois

Lois's letters always bring a history of colourful names. They sound as quaint as old gravestones. They are documents of buried lives at some lonely crossroad or hidden under wooden crosses in unmarked graves. Strange characters with even stranger pasts.

'I'm from convicts,' Alice says, raising her voice from the bedroom.

Max isn't interested. He's in the kitchen, crushing vegetables, practising his tech homework. He yells back over the sounds of pounding meat.

'You've only got half an hour to get those mushrooms from Coles.'

'Yeah in a minute! Soon as I've finished reading Lois's letter. My ancestor Robbie James stole shirts and chooks.'

'Ha!' came the trumpeted call back.

Alice, miffed by his laughter, calls again from the bedroom. 'Everyone knows they were sent to Australia for stealing because they were hungry. *Dummkopf*,' she says, quietly into the letter.

She opens the four pages. Lois's calligraphy of the family tree and penchant for description paints a nineteenth-century England, including beautiful women's names like Hannah, Jesse, Sarah Jane, Annabelle, Louisa and Isabella. The family lineage is a staircase of faces flushed with pearls, women dressed in bonnets and bows, flounced sleeves, long flowing dresses. The men in waistcoats, cravats and billowing, hooded overcoats.

Alice tucks the pages back into the envelope. For an instant, her realities merge. One minute she is sitting in an English class laughing and joking with other women her age, the next she is watching a Dickens-type Fagan running from police in a stribbling rat-infested lane.

Max stands at the door, leafing through twenty-dollar notes in his wallet.

'Okay, I'm going now.'

On the way to the shops, it really annoys Alice that he hasn't responded at all about the news, his face expressionless when it came to notions of history. The part that really infuriates her is his constant bitterness towards family, no matter what side, no matter how notorious or interesting.

Max's new building project nears completion, four units requiring Alice's help. After a fortnight of choosing tiles, gas cook-tops and stoves, she mops, dusts, polishes the woodwork, washes curtains and sprays the oven. She can't bear to think about her home rented, her recently manured vegetables, spring blooms coming on. She sees them trampled, or dying from lack of water. The sewn patio cushions, creepers on timber trellis, her wire baskets of pink impatiens, all that work that has become a sense of rhythm, lost.

***

In the remaining weeks at the house, Alice continues to study for an English exam. She's in Maggie's old room, and feels that she's engaged in a similar struggle. She can still see Maggie bent over the desk, drooping under a study lamp, Milo and toast getting cold. Max hasn't observed how important this space is for Alice, as a past reminder of children, a quiet outlook on the back of the house, the garden plaiting its colour around both windows. She is leaving a future: plans to renovate the patio, making one half a sleep-out, the other a latticed veranda with more vines to keep out the sea-wind.

Late spring and Alice paces the pathways, staring up at the sky and birds. A plash of rain penetrates her cottage garden. She is depressed and worries that the snails will devour her tomatoes, lettuce, and herbs. The extra work makes her tired. The scenario of a future dark and dirty house, slow-combustion stove scuttling soot in all directions, imprints on her dreams.

There are several things she might do at the new place: buy a cane rocker, install a potbelly that would fill the space with the aroma of boiling soup, plant a host of other smells that trail in from a herb and lavender garden. She imagines Vivaldi on the hi-fi, a beautiful dawn filling her with primary reds and yellows.

Helen Hagemann

They shift into the unit close to Alice's birthday. Instead of getting a furniture removalist, Max uses their Mitsubishi van, taking over two weeks. The move is street theatre. Neighbours spying through curtains. The frowning couple. A dialogue of steamy words. Conflict over *what went where.* And, of course, the villain, a scrappy little Silky Terrier snarling at the postman's motorbike and other legs that scissor by.

The Third Road

Memo 22:   *A dog is man's best friend.*

Alice constructs a wooden gate using market crates. It falls over in the wind. Bailey gets out, constantly roaming the streets, barking at neighbours, visitors, tradesmen, couriers. After a week of chaos in the house, Max tells her he's had enough. 'We're going to get rid of the dog.'

'No we're not. He's just doing his job.'

Alice saw Bailey's antics as humorous, running from backyard to front door, climbing on furniture, gnashing his teeth at window glass. He's never seen so many visitors. But Max can't deal with the incessant barking. 'We're going to do the deed, today. I don't want any arguments, Alice. What if he bites a tenant? This is a business remember. It puts food in our mouths.'

'You take him to the bush, yourself.'

'You have to come with me, hold the dog on your lap. I can't drive and hold him at the same time, na?'

'What do we tell the children?'

'What do they care? They only ring up when they want money.'

***

The car bounces its way along a furrowed trail into the pine plantation. The area is filled with neglect; potholes dipped in patches, and on higher ground loose limestone stretches powder-like under the trees where larger rocks border hummocks of pine needles.

Alice enters the pines like a child, prodding her feet slowly across the ground as if some animal trap or sucking quagmire lurks beneath. She unclips the dog's lead, letting him run further in. The car boot creaks and Max rattles metal before slamming it shut.

She watches Bailey sniff in the rye grass, cock his leg on the base of several pines. As his scrawny body darts to the left, his coat like the bush around him is grey like coalsmoke.

On the way from the highway to the plantation, the road verges splashed colours of dry mustard, the passing farms revealing green corn stalks or fields of dahlias. Now in the undergrowth of tall trees, the day turns dark slate. The whole pine forest seems to take on the same hue. When a tree spits its needles onto her shoulder, she stumbles down a soft incline. With the help of an exposed piece of metal, she pulls herself up. Clinging to its crossbar, she eases her body around it. Taking two more steps, Alice discovers buried car bodies mounded like a cairn of tree and leaf litter. There are two cars, the chassis and axle of one, and the other an upended Falcon station-wagon, exposing its rusted wheel rims. A small eucalypt has managed to flower in between the wrecks, giving it a horticultural air amongst tortured metal.

Alice stands for a moment brushing her skirt, watching her husband in disbelief. Max, snorting and spitting, carries his rifle over his shoulder, his old Akubra drawn down over his eyebrows, making him look like some bounty hunter. She is trapped in a bloodthirsty movie. How have they come to this? Why is she meekly going along with his plan? What if he misses when firing the gun? Thinking now, she wishes she'd taken that piece of crate wood — that makeshift fence with a hundred rigid nails — and whacked him across the back of the neck. Alice's mind is back in her yard; hammering him into the ground, burying him beside the petunias while the animal sits, tongue lolling with contentment, watching her sip sweet, iced lemonade.

The backyard cuts its way back in. 'A simple gate, Max. That's all.'

'No, I said. What is the point spending all that money on a brick wall and jarrah gate, when I'd have to pull the whole thing down? How many times do I have to repeat myself, Alice? The dog is a bloody nuisance.'

Alice mulls about the last few days, Max pacing the driveway, the ranger giving him a notepad fine, tapping out a warning with his biro. Bailey had bitten a neighbour's child, her face swelling into a bruised third cheek. The little girl had glared at Alice on occasions when she walked to school. She wishes they'd never bought a silky terrier; a docile Labrador would have been much better. But his cuteness won her heart; a pint-sized guard dog, territorial, and not much bigger than an ankle.

Alice recalls the day when they first collected Bailey, going to a workmate's house, the litter of puppies running around, stumbling in and out of their basket; the feisty one licking her hand. She should have got the last of the females, but the little ball of energy made her laugh, and he'd jumped up on her lap. Now it's his last day on earth. Hell, she thinks, I can't do this.

Max says something, but she ignores it. Then he nudges her, rolling two bullets into the palm of her hand. He's already loading. How these things can part and bleed flesh. They look so innocent. A little gunpowder, a copper casing and a life ends as quickly as saying, '*auf Wiedersehen*'. Perhaps that's it, that Teutonic streak in him. It comes out now and again like some Aryan dogma he has to follow. Although he denies it, he *is* like the rest of the Klauss family men, hard and unrepentant, especially when handling women. Max has never treated the dog like a cuddly family pet, and now Bailey's time is up. That is that. *Finito la musica.* Max has repeated that all morning.

They walk silently into a glade and a large field opens up holding the remains of a Massey-Ferguson tractor. It sits clogged with branches, collapsed like an old workhorse. The seat sprouts tufts of horsehair between cracked leather and stitching. They cross another limestone track. 'Too exposed,' he says. 'I want to go further over there.' He points towards the old growth trees, past hedges of new plantings.

The day darkens with the threat of rain clouds. Lightning hisses and splits the sky somewhere over the distant hills. It quakes once and then again soundlessly. Alice takes a large gulp from her water bottle. The liquid seems to stick somewhere in the stream of her throat. Suddenly it comes back up and she is choking and spitting water onto the ground.

'I feel sick,' she says.

'It won't be long now. See those thick woods over there. That's where we'll do it.'

They both stop. Max holds back the top of her shoulders with his arm. The drone of a two-stroke engine rises and falls away, topping a hill, then disappears into a gully.

'Damn trail bike,' he says.

Max scuffs and stomps his black boots into the pine needles, an angry line of sweat dampening his sideburns. Alice wonders if that nervous tic in his neck is some indication of more trouble. He's flicking out a hanky from his pocket, wiping the band's indentation on his forehead, replacing his hat and scowling. 'A person can't even take a stroll in a bloody pine forest without some hoon trailblazing. On a Tuesday, for godsake.'

Max stares at Alice while she drops her eyes. 'Bastard! We'll have to wait until he's gone.'

'Hide the gun,' says Alice.

'Why? We could be shooting rabbits.'

'I hate this. Let's come back another day, please Max!'

And to herself she's thinking she'll ring the Animal Haven; have the dog picked up straight away. Perhaps that dog-sitter, Bill somebody-or-other will know what to do.

'Where's the dog gone?' he asks.

'He was here a minute ago.'

'I told you to keep him on the leash, Alice. You can be so stupid sometimes.'

'This is not exactly my idea of fun. I'm going back to the car.'

'Oh, so now I have to fucking-well find him.'

'That's your problem.'

Alice turns from the deep ruts of pine needles, the carpeted vehicle wrecks, and walks back along the dirt road. She is slightly disoriented. Where is the car? Then an inbuilt sense gives her the number three. Yes, they have crossed three tracks. The car is sitting back there on the third road.

She hurries through the pines, and reaching the second limestone track past the open field, turns around. Max is nowhere in sight. The forest sulks to a dark grey, and an evening mist wheels its way in. She shivers, feeling the cold air on her arms, slapping herself warm. She wants to run, but can't. The forest floor is dense, opening up like a part of hair as she treads through. She's in the darkest part of the plantation, and the haze continues to wrap itself around the trees like a long grey scarf. She hears something like a voice, a kind of rustling. She sees a misshapen figure further up.

'Hello,' she calls.

She sweeps an arm into the air, and waves. Only an eerie fluttering returns. The haze thickens and the distant trees stand like cold alpine sentries. Alice's legs ache from standing too long. She shifts them from side to side, and wonders why this person is taunting her. Defiant, she yells out. 'We're killing a dog in here, today. What do you think of that? Be careful, he's got a gun. He might kill you. He threatened to kill me once, if I ever left him.'

She watches and waits; her voice winding down to a pathetic moan. 'Well go on, disappear then, don't try to help.' She calls out again. 'He's got four guns, a double-barrel shotgun, a BB gun, a Smith and Wesson revolver, and a 22 rifle. It's a marriage of guns and bullets, living with a bully. And what do you think I am? A quiet hick-town mouse, huh? Never amounting to anything, huh?' Alice lifts the fur of her collar, and puffs on her fingers.

'No. I got to university,' she says, slowly. 'Hey, you over there.'

Alice grows tired of waiting. And then a bounding sound and a crackle of leaves amongst the pine litter forces her to stretch her eyelids as if focusing binoculars. First she spies a large kangaroo, then another with a joey trailing behind.

'Bloody hell, I'm talking to a bunch of kangaroos.'

She moves away, muttering to herself that they're not interested anyway. Along a dirt track, an iron bed frame comes into view, its springs skewed and rusted. Carloads of rubbish line the side of the track, old televisions, lounges, cardboard boxes, auto-parts, and a spread of mildewed carpet and cracked ceramic tiles. She crosses over onto the final road and can see the car ahead, stark white against the dusty green trees. A loud phalanx of Carnaby cockatoos erupts overhead and a strip of sun brightens the ground, warming her back as she walks. She hasn't notice them before, but the car is surrounded with patches of apricot spider-orchids. She gathers a handful, and unintentionally pulls out bulbs, and shakes the peaty soil from the stalks.

A loud crack rings through the forest. Its short burst detonating the air like the first *whack* of a whip, cutting the day in two. First a sharp menacing sound, then a hollow silence follows. Alice leans against the car boot, and slowly slides to the ground, her auburn hair catching on the bumper-bar. She gathers in her pleated skirt, wraps her arms around her knees, buckling her stomach in. With the finality of the bullet sound, everything tightens: her hands, neck, calves and toes. She shuts down, then rocks and heaves and moans.

Then of all things, while her coat is pulled up over her head, Bailey is there underneath licking her face. Tears stream down her cheeks as she wraps the dog in her coat sleeves. 'Bailey, oh, I'm so glad to see you. He missed hey? I'm so, so sorry.'

'What are you doing?' Max says, peering in at Alice sitting in the back seat, an old car blanket wrapped over Bailey, trying to hide him.

Alice squirms, raising herself up slowly. 'I'm staying here, I feel sick. Just get going. I want to go home.'

'Don't ever ask me to get another dog,' he says, shutting the car door. He flings the gun over the back, almost hitting Bailey. 'That is the worst thing I have ever had to do,' he says, revving the engine into first gear.

The car bumps its way out of the pine plantation. Alice's heart is pounding. She clutches Bailey tight in the blanket with only his small face showing. The traffic is heavy and noisy along the freeway and as they turn into the last three streets Alice decides to reveal the dog. 'You missed,' she says, opening up the blanket so that Bailey gives a little yelp, and continues to lick her face. She looks long at her husband, at his rigid stare in the rear view mirror. She can see his anger, his black heart.

***

Alice waits a month before either delivering the dog to the original owner or the Animal Haven. She returns to their usual morning walk, sneaking out at six thirty, completing two laps of the park with the early dog walkers. Alice is happy knowing Bailey's life is saved. She doesn't want to give him up, but it's inevitable. In the last few days, Max has arranged for their dog-sitter to adopt him. He loves Bailey and together with his other two dogs, Alice knows he will have a good life.

She is a little miserable this morning as Bill is collecting him in the afternoon. They enjoy their walk, until the traffic accident. Two cars have gnashed bumper bars and teeth together at the corner stop sign. Glass everywhere, the jaws-of-life has released a bloodied woman's body from a squashed Datsun. She notices a young boy's ghostly face, police moving about, waving them on, so she hurries across to the park. The old chap with his trained German shepherd shuffles up behind her.

'Terrible,' he says. 'They couldn't get her out at first.'

'They said the driver of the other car just got out and took off.'

'That woman was cut up pretty bad. So, you still have that larrikin dog of yours I see.' The old fellow continues to walk beside her.

'Oh, yes.' Alice pauses not knowing what to say. 'Not for long.'

The man gawks at her with bulbous eyes. 'Oh, shame. He is only a young-un. Badly behaved, hey?'

'I have to give him up. I don't want to talk about it, really.'

He turns and leaves. Alice looks across at the old chap, bending down near the swings, releasing his dog from a choker to run in the trees. Four dogs run across the oval, two owners spot her, wave and notice she still has Bailey. She can't think of anything she might say to them, only. *I feel sick.*

On the last turn into her street, the stooped lady with the Jack Russell and pug says she's heard the story about giving up the dog. She knows what it's like to lose a dog you love. 'Well darling, I have just the thing,' she says, untwisting the dogs' tangled leads. 'My next-door neighbour, young single mother, you know not much money. Well, she has three kittens. I can get you one if you like.'

'Uh? Oh, no. Not yet,' says Alice.

***

Alone on her morning power-walks, Alice doesn't look up or speak to the dog owners. At the end of the week, just two streets from home she encounters Gladys and the kitten scenario again.

'Be no trouble, darling. They're free. I forgot to mention that.'

'Well, give me the address and I'll go myself.'

Alice's mouth curves into a dry smile. Of course, she's not going, already tracking a new route in her mind. This time, the golf course, school grounds, back through the park where there are plenty of dense grass trees.

Her plan works. Alice and the motley dogs and their owners are fields apart. She returns humming, listening to her Walkman. The roller door clangs to the roof as she walks down the path. Max is in the sunroom with a stubby in his hand. She hears a scraping sound but can't work out the noise. Untying her sneakers, she picks off a burr lodged in her sock. Max appears fairly composed, even with the commotion going on inside.

'You've had a visitor,' he says, through the flywire. 'Come and take a look at this.'

A young cat is pawing at an aluminium bowl in small increments across the floor tiles. In the shade he's pale grey and white. As he moves towards an angle of sun, he shines silver rays of angora fluff. His pointed ears flick up like antennas when he catches sight of Alice, spreading them to the sides, as if checking all left and right angles. He jumps twice, arching his whole body forward beside Max, and claws the cane leg of the chair.

'Some woman dropped him off. Said you'd take one of her kittens,' he slurs. 'What on earth did you do that for? You know I hate *cats*!'

***

Alice makes another adjustment. She no longer walks around the familiar suburban streets. She takes the van on certain days, and spends fifteen to twenty minutes strolling along the foreshore from Sorrento to Mettam's Pool. Maggie takes the cat. She'll either keep him, or find a home. She doesn't miss Bailey, nor does she find the silence strange.

With Max busy tiling the units every day, Alice is free to do whatever she chooses. Some days she listens to Radio National, sorts out business files in her office, or simply daydreams on a banana lounge. Her mother has written a three-page letter, her dad visiting in six months' time. His new friend Barry is bringing him, but Alice knows it's the drugs that are spurring him on. Her mother writes that her father only smokes outside now. Alice knows that his emphysema is killing him. She makes more mental notes. 1. I'm so depressed. 2. Stay sane. 3. Use humour and wit. 4. Reverse psychology. 5. Mark, I miss our fish and chips. 6. Dad, I'll visit *you*. 7. Bye Bailey.

The Parmelia Hilton

Memo 23:   *And the load doesn't weigh me down at all. He ain't heavy, he's my brother.*

Alice walks through the front courtyard to the top unit where Max is storing broken pavers in a corner. 'Here's a letter. It looks a bit different from the rest of the bills.'

She stands and waits while Max wipes his glasses. Earlier in the day, he finished painting the last two units, airing them, leaving doors and windows wide open. He dug ditches, unearthing building rubble, carting it in a wheelbarrow down the drive to a dumpster angled on the verge. The green bin spills with an overload of weeds, plastic wiring, broken bricks, guttering and all matter of concrete and cement. Now his checked shirt is powdered in red dust. 'What about the rest,' he says, sloshing water at his face.

The paving contractor left his bill. There's a letter from the bank, Midland Brickyard sent a credit note. The usual, telephone, water. I can get them if you want.'

'No, but you can get me a beer.'

Alice flips out. 'No! Just open the bloody letter. You can drink later.' He folds it in two, securing it under a paint tin. She waits while he removes his shirt, shaking out the building dust. Blowing hard into a large hanky, Max rolls his head around. 'I can't keep up with all this.'

'Well, I'm helping. Took me hours to vacuum this morning. But I'm not stopping for a beer, am I?'

You're so argumentative lately, Alice. I can't even have a beer any more. Always on and on about something.'

He passes Alice the dribbling hose, motioning her towards the tap. 'Oh, Jesus,' he says slowly, opening the envelope. 'It's a letter from Steb. He's in Perth and wants to meet me. He would like me to sign some papers. Fucking hell, the Parmelia Hilton! Where is he getting the dough for that.'

'I'm not going.'

'Well, you have to. I want you to read the fine print before I sign anything, and he has some news about father. Besides, Yvette is with him this time. You two can have a nice chat.'

Alice and Max enter the giddy pull of revolving doors. The foyer is decorated in a medley of brass, mustard leather and mahogany.

'Do you have any luggage, Sir, Madam?' asks the porter.

'Oh, sorry, no. We're only here to meet a relative,' says Alice.

The porter swoons his body into a gesture of submission and points towards the check-in counter. 'Over there,' he says. 'Amanda will help you.'

Standing in the sun-washed entrance, the highly-polished boots of four American servicemen press a regimental squeak into the slate tiles. One catches a set of keys whisked through the air by an officer just finished at the desk. A professional man with an attaché case, and shouldering a suit in zipped plastic, queues behind three elderly ladies already sending a shrill octave amongst the waiting guests. Max and Alice move ahead in small increments. The foyer fills with the crush of more US sailors, shouldering duffel bags. Alice and Max stare at one another. Pounding jackhammers chip into the hotel's road edge, and everywhere white sailors' caps converge from taxis and stairs. Alice counts another head pushing into the line, as Max coughs, directing the fellow to the end. She shifts from side to side, hoping that by some chance Steban and Yvette have left Perth.

Alice no longer cares for Max's family. It has been four years since any contact with Steban. Max offloading stories about his peacock stance at Rainer's funeral, always the showman, lacking sensitivity. Max has questioned the family why Rainer died from breast cancer? Didn't they know? Now they're both hesitant about this meeting. Alice, not wanting to talk since the Adelaide holiday, and Max remembering how Steban belittled him for years on building sites. At Rainer's funeral, still calling him, *little brother.*

When the queue separates Max slaps his keys on the top counter. He shifts the bunch from side to side. He turns to Alice. 'She's deaf, of course.' The young blonde writing in a large journal looks up for a moment. 'It's about bloody time. Please advise Steban Klauss that his brother is here to see him,' Max says, quickly.

She takes no notice. And with someone accustomed to all matter of interruptions, swivels her chair to face a tall potted ficus, telephone in one hand, blocking an ear with the other. When Max rings the bell on the counter she removes the handset. 'Sorry, it's London,' she says, in a shrill English accent. 'Apologies!'

Alice passes a piece of paper across the desk, and smiles. 'We'll be waiting in the bar.'

Resting an aching foot on a chrome rail, Alice orders two drinks, a schooner for Max and a lemon-lime and bitters. Popping a peppermint into her mouth, she catches Max wiping a corner table with a scrunched-up napkin. She can hear him grumbling about the full ashtray as he transports it to another table. Straightening his watch, and placing coasters under the drinks, he grizzles further. 'I bet the bloody bastard will keep me waiting, just to get his kicks.'

'Well there's not much we can do, except wait. We have to be here, find out about your father.'

'I just hope that Steb has done the right thing. Not put father in some crappy nursing home. I told you, didn't I? He stole three thousand dollars from him in 1984 when he was about to come to Australia, eh?'

'Yes, several times.'

'Emptied his bank account.'

'I know.'

'I don't trust him. He's up to something.'

A weathered face in a khaki safari-suit raises a forefinger. Alice leans into the table. 'God, do you see what he's wearing.'

'Hi!' says Alice.

Max stands.

'*Wie gehts, Bruder*?' A hand comes out to shake Max's, but Max just stares him down for a second.

'Let's stick to English, brother. We're in Australia now. No need to speak German anymore.'

'Sure. And how is little Alice?'

Alice turns and moves closer to Yvette, extending a quick kiss either side of her face. 'Are you enjoying your stay in Perth?'

The woman shrugs her shoulders.

God she's strange. Born in Australia, but completely gone over to a German mute. Alice notices her stoop and the way she stands behind Steban, as if there might be some way of tapping into the energy of his shade.

After a long silence, Max returns with more drinks and lifts Steban's chunky gold chain from beneath his collar. 'I see you're doing well, Steb.'

'Of course, it's a business trip, Max. But I had to see my little brother.'

'Don't little brother me. What do you really want?'

'Like I said on the phone, father is dying.'

'Of what?'

'He had a seizure. A turn. Similar to Mae, but his brain is still sharp. It's his right hand. He can't feed himself now. And that woman of his, Naretta something, just packed up and left.'

'What happened to Mae?' asks Alice.

'Oh, doesn't she know?' he says, turning to Max.

'I didn't tell you, Alice. But Mae…the letter was very strange. Father told me not to tell you. But he said Mae went all funny and hung herself in the attic.'

'What?'

Alice can't believe what she is hearing. Something has to buffet this news, her eyes filling gradually. Silent images of a sky-lit attic return where she once hung out the washing, her mind clicking and clicking imagining dear sweet Mae, dangling from a rope. For a moment, she sees the old man clutching a coiled lasso, handing it to her, teasing and tempting the woman, telling Mae like some brutish herald from heaven that it's time to go, then hearing the same words over and over, like she did four years ago, that Mae was a crazy no-good-for-nothing mad woman!

'What pray was Heir Klauss doing while Mae was suffering in the attic?'

Steban recoils and looks towards Max, resting his shoulders into the curved back of the chair. With a slight smirk on his face, he leans forward, then slaps his hands on his knees. 'Ha! He was outside polishing his latest Volkswagen Golf.'

'It's not funny,' says Alice.

'Never mind. It's getting late. What I want to know is,' says Max, 'how's father, and where is father?'

'He's with the nuns in St. Pauli. I had to arrange it very quickly. It's a little expensive, but efficient. Doctors come and go twenty-four hours. The deal is, they take part of his pension, to take care of him. So, that's it, na? Not long to go now.'

'The old boy's been dying for as long as I can remember. It will take more than a stroke to kill him. You're not thinking of handing him a rope too, are you brother?'

'Max, Max. Who do you think I am? If it wasn't for me little brother, father would be still lying with his face in spit. I was there. I got the ambulance. I saw to everything. Man, Man! I didn't even get to my business appointments.'

For a moment, Alice imagines her father-in-law, face down on the floor, pressed on his heart. She sees a dark hole spilling blood, his body unbuttoning its cardigan, exposing a large, over-cooked rhubarb muscle, palpitating, thump, thump, thump. Boom, boom. Kerchunk, kerchunk, louder and louder. It won't give up. He's so clever. Look at him now, watching a trained uniform beside his hospital bed. He's so clever, pretending to be a nice old man. It's just like him to watch stockinged legs, fat bum swaying side to side, Nurse Betty singing, humming, fluffing pillows, lifting his chart from the rail; walking the curtain around his bed, doctors in confident voices prising out his dribbling tongue.

Alice is light-headed. She wants to go to the Ladies and wash her face, but a faint rolling sensation down her right shoulder tells her that an earring she casually twirled has rolled somewhere on the floor. On all fours beneath the table's raw wooden surface, Alice pinches Max's ankle.

'What the...? What are you doing down there, Alice?'

'I'm looking for my earring. Help me find it.'

Between chair and human legs, Alice grabs Max's shirt collar, pulls him in close, hissing through her teeth. 'This is a pain in the arse. I want to go, please!'

A phone rings, startling Max so that his head hits the corner of the table. He tries to negotiate his paunch and bent legs through two stubborn chairs. 'F... hell that hurt,' he says, standing and staring at Yvette.

She brushes a quick smile across her face.

The remaining three sit at the table staring at one another, conversation distilled now by a commanding voice in the corner.

Steban falls back from the wall where his chair has leaned, and places his mobile into a small leather case. With his voice still high on the adrenalin of 'changed directives and outcomes', he flings dollars at Yvette for more drinks. 'There's a good wife, na?'

'So,' says Max. 'You haven't told me yet what you're into?'

'Wall beds. The ones that collapse and fold away. Here, this one's the Chalet. That's the Presidential.' Steban opens more brochures and passes them to Max. In turn, the pile is handed across the table. He points out the dynamics of their spring-loaded mechanisms, beds of all sizes and descriptions hinging back into wall units, cupboards and alcoves.

'Just the thing for greater space. They are excellent for bed-sits, small flats and apartments. I've borrowed heavily, but I know that Australia is just waiting for this invention. It's revolutionary!'

'Steb, Christ,' Max says. 'This is Australia mate, the wide brown land. There's plenty of space, houses are huge, four bedrooms, two bathrooms. Australia doesn't need to economise on its bed space. It's not cramped living like Germany.'

'You'll see. It will take on like wild fire. I'll make a killing.'

The four stand. 'I've got things to finish,' says Max. 'Come to dinner tomorrow, my treat.'

Steban and Yvette turn towards a small flight of stairs and wait on a landing near the lifts. Yvette glances back at Alice, a little apprehensive about waving goodbye. Alice hears their muffled arguing, Yvette giving Steban a certain scorched look. He bundles her into the lift, his unconcerned air still floating after him.

At eleven-thirty the table is set. Max ceremoniously cooks the midday meal, clamoring and swirling stainless steel. At one stage, Alice got in the way, and so he told her to piss off. She knows today is going to be a scene of black comedy. He's got flour in his hair, and the barbecue apron with the plastic tits looks bizarre as he sways from room to room. She's not unhappy, but Max's angle on this role reversal is teetering precariously, in more ways than one. It's hard not to feel the strain of it. One minute he's in high spirits, the next pumping out complaints. So, with a sigh of relief she's giving the house her personal touch, sweeping the pavement, pulling out weeds and snipping potted fern to make an arrangement on the coffee table.

Alice hears the phone in the living room, Max's voice breaking into a laugh. 'Ha, that was Steb,' he says, coming back into the kitchen still whisking his vinaigrette. 'He went to the old house, what a nerd.'

'But we gave him our new address.'

'He wants to see what kind of house Max Klauss built, na?'

'Stickybeaking, more like.'

On the other side of the street, Yvette gets out of the taxi. She's dressed in a tartan pleated skirt and plain white blouse. Alice can't get over how old-fashioned they look, Steb wearing faun socks and Bermudas, his square haircut ruffled in the wind. As he wanders up the path, briefcase under arm, he's got his nose in the opposite unit, pointing, mind-clicking the word 'four' in his memory bank.

'Is this all paid for?' he asks Max, as he enters the front porch.

'Give it a rest, Steb. Why did you go to Swan Road? I told you we're in Butternut Way.'

'I'm impressed little brother. So, do I get the guided tour?'

'Later.' Max interrupts the women's conversation, 'Snook, can you get the wine and the opener?'

Alice darts about the room. She still hasn't got used to the kitchen. She knows she should learn where things are, but Max keeps moving everything, especially the utensils. The whole kitchen is cluttered with his new pots and pans and stir-fry gismos. Eating used to be a pleasure. Now with Max cooking, there are problems.

'Voila! My pièce de résistance,' says Max, bearing a large dish of crumbed chicken fillets, neatly arranged on red and green vegetables.

'The mat, Where's the mat, Alice? I told you to get it out.'

Alice forces the place mat under the hot dish. 'Well, don't get your jocks in a twist. I put the board there for that.'

'Listen,' says Steb, with a raised fork. 'I hope you killed it first.'

'Funny bugger, aren't you?'

They serve themselves and eat. Alice watches their chins, chewing rhythmic revolutions, opening and closing. Each person looking ridiculous, pecking at green leaves, snarly like birds. She'd love to be with the tennis girls right now, giggling, laughing wildly over some crude joke or a vulgar sex scene from a movie. Her mood is tense and on the outside there's a flourish and wave of hands, a sort of forced, pretentious cheerfulness. At least, Yvette has helped her with the sweets, moving plates around to make way for the jug of chocolate sauce.

When the ordeal is over, Max responds with a quick kiss to the back of Alice's neck. He tells her he's satiated, feels relaxed; the black-forest cake giving him that warm *gemutlichkeit* feeling.

Max washes his hands at the sink. 'See the way they tucked into my chicken and potato salad?' he says, lowering his voice. They both move through the smaller spaces of the kitchen and around the bench top, scraping plates and swishing them under the tap. The kitchen is Alice's place for thinking. She opens the fridge and places a stubby in Max's palm, waving him outside. 'The vegetables were just right, crisp, not over-cooked, like you do Alice,' he continues. 'But what a stupid question? Did I make the black forest cake? Man, man. I'd like to see him put a hand to all this, study, pass all the tests. I betcha he couldn't spell 'streptococcal' or 'staphylococcus'. But what a dickhead, na? Nearly had Yvette bawling in my lap. Poor woman desperately mopping up her spilt wine. All the time, he's jawing in my ear, on and on about bloody collapsible beds.'

'Max, shush. They'll hear you.'

Steban enters the glass slider from the outside, and places his can of beer on the garden furniture. Both Max and Steban, buoyed by their tipsy state, discuss the project and their new sunroom. Alice watches the two from the family room slider, Max gesturing his brother to sit and relax. She notices that since arriving Steban's been complaining about the flight, airline food, slow taxis, or lack of airport staff. When they previously circled the units, he was like that crocodile pursuing Captain Hook – tick, tick, ticking the whole time – gasping over any expensive bathroom accessory, kitchen appliance, cupboard, or interior face-brick; his voice rising on a higher chorus of *Man, Man, Man!* or an *ooh là là'* when Max shows him the bore and reticulation.

Alice is revved up. She's practically drunk a whole bottle of red and doesn't care. She knows she's rambling while doing the dishes, asking Yvette about the children, telling her about Maggie and Mark, discussing the day they moved out, her visits to their Como flat near the university. This background information seems to strike a new melody with Yvette. They enjoy a companionable moment at the sink. She has two girls. Marguerite's in the police force and Tiffany's at home with the baby. No boys? No! Alice realizes that Mark is the only one carrying on the Klauss name.

'That doesn't matter,' says Yvette. 'If you have enough money, you can have a very comfortable life, and not worry about that sort of thing.'

'I've just passed my TEE. I'll be starting a Fine Arts Course at university in a year's time. In the meantime I have to defer and help Max.'

Yvette holds her tea-towel still for a moment, not saying anything.

Outside, Max is curled up on the sofa. He's sleepy now after several beers, the midday meal and the constant talking. He keeps rubbing the back of his head, trying desperately to stop its drowsy pitch. He's got several papers on his lap. 'I'll have to get Alice to read it, Steb. I am not *that* good at English.'

'Max, Max. It's just a release form, for when the old man gets better. You're just another family witness, little brother.'

'Yes, well how old is he now, eighty-nine? He's not going anywhere.'

They swap workable pens, and Steban clicks his case shut. 'Now that the business is over, I have a small present for you.' From a cooler bag at his side, Steban produces two Löwenbräu beers from a six-pack. 'They're imported from Germany now. I can't drink that Coopers 'suppe'. It gives me a constant headache, na?' Steban waves to the women inside. 'Come out ladies and join us. Yvette, where are those chocolates?'

Despite the difference in their ages and temperament they begin to enjoy the latter hours of the day. Steban and Yvette talk about their trip to Munich, Rome and Paris, their thirty-fifth wedding anniversary. Alice begins to feel annoyed. They're talking about fountains; afternoon walks in the piazzas, buying music boxes in Amsterdam. They have a mutual love of travelling, and their eyes are afire when they talk about the canals in Venice, planning their next trip. Alice feels like a ship in a bottle not going anywhere. She feels like she's experiencing an uncontrollable grief. Maybe it's the wine, but she knows that this matter-of-fact husband of hers when he drinks only goes one place, into his mind, back to his miserable family history.

Sitting on the toilet, Alice can't move. The little room is spinning. There's a powerful voice coming from the next room. It's Steb getting furious about something.

'Sneaky bastard!'

'Let's leave Stebbie,' says Yvette. 'Max is asleep. Alice is nowhere to be found. I'll ring for a taxi.'

Alice can't quite make out their conversation. She wishes she still held her wine glass to listen against the wall. Their voices are fractured, lowering at certain points. She can just make out Yvette's moaning.

'I'm not so sure, I... I wish I was...'

'Yvette, don't you see...?'

'I want...to the girls, Stebbie.'

'Have a look around you, what do you see, na? Money, na?'

Alice can hear Steban and a noisy slap of hands on something. Conversation moves back and forth, dips then heightens, but it's Steban's voice Alice hears.

'Father's money, na? Bastard. Bloody bastard. I've risked borrowing thousands for my business venture and Perth has, well... What? What? I've been double-crossed, I tell you. That big house around...Ja, ja. What? You thinking like me, *Liebling,* more for his kids, eh? Been in cahoots with *Fater*, na? Man, Man. I should have guessed this from the start.'

'I don't... Well, it certainly...'

'Of course, money from Germany, na? How else...the bastard... afford all this?'

Their voices lower and Alice hears the rustle of plastic. A slow contagion of misery fills her. Family. What a family. All they ever think about is money. She knows she's pissed. But it's that old swansong again. She wants to stop thinking. She wants them to leave the house. 'Bloody leave,' she tells herself. 'Go on piss off, back to Adelaide. See if I care.'

The front door clicks to the sound of a running motor. The changing sound is like the echo of her life. Go on then, back to your travelling, back to sweet Paris in your *Lederhosen*. Fuck you! Fuck the whole fucking lot. Hope your fucking plane crashes. Hope your fucking family gets the pox.

'Including the old fucker,' she mutters, lifting the Terylene curtain at the front window.

Murphy's Law

Memo 24:   *Charity begins at home.*

With the units completed and rented, each Sunday Alice and Max take up cycling in King's Park. Mark has come this weekend, and there's plenty of insane racing down the hills, the throat gulping when Alice brushes through scrub and nearly cleans up an army of seniors walking leisurely from overhanging trees. After the last steep climb along Thomas Street to the restaurant, she curls up with panting breaths, staggering to the car. She's buggered. At home, more laughter, going over the morning's workout of lungs and pedals. Mark is surprised when Alice tells him she's reading *Women*, by Charles Bukowski. 'I'm just getting up to date,' she says.

Alice sees a change in her son, he's no longer a boy, but a man. His busy life divided into work and social events, and now he's counting the days until a government school project is finished, assuring her that his design will lift eyebrows. Three diamond-shaped buildings, similar to a Glenn Murcutt design, remain a secret until the Premier's opening night. There's a brightness, too, in his outlook, and when he stares into her face she sees the same sensitive little boy, football beanie pulled down over his ears. He leaves smiling with his ambitions tucked inside his head.

***

Mark is absent for longer periods than Maggie who visits often. Alice remembers the last time, the rearrangement of furniture. The argument. Max shuffling in his chair under the table, a broken slat in the pine.

Alice had watched the pair in the house, tempers brewing like coffee. The familiar trill in Maggie's voice as Max grabbed her wrist, flinging her to the floor. At first, Maggie had sighed deeply, snatched up her house keys, rattling the sunroom's door behind her. Outside, the flooding tears, the whole scenario of her father not helping out with a loan, lost on her. She had wandered around the backyard, worrying about getting to work. Alice noticed a nick in her leg, bleeding. 'Bloody hell. What a wanker!'

Now Max keeps reminding Alice about her visit. She hears it for days, girls and their tempers. She knows the car started the argument, but the spark was calling Max a stingy wanker. What does he expect? They get in a heated conversation about investment and money, and he pulls the devil from under her. Later, he expects her to be nice. No wonder she called him a cunt in retaliation.

'Poor little Daddy,' she had said.

***

'Where's the car?'

'In Nollamara,' says Maggie.

Alice remains fearful of Maggie's determination to buy her first car. Sitting in the sunroom, they discuss how to get the finance. Alice has already spent an hour going over the problems at the bank, guaranteeing the loan. Maggie's little plan makes her heart pinch. On the one hand, she wants to help, while on the other she has to lie, and go behind Max's back. Families, she thinks. All the previous squabbling about money. 'She hasn't any,' Max had said. 'I'll buy her a car for five hundred, no more.'

At first, Alice had said 'no' to the idea. Now Maggie is dragging her through suburban streets to see a 'fabulous' Datsun 200B.

The car is a shock. Bending and looking in the tinted windows, Alice knows that three thousand dollars is too much. The only good thing is the set of lambswool seat-covers. The duco is dark green, faded in patches and the venetian blind at the rear twists into itself. The Asian fellow opens the bonnet and points to the engine, carburetor and radiator. 'All new,' he says, smiling. 'Good car, very, very cheap.' *But what about the ding in the side,* thinks Alice.

After the test drive, Alice is sweating. The car previously parked on the gravel drive has baked in the sun. 'There's no air-conditioning, Maggie.'

'I can get that later. Well, what do you think?' she asks, turning up the radio's tempo. 'See, twin speakers front and back.'

Despite the terrible green, Alice is at least pleased that the Datsun's gears are smooth, the motor quiet. 'Okay, we'll get it,' she says, finally.

When they arrive at the local shops, Alice begins to think she's made a big mistake. She never wants Max to find out about Maggie's car loan, or going guarantor. She leaves strict instructions at the bank not to send any of Maggie Klauss's dealings or correspondence to Butternut Way. All letters must go to her Mt. Hawthorn address.

Remember Murphy's Law? *Anything that can go wrong, will*. The bank ignores Alice's request and sends the letter of authority to their new units. This all happens two days before Alice is due to fly to Sydney. On the first reading of the letter, Max struts and waves the paper around. How could she do it? How could she go behind his back? What got into her? Alice doesn't want to answer, but eventually does. 'Why the hell shouldn't I help my daughter? I trust her to repay the loan.'

'It's not a matter of trust. It is the principle of the thing. You have gone behind my back, and now I can't trust you.'

'Why didn't you help her, when she asked?'

'Because she has to save and learn the value of things. It doesn't come that easy.'

'It would take a million years for Maggie to save the money. She needs the car right now. She's got a job, she can afford it.'

Alice can understand the pressure if her family is poor and destitute. Living as some people do, dead on the borderline of poverty. Subsisting in long employment lines of a hundred people queuing for one labouring job. She understands if a man had a high-pressured job, coming home at nine o'clock in the evening, taking it out on his wife who nags him about being late. Slapping her around instead of smacking the boss in the face. She can understand Max not wanting to help a friend or neighbour going guarantor if they're not part of that close family. But why can't he help his own daughter? Get out of that bloody mindset. He is typical of the Klauss family men, steel hides. Hearts as hard as the corrugated back of a frying pan.

She should have hit Max with a frying pan when he gave Bailey away. And now he's punching her with his fists. Holding her over the sink with one hand, slapping her arms and legs with the other. He knows where to hit. Not on the face, or eyes, just on those soft parts of the body, covered by clothes.

Alice is glad he stopped after ten minutes.

***

Going guarantor for Maggie's car is a big issue in Alice's life. If she can't help her daughter, then who else can she help? Nothing makes sense. Going behind Max's back begins her first step in defiance; a husband whipping her arms and legs with his fist is the death of love, the last tuft in the straw. She is a bawling mess of emotions with nothing left to spring back. She has betrayed him, so he says. But the shroud of bruises means she has failed. Failed her mother and father for her choice of a husband. Failed her son and daughter for giving them a cruel father. The purple swelling on her legs and arms lasts her whole holiday. For nearly three weeks while in her mother's house at Sanctuary Point, she keeps reminding herself that Max is the biggest embarrassment. How has she reached this stage, not even wanting to tell her mother? At the airport when Maggie picks her up, she says she's tired of Max's cruelty. 'I'm planning on doing something drastic, Maggie. I just can't take it anymore.'

Home from the holiday, Alice avoids their nightly battleground. The only time to concentrate on the cashbooks is in the midnight quiet, her printer quickly spitting out figures. Before Sydney, she suffered the ritual of Max's slurred demands. His foot making announcements at the door. 'Write this letter to the bloody executor - that email to the lawyer.' Often, in their wild arguments, post-its and letters on her pinup board disappeared behind the desk. The doors between study and passage slammed back and forth, loosening handles and hinges.

It sickens Alice that tonight he's up late, on his second bottle of port. Her head is dizzy from all the tasks. The German Lawyers calling for twenty thousand dollars. Bank statements to enter. Max not apologizing for a previous argument, making her cry for days.

Slumped against the doorjamb, Max belts the back of the door with his boot. 'Are you going to stay in here all night?'

Alice stiffens. 'I'm working, so leave me alone.'

'Fuck and shit. And you think you're so smart.'

'Just fuck off. Do something, besides obsessing over your brother!'

Max stands, swaying, watching her, his eyes like the watery flesh of a fish. She is careful not to speak further, quietly returning to a stack of mail. Alice hears the crash of his wine glass on the kitchen's ceramic tiles. She thumps her computer keys, bites her lip. Groaning, she bends the nib of a pencil. Ungrateful prick. She shrinks her body into the chair, trying to control her breathing, her tucked stomach experiencing a sudden pain. In her mind the unbearable images of Bailey playing with two other dogs,

Max's evil brother, and waiting for her bruises to fade. She puts her feet up on the desk, thumps hard, and bawls.

It's All Going Up in Flames

Memo 25: *No woman should have a memory.*

It annoys Alice that night after night they argue about Steban, not settling the inheritance. Max believes that Steban has used their share of the will to pay off business debts. They're defeated and that is that. Max has to face up to the realisation that his brother has never intended passing on his share. He's been working on the plan while they sleep. The inheritance wrangle, visits to their German-speaking lawyers, fruitless trips to the German Consulate all sink Alice into a deep depression. Her moods become darker and while Maggie suggests reverse psychology or AA, nothing helps. Her only recourse is to talk over matters with a sharp tongue. 'I want you to give up drinking. You're two different people. You can't remember anything you said to me last night. You drank my cooking sherry.

God! You're okay now, nice as pie. But I'm sick of it, Max. I'm telling you, I want you to give up drinking. I hate it!'

'It's because of my brother's corruption, holding back my inheritance that's why,' he blurts. 'I can't understand why my father ever made him executor. Steb stole three thousand dollars from father's bank account, when the old man wanted to migrate to Australia. I haven't told you that, have I?'

'Yes you have, over and over, Max. I don't care. Money, money! That's all I ever hear. Stop it. Your brother's a crook. He stole your share because he's evil. How can you fight him? He still has the language. You don't. How are you going to deal with German courts when you can't write High German?'

'It pisses me off that I can't read this solicitor nonsense. Here, look at this word *Nachlaßgericht,* see what I have to put up with. I never even finished school.'

'Well, there you go. It's a pointless exercise. What about karma, Max. Life will pay Steb back.'

'You hate him as much as I do. That's why I want him dragged through the courts. You know that I'm right.'

'Max, I'm so tired of it all. Yeah, I hate your brother. What he's done to this family. But what kind of life is this? All we do is argue. I'm sick to death of your moaning.

DRINKING! I can't stand to be in the same room with you, watching you get stupid. I've had a gut full.'

Alice is charged, the adrenalin kicking in. She watches Max in his silent brooding flick on the stereo. Two beers and he'll soon be frowning, cursing, giggling, there till midnight, settled in his usual binge drinking. What is the point? She wants to piss off.

***

Alice hasn't spoken for days and avoids his wolfish glare. From the family-room slider she gazes at the immense sea of red brick and asks him to build her a fish-pond. Instead he asks her to come and sit with him for a minute at the kitchen table. 'I have an announcement to make.'

'Oh, good! You're giving up the drink.'

'Get off my back, please Alice.'

'Well, what brilliance have you come up with this time?'

'I'm burning everything that's German in this house.'

'You what!'

'You heard me. Presents, photographs, letters, tapes. Come with me.' He drags Alice by the arm outside to the barbecue. Placed on the ash and coals is the painting of the

Spthe house. It sits there like an offering. Alice begins to tremble. How many more things is he going to take away? 'It's innocent in all this, Max. It's just a house. We had a lovely holiday there.'

'I don't care. It's all going. When I'm finished with this lot, we're going through everything. I don't know why I keep these shitty reminders of why I left bloody Germany!'

Alice's face tightens as Max smashes the painting with an axe. He's doused everything in kerosene. It catches alight and hisses like a firecracker. She broods in silence, a trickle of perspiration forming under her fringe. Flakes of charcoal waver in the air, the fire travelling quickly through the roof lines of the house. The oily residue smells like burnt carpet. Aunty Gerda and Mae's soul smoldering in the flames. He is killing all the lives that ever lived in that house. The sadness overwhelms, sparking her eyes, dribbling mucous from her nose. He's burning "their" life. She runs towards him, angling her shoulder into his, screaming. 'I hate you. HATE YOU!' With his full weight, he bumps her hard into the shrubbery, her body toppling sideways. She stays there curled on the ground, blood and snot dripping, clutching her arms into her stomach.

'You're hysterical. Go inside and calm yourself down, Alice. Start by looking for the photographs.'

Inside, Alice locks the bathroom door and runs the shower. She stares at herself in the mirror. 'This is it,' she says, looking at her red swollen face. 'It has come to this...damned rotten...' Still holding her stomach, she eases herself onto the porcelain bath listening to the water sputtering down the drain. In the long nights and days she has spent with him, she thinks of rooms she has dusted, vacuumed, decorated or slept in. Her body wants to shriek out with the agony of all the roses she pruned, walls and stoves she scrubbed and all the curtains she made. A headache emerges, whopping at her like a helicopter. The blades are spinning a steady rhythm in her head. The blackbirds in King's Park come back to her, and she imagines them swooping and pecking at her father-in-law's head. She sees her brother-in-law stealing pies, birds straddling fences in King's Park, memories of an old man on a bench, staring at the river in silence. Then the chaos subsides and she pushes her hands down through her clothes.

She glides silently into the kitchen and hears Max talking to himself in the lounge room. He is already half way through a bottle of beer. 'You look like shit,' he says, smiling, his bleary eyes out of focus.

Alice looks down at him and pokes his shoulder with her index finger. 'I want a divorce.'

'I'm never going to get that inheritance. My own brother! I just can't believe it, na? Steals one point two million Deutschmarks and gets away with it. So what is my lawyer in Germany doing? Absolutely bloody nothing. It's criminal that's what it is.'

'Are you even listening? I want us to split. For good.'

'If we split we'll do it right. We can have a nooky from time to time. I'm not going to give the government everything that I've worked hard for. You can have the front unit and I will have the other three. Father's money helped build this, na? Including Swan Road.'

'Fuck the money. It's blood money. Tainted. Shares, stockmarket, assets, rental. That's all I ever hear! What about life? What about doing something? You just sit there and thump your lips. What about all your big promises. England. Canada. The big cruise. What happened to that? Still at sea, is it? Fucking shit.'

Alice opens the glass doors of the wall unit. 'Seems to me all your ideas bottom in a beer bottle,' she says, removing a stack of CD's.

'I'm taking this, this and this. Yes, I'll have Queen and Annie Lennox. Goodbye Dylan, Lionel Ritchie, Diana Ross. Hello Sting. You've got a better place to go.'

The man with the glazed eyes stares ahead. She isn't sure if that twisted look is sadness or warped delight. He keeps on mumbling. She isn't even in the room.

A Better Place to Go

Memo 26:   *Parting is such sweet sorrow.*

Each day she fills shelves. Puts her notebooks, photographs, and new sketches in one of the end rooms. The three-bedroom, one bathroom, is conveniently spaced with no common walls. With the ex-Vietnam vet moving out, the paintwork has been touched up quickly and the carpets cleaned. She wanders through the empty rooms wondering how she might fill them.

The unit, half the size of her old house, has winter sun on the northern side, an L-shaped lounge, dining and neatly tiled laundry and kitchen. It has a little portico at the front door and the outdoor courtyard blooms trellises of mauve, lilac and purple salvias. Ferns and canon lilies dominate the bricked flower boxes and tiny sentinels and geckos sun-bake or run along the brickwork. She moves and listens to her own conversation coming back as a grateful collaborator. She hears sounds of the roof cracking, doves bobbing and cooing in pairs on the roof. The large mirror in the bathroom shares her complexion as a bright smile joining her raised eyebrows. She's in the hall, making a fist at her reflection. 'Yes, yes!'

Her departure has been a quiet affair, almost too good to be true. She carries small household items and clothes in boxes or wire baskets. Max uses the wheelbarrow to cart one of the sofas. Later, he leaves their dining room furniture at the front door. In the coming weeks, she informs him about a few things in the shed. 'I need that old dressing table with the winged mirrors, and the chest of drawers,' she says. 'Before you chuck them out.'

Silence fills the house. He flaps out his newspaper. More silence, until he tosses her a letter from his German lawyers. 'How am I going to answer them now?'

'Usually it's done in English,' she says. 'But why bother.'

'You could at least help me a little bit.'

'No! When can I get the dressing table?'

'When I'm good and ready.'

On the weekend, with Max out, Alice quickly crosses the path to the shed. The crammed interior has a musty smell, an assortment of building materials, papers, clothes, and camping equipment. Their blue canoe hangs from the rafters. She opens a wardrobe, finding an odd saucepan, frying pan and crockery. The lacquered chest of drawers is piled like kindling in a corner, as if recently chopped. She shifts boxes of tiles from the winged dressing table. At least, that's still intact, although the mirrors are pitted at the edges. Grunting now and again, the table is impossible to move. Each time she scrapes the bottom over the concrete, one of the wings swings around loosely on its hinges. She tilts the table to the side. Again it's impossible, the mirrored wings batter back and forth like a glass moth. Finding string or rope that will do the trick. There! Alice spots the silver sheen of gaffer tape in Max's toolbox. He'd used it to tape up the rust on her car, now she needs it to fasten the two arms together. Eventually, the dressing table sits in the middle of the backyard looking like white wood in a straitjacket. Sliding a piece of carpet under the base, she jiggles and pushes the piece of furniture from side to side, moving the heavy weight in small increments. Embarking on the final leg across the driveway, Alice finds the downhill slide the easiest. Halfway across, she stops suddenly, Max cornering her in the van, almost side-swiping the dresser. 'You couldn't wait, could you?' he says. 'Get the other bloody end, and we'll get it inside.'

Days later, Alice watches her silhouette in the window, crossing the pavement, an afternoon breeze ruffling the outline of her hair. In the kitchen, she quickly opens cupboards, slipping an odd utensil or casserole dish into a canvas bag. She boxes the vacuum cleaner. Nothing in her manner suggests that she will ever go back to him. Her body language says stick your marriage vows. 'For better or worse' – what a joke. So, she makes another announcement. 'Max, I've seen a lawyer at the Citizens' Advice Bureau. A divorce is easy. It's just a matter of a JP and you signing the paper.'

'Yes, on paper it will be a divorce.'

'No, I'm talking about a real divorce. Not what you think.'

'Yeah, split incomes. Future single pensions.'

'No! I told you before, but you don't seem to be listening. If you'd just stop drinking, you'd bloody-well remember. Read my lips. It's over. *Finito la musica*.'

'Why? Haven't I done everything for you? Haven't I given you everything you have ever wanted? I know I'm not the best person to live with, but we can have a cuddle across the way, now and again. I will leave you alone when you want.'

'No! I want my peace. I can't stand being with you. I hate this Jekyll and Hyde crap. The marriage is over. DEAD!'

He just stares into his glass with a sorrowful, bloodhound look. She isn't sure about his brain cells, if he has any left at all. But she knows that any talk will be about property division, a question of money, his innocent-victim mentality fuming on repeat, questioning *her* madness. Max's silent nodding shadows the house.

'It's not my fault that I have a rotten family.'

'I need to take some things, like the microwave and the blender.'

'You're not having *those*!'

'Well, we should make a list.' Alice fetches a pad and to writes. The air is frozen. Alice suspects that at any moment he'll exhibit a meltdown or a wild avalanche.

Max leans over the table and rips the paper. 'Here, this is what I think of your bloody list.'

'Well, I'm going. Let me know what I can have when you've calmed down. I don't want all your fucking cooking utensils. Just give me what's fair. Know this, I'm not asking for half of the property, so I think I'm entitled to that thirty-year old piece of shit, we call a washing machine.'

Part V

The Boyfriend

Memo 27:   *There's no fool like an old fool.*

In the four years of Alice's part-time course at university learning to paint and draw, she often wonders how many like-minded souls have found the same sheer joy in art. How many attics, garages and spare rooms have nurtured a therapeutic nest of cardboard, paint, brushes, clay and canvasses covered in cloth? She has immured her art inside the shed's brickwork. Her beginnings glow beneath satin gloss. Lately, she is taking her work to deeper metaphorical depths. She sketches elbows in laundry troughs, long fingers threading needle and cotton, arms bonneted in rubber gloves.

Since the 'fifty cents' episode with Ryan, Alice has tried to make friends. In the gift-shop, she caught him behind stands, saying, 'we shouldn't go on meeting like this.' When they were in the library, she managed to get a smile from him now and again. Sometimes his mood was dark almost volcanic, other times he withdrew like a moth into a dark cocoon. She knew he was different and the most talented in class. On certain days his head drooped and occasionally his eyes would emerge from tiny pinpoints to plot a stare at her across the room. The geography of his hunched body intrigued her. Was it from a heavy workload? She didn't suspect drugs. He didn't show signs of rubbing his nose or the presence of reddish rims on the eyes. Alice could see the internal workings behind the armour of his sad face. How his eyes, with dark curling eyelashes, reached out then sank back when she spoke to him against a door, or commented on his ink-wash drawings. At first, he hesitated to be drawn into any conversation, lacking the sparkle of the young. He was like a beautiful black butterfly, dark and moody, struggling to be noticed, hovering in the shadows, until finally she allowed him under her light and pastel watercolours.

When the group gathers in the arts coffee shop, Alice discovers that Ryan is interested in philosophy. Plato, Socrates and Descartes are some of his favourites. Alice listens intently as he quotes, *I think, therefore I am.* She is amazed at his memory, reading Dante at the age of seventeen. She doesn't have a desire to speak, just to listen. 'Ryan,' she says, 'you're a mind of information.' So they read Heidegger together, make coffee rings on notes, offering suggestions for their next art project.

After four weeks of slimming, Alice is back eating M&M's, sausage rolls and potato chips. She is lightheaded when she's with Ryan. He's cool and easy going. Lately, they find a space where they can be alone, and he fills her in on things about the Gulf War history she missed while in hospital. She thinks he's a born comedian, too, ending his emails with, *Keep the Sabbath dream alive!* In a recent email, he's invited her on a mystery tour of a wrecker's yard. Did she want to go?

The next Saturday afternoon in good clothes, Alice enters Bob's Wreckers. Like an ironclad automotive depository of old ghosts, rows and rows of Commodores, Fords, engines, mufflers, tyres, and unrecognizable car bodies huddle together like sad relatives. Ryan points to a doorless red Toyota. 'See!' He springs to the rear of the car. 'Your new hatch! Just a bit of surface rust, but I can paint over that.'

'Oh, I thought...'

'You can't keep your window taped up forever.'

Alice watches him tossing bits and pieces of car bodies around, throwing keys into old car wrecks, taking off her rusty hatch door and replacing it with the red one. She views his actions and energy with an amused grin, laughing at his choice of swearwords when something doesn't quite fit. He keeps telling her that the old one is dangerous; how any man could let his wife drive around with so much rust he didn't know, she could have been pulled over, the Police slapping on a Yellow Sticker. 'Any longer with that thing, and the glass would have slipped and crashed onto the road. It only needed a little work, not automotive insanity!'

Later, they sit in a harbour restaurant. She shouts him a hot chocolate and a sandwich. She wants to make up for the hard work and effort he's put in. The inside of her chest tightens, contemplating that old beery breath of a husband ready to sell, discard or give away her car, her freedom.

'I can't tell you how much I appreciate the new door, Ryan.'

'It's nothing.'

The virtuous young. He would never understand how much it means to her. She needs to concentrate hard, move away from old feelings.

Seated on the harbour decking, Ryan's mind makes a sudden connection. 'That's what I have, nothing,' he says. 'I don't even have a girlfriend.'

'But you will.'

'No,' he says emphatically. 'No, it's never going to happen.' Telling her now that he fails when it comes to girls, how depressed he got when nothing ever works out, that he's a virgin at twenty-eight. Laughing almost in tears, looking into her eyes.

How vulnerable he is, thinks Alice, so young and so insecure. 'But you're a nice guy. Any girl would love to be with you.'

'I don't like these skinny chicks, Alice. They're weird. They eat nothing and look like stick insects. No guy wants to be with a set of bones. Look at me. I'm skinny! It would be, 'so let's get down and do the bone thing, baby.''

'You're funny. So you're saying you don't like the young girls?'

'Oh, some of them are okay, but there's nothing happening in their brains. Man, I'd rather have a MILF.'

'What's a MILF?'

'A round, rosy mother with a baby in the pram. At least you know she's doing it.'

'I've never heard of such a thing!'

Ryan shuffles his chair closer; spelling out the acronym in her ear, couching himself back into the chair with an amused grin.

'Oh, heavens,' says Alice, giggling into her hands.

'See, it's really like this, Alice. We draw shapes don't we, not pencils? I like older women for that. They've got back, curves, big hips. They've experienced life. They know what they're doing in bed. Guys get turned on by that!'

Alice stares out across the water. They sit in silence for at least five minutes. She looks back at him and he gives her a quick breathy cry, as if he's trying to tell her something, but didn't quite know how. She can't pretend that she's curious about his ideas on women, that all of a sudden here is a new education on the young, someone who lives by a different set of rules. How unusual that this young man dislikes skinny young girls, preferring round women with puppy-dog tits!

'My husband used to call me fat.'

'Man! What a prick. You're not fat. You're a woman and that's how I see you.'

'He called my legs oversized drumsticks.'

'Where is that son-of-a-bitch? I'll pierce his eyeballs.'

'Ryan…'

'Yeah?'

'You're not presuming something about me, are you?'

'I like you. I know that for sure.'

'We're just friends, right?'

'Yeah!' He gave her another quizzical look.

Alice's head is growing hot, and raising her held coffee cup, she tries to shade the burning sensation in her face. By now a chill has hit the deck and in her sudden physical drop of temperature, the late afternoon air makes her body shake. He wraps his jacket around her shoulders, and in the hub of different bodily depths and temperatures a coil of sensuality begins to burn.

They stand inside the narrow passageway between two cars. He reaches for his jacket, and in the pull of the garment his warm hand brushes her cheek. 'You know if you ever need anything mechanical or Faber Castell, I'm your boy!'

Alice straightens, then climbs into the driver's seat. 'Come visit me sometime.'

'Right, it's a deal,' he says, slapping the roof of the car.

A week later, on the Saturday when Maggie attends an all-night gig, Alice invites him over for a beer. She thinks about intimidation, his emails and buying new slippers. She mines a trail from the wardrobe to the bathroom mirror. She plays his *16 Horsepower* CD and decides *Goldfrapp* is better. She tries different shades of lipstick, and can't imagine a young man not feeling the flesh of a woman against his skin. For her, too, it's been a long time, and ages since she's experienced the *holiday of a lifetime.*

She has thoughts about his clear skin, brown hair spiked with blonde tips, and has visions of just the two of them alone, his softness, fragrant neck and that warring landscape of dark hairs on his arms. 'I'm caught in your second-day growth, doe-eyes, feeble laugh, your windchime voice, kinky K's in your notepad. Yes, I won't deny it. I'm tired of memorising what it's like. So what's a few fucks, anyway,' she repeats to herself.

Ryan arrives half-an-hour early. Alice already has drunk a beer and since she really isn't a drinker it has gone to her head. She feels loose and carefree and they laugh on the lounge over his Munster jokes. They down further beers. Alice is on her third as they watch television, deciding finally that it looks better switched off. They sit close together, pointing at some of the best work he has brought on Goya and Bosch.

'You have awakened my mental sharpness,' he says, moving in closer, so that their legs touch.

'I like your pencil drawings. The one you did last week was especially good, with that lady reclining on the bed. It was in perspective, I thought.'

'The gal with the big bottom,' he laughs with killer eyes.

'Are you a tit man or a bottom man?' Alice slurs.

'Hell! Bottoms. There's something about them. I just want to grab them.'

They both laugh and drink some more. Alice thanks him for his emails. She likes his idea about her taking a job as a secret counsellor, that she isn't just being charitable and doesn't mind knowing about all the stuff going on in his head.

'I just like talking to you,' he says. 'Hell, it's better than a movie or going to the shrink.'

'It's nice, just to talk. We look at things much the same.'

'Yeah. I was afraid you might've interpreted certain things a bit different. You know what I mean. It bugs me, you know, about my lifelong suffering.'

'Your lifelong suffering. You mean not having a girlfriend, is that it?' she says, moving a fallen hair from his lip.

'Kinda. It's the other thing, though, the big thing. I just don't know when it's going to happen.'

'Do you want it to happen right now?' Alice pulls the stubby from his lips and places it on the coffee table.

'Uh, you mean…?'

'Yes, I mean, you and me, right now.'

'I'm totally shocked,' he says, quivering.

'I've said the wrong thing, then.'

'Oh…no, it's just that… Man, I'm blown away!'

Alice pulls him slowly from the lounge and in front of the bed still holds his hands. 'Sorry, this is all I have. Maggie's got the big bedroom with all her music gear. And she's got a boyfriend, I haven't.'

She cuddles him in the small room filled with books, teddy bears and throw rugs. 'I wasn't going to, but…' She starts to undress and he climbs in beside her, fully dressed. She places his blue hand on her breast. Then the room fills with his presence, her job at the library, and keeping all this from Maggie. 'Don't worry about anything. Just hold me.'

'I'm sorry,' he shivers.

'Just relax. It's natural to feel nervous.' Alice watches the way he looks at her body; sees him flush and then she unbuttons his clothes. His mouth is dry, but she begins kissing him all over, soft wet orderly kisses. Then he giggles into her ear as if it's playtime. She hasn't known anything like this before, and the distraction of him nosing her cheek with a kind of pigeon cooing suddenly makes her snort with laughter. Somewhere deep down in the tangle of bedclothes, amongst the frolic, side-stitches and tears, serious sex no longer matters to Alice. He is hilarious.

Ghost Town

Memo 28: *Up ahead is another town: circa 2000*

Alice is on the back seat, returning home. Kevin and his latest girlfriend puff on cigarettes, their tape deck filling the cabin with steely rhythms, the invisible meander of the music's last note trailing off into a dark chasm of trees.

They leave the highway and head down the mountain pass. Alice ratchets the window of the old Chevy down another notch. The odour of tobacco reminds her of her father's smell, the stale Vanguard, pumping its brakes at the bottom of Bull's Hill.

'I'll never forget Dad's antics. He got a kick out of driving down the hill in angel gear. Once he teased me, about drifting. Of course, back then I didn't know the difference between 'drifting' and 'coasting'.

'I don't remember that,' says Kevin, 'I was too young.'

'Yeah, he reckoned only yachts drifted. Dad and Jimmy made a big deal out of it. Stirred me forever after that.'

At the end of the inlet they cross the bridge, the road meeting the railway's flat line. Dark shapes of grass trees and light on the water remind Alice of another road trip, watching the scrub slowly darken at dusk, a congested car club rally all the way to Sydney. She remembers the boredom; her cardigan stretched one way, then another. Her two brothers, Kevin and Jimmy in a tussle behind her, pulling hair, pinching thighs. Flash. Flash. The old town's memories turning like bike wheels left in sand. She thinks about Somersby, bombing the falls, the valley filled with the chinking sounds of bellbirds. Jimmy and his school mates disappearing into the tall grass while Alice is left behind.

Leaning out the window, the bird's chiming is like a recall at the age of ten, racing the Green Point train, watching the last carriage snake away, puffed out only after five minutes of riding. 'Remember the jetty baths, the stingers?'

'Yeah, the baths. They're still there,' says Kevin. 'Green Point's still the same, so's Temple Bay. We'll show you the old haunts.'

'I used to live in Glenrock,' says Sonya.

'Really? We passed the station yesterday. Much bigger than I remember more houses.'

'It was nice there. I liked it,' says Sonya, rubbing Kevin's arm. 'I owned an old fibro, half-way up the mountain.'

'When we arrived on the train, I got a bit teary seeing the old place, the blue jacarandas, showing Ryan the big rock in the bay.' Alice is aware that Ryan is giving her quizzical looks. 'The green, green grass of home,' she says, watching his thin face pan into a smile.

He smooches close. *'Then I get out of my car, coz that's where you are. And there's only Alice,'* he croons, raising his eyebrows.

Alice pushes Ryan's creeping hands away. 'Is Ridge Street still a holiday house, Kev?'

'Not sure.'

They park on the Esplanade close to the beach. Alice sighs into a vision of change. She can't believe this landscape's hijacked face: paddleboats, canoes, the Sea Breeze Café all gone, the bulk of water in the bay replacing plump dunes where she built cubbies in the lantana. Those warm shelters where she slept on a towel after a freezing swim, waking up only by the noise of holidaymakers shuffling past. Everything appears smaller, pathways, jetties, the deck of weathered cottages at Peaceful Bay. Alice takes her time photographing sandbars, a lone pelican, pair of catamarans, a cruiser and a sailboat. She's drawn to the street trees, the few remaining pines and one Illawarra Flame stilled carved in sixties' initials.

Heading towards the ocean beach along the coastal strip, Kevin suggests they have lunch on his new boat at Hank's Jetty. 'I need to check a few things. We can look at Ridge Street later, Sis.'

Facing the headland with the wind catching Sonya's sun-frock, Alice groups the three together. She knows she's eccentric taking shot after shot, but her new camera is nifty. She can edit to her heart's content, or click 'replay'. The small islands, the Peninsula, Warrah Head and scenic views of the foothills of Temple Bay materialize like silent ancients guarding the blue bay.

In the shade of the Surf Club before the flash pops, Kevin picks at his teeth, 'Gawd! Never had me photo taken this much before.'

'Smile,' says Alice. 'I don't know when I'll be back.'

'I'm getting the tummy rumbles,' says Kevin.

They circle back past the dunes and enter Temple Bay's main street. Leaning against the car, Sonya winces at the size of the new high rise, a glass spectacle of nine levels, occupying a whole city block. 'My God, I think that's really, really ugly.'

'They were building it last time we were down here, remember?'

'Yes, but I didn't know it was going to be that large.'

'I had to avoid it down the Esplanade,' says Alice. 'There it was in every frame like a cataract on the eye. When I moved, it moved. How on earth did they get that thing passed?'

'Usual way,' says Kevin, flicking his cigarette. 'Shifty.'

'Where's the RSL Club?'

'Swallowed up inside, somewhere.' Kevin points to a small row of shops. 'They moved the old diggers over there. Business, not as usual. Recognise the agents across the street, Sis?'

'Well, I'll be. Jeff Hawking's Real Estate!'

'Yeah,' says Kevin. 'Still here after sixty years.'

'They were down there near the cake shop.' Alice snaps her fingers and points. 'Next to the Commonwealth Bank.'

'That little box thing? Nah! That was the Rural.'

They talk for a few more minutes about old-style shop frontages, the pokies and returned soldiers. Alice can't disguise how she feels, the conversation moving to the eighties' corporate cowboys and WA Inc. A hot flush creeps into her skin. The RSL Club was big enough when she left town, but this was ridiculous. Memory, too, was giving her visions of the past like a sixties' replay. How could they turf out the RSL? How could they let the owners use up a whole city block? She was sure the townies wouldn't have wanted such a Gold Coast-styled complex. 'I wish you'd told me about it, Kev. I could have written a letter to the council.'

'Let's get out of here,' he says.

On their way through the streets, Alice nudges Ryan at every turn. They pass the mini-golf site, disused vegetable store, and carnival grounds now subdivided into units. 'Oh, look. There's my old milk-bar, The Rendezvous.'

'The one where you played 'Roy, the Boy',' chuckles Ryan, digging her side. 'And The Animals and Donovan.'

Kevin idles outside the new build of restaurants, markets and cinema. 'We saw *Rabbit Proof Fence* in there last time, didn't we, Sweets?'

'Yep, good movie. Seats were comfy. Very art deco.'

'It used to be the Sands Motel. Remember the fire, Sis?'

Alice is silent for a moment, not answering. 'Did you ever see that Italian movie *Cinema Paradiso*? They saved all the filmed kisses that were banned by the town's priest. At least this end of town has *good* karma.'

On the jetty, Alice turns and aims her camera towards the foreshore. 'Bloody hell, I can't believe Hank's Boat Shed is still here. Amazing!'

Kevin lifts her into the rear deck of the cruiser. 'Got the boat moored here 'cause it's cheap. I'll be taking it back to work soon. Need to do some running repairs.'

'It's bigger than the last one.'

'Yep, she's a thirty foot Nova. Cost me a packet, too.'

Alice watches the way he proudly points to the mod cons. Toilet. Bunk beds. Small kitchen. He pulls out a tray from the gas cooker. 'This is where Sonya cooks the fish.'

'It had to be self-sufficient,' adds Sonya. 'We work all week, so we didn't want any fuss.'

'Yeah, 'specially having lazy weekends on the Macdonald River.'

'Isn't that cheating, having an Echo sounder?'

'Nah,' says Kevin, screwing up his nose. 'Ya don't waste any time with this thing, not when you're after a feed of flathead. Talkin' of food, me stomach's growling.'

Up on the fly-deck, they unravel butcher's paper filled with fish and chips. Slurping cans of Coke, they discuss prawning, cycling to Dillon's Farm, horses at the Dude Ranch. 'You remember riding that pregnant mare?' says Kevin. 'Slow as a wet week.'

'So, what happened to the beautiful beach?'

'Silly buggers in the council removed all the tea-trees, didn't they?'

'There's hardly any sand to walk on. It's just not the same.'

'Like the Club, Sis, nothing stays the same. It breaks my heart that Mum and Dad moved out of here. It was all because of that night, Dad driving to Woodford. It was a bloody miracle he didn't crash the car over the cliff.'

'What happened?' asks Sonya.

'The police found him the next morning, slumped on the wheel. He'd drunk a whole flagon of wine. Scared the life out of Mum. God, did she go crook. The police threatened to take his license away, so he stuck to beer after that.'

In the late afternoon, Kevin drives through town and around familiar avenues. Memorial, Cove Avenue and Orange Road. He returns along Beach, down Box and into Carramar Road. 'Remember the billycart race? Mrs Blanks in Bourke Road? She outlived grandma. Did you know Mrs Gettoes had a heart attack?'

'Nah', says Alice, as Manning's store and Judith's house enter her side vision. She'd like to get out, go inside, pry open old doors. The Doctor's comes into view, same trees, but it's no longer Fox's surgery. Alice is glad to be back in her old town with her new guy. 'I knew you'd like it', she says, pressing her face into Ryan's cheek. 'So what happened to Betty Parker? Is she still around, Kev?'

'Oh, no, she died a long time ago.'

They drive slowly down Ridge Street. The road verge weaves its greenness from loose gravel stones into moist front yards. Late spring rains have left small ponds on the grass. The Chin's veranda-style weatherboard, re-built after a fire, is now brick and tile. A hedge of bushes hides the exterior of Number nine. A healthy cypress fans the front roof, and a spindly jacaranda drops little blue slippers on the lawn. The letterbox struggles with junk mail, paper dangling out like legs from a nest. Wooden blinds are brown-eyed slits closed on a hundred year-old house.

Alice catches Kevin's face in the rear-view mirror, and a quick sting like 7-Up sparks her nostrils. She can't bring on the waterworks. Not now. Not in front of Sonya. She blows her nose and cuddles close to Ryan, squeezing his hand. Alice senses time ticking away, but can't be bothered knocking on the past, or the house's aqua face. The sunken and broken concrete drive gives an even poorer feel to the place. The two small windows, her brothers' rooms, hedge and fence, a purple haze glowing inside the screen door, all have a shoddy air about them. The old fibro and weatherboard house has finally shed its skin. 'It looks so different. So worn out, as if it was never ours,' says Alice.

'It's just a rental now, Sis.'

At the Farm

Memo 29:   *You can make anything happen*

In the evening on the veranda, between Kevin and Sonya, Alice and Ryan laze back on an old sofa. Jack and Mia, the two young kelpies, nose their palms for biscuits. Relaxed in Ryan's arms, Alice hears bush sounds; the constant calling of birds, the wind whopping the tree tops. She feels pampered, Sonya springing up now and again, serving tea and nibbles. She's spent two days now on this veranda, the reverie coaxing her to enjoy the panorama, the smell of fresh earth and mown grass. Inland shapes of mountains, bush and track appeal to her artistic flair. Looking beyond potted succulents to a small orchard, her eye catches the pastel forms of peach blossom and apple-green. She watches the evening's flash of parrots in the gums, thinking about Kevin's sanctuary, his terraced view from the

veranda to the sheer drop of valley. She is experiencing his
dream, a twenty-acre farm, three sheep grazing in a yard,
only one neighbour four kilometres east. The property
suited him. The Hunter Valley to the north, dirt road in, no-
one to complain about the dogs.

A light aircraft gurgles low over the valley. 'Do you
get many planes out here, Kev?'

'Yep, a few. Don't notice them during the week.'

'Drinks!' chirps Sonya, swinging out through the
French doors, tray in hand.

'This is paradise,' says Ryan. 'I could live on a place
like this.'

'Yeah, lot of work, though. See that felled tree down
there. Took me two weeks to lop it. Still got a few to go.'

'So, what's down there?' asks Ryan, pointing to the
cleared land.

'Oh, gotta build a garage. Plant some more fruit trees.
You want loquats, don't you, Pet?' he says, reaching for
Sonya's cigarettes. 'We've got a dam in there, past the
sheds. It's just a short walk. Gets a few ducks and wild
geese.'

'I planted those roses. There was nothing here
before.'

'They're beautiful, Sonya,' says Alice. 'And I love the trees, and the space. You're so lucky, Kev.'

'Oh, I don't know. You can make anything happen if you want.'

Acknowledgements

The Five Lives of Ms Bennett is a work carried out as a Masters of Writing Degree at Edith Cowan University (2006). I am indebted to Dr Susan Ash whose supervision of my candidature was inspirational and, although belated, I thank her for her writing guidance, support and encouragement.

I especially thank Lucas North (1973-2013), Bronwyn Thomason, Glen Phillips and Sharron Quayle of the University's Friday Critiquing Group for their support, time and encouragement. The lunch sessions helped tremendously, way back when. I have fond memories of Flora's Smith school teacher charm reading my work and the MA thesis essay (1947-2023). Everyone will miss her dearly, especially her poetry. A special thank you must go to author Bruce Russell for his chapter reading, advice and good wishes concerning the novel.

A thank you to the love of my life, Lucas North, I will always miss him. My deepest gratitude to my family and friends for their ongoing kindness and support.

About the Author

Helen Hagemann lives in Perth, Western Australia and is published in Australian literary journals including Southerly, Westerly and Island magazine. Her work also appears online, in an international Chinese publication, and recent poetry can be found on Phillip Halls' Burrow – an online poetry journal. In 2004, Helen received a poetry mentorship award from the Australian Society of Authors studying with Jean Kent, a NSW poet. In 2008, she won a Macquarie/Varuna Longlines Poetry scholarship resulting in the publication of a chapbook *Evangelyne & Other Poems* published by the Australian Poetry Centre, Melbourne (2009). Her second collection *of Arc & Shadow* was published by Sunline Press, Cottesloe, WA (2013). Helen holds a Masters in Writing from Edith Cowan University, has taught prose and poetry in Fremantle in association with the OOTA Writers Inc., and has been accepted into writing residencies throughout the world. Helen has two novels published *The Last Asbestos Town* in 2020 and *The Ozone Café* in 2021. This work is published under the Imprint of Oz.one Publishing © and her books can be found on her website.

Visit Helen at https://helenhagemann.com/

https://www.facebook.com/AuthorHelenHagemann